A HOPE
at
THE END
of the
WORLD

ALSO BY SARAH LARK

In the Land of the Long White Cloud saga

In the Land of the Long White Cloud

Song of the Spirits

Call of the Kiwi

The Kauri trilogy

Toward the Sea of Freedom

Caribbean Islands saga

Island of a Thousand Springs

Island of the Red Mangroves

A HOPE
at
THE END
of the
WORLD

SARAH LARK

TRANSLATED BY D.W. LOVETT

amazon crossing

Text copyright © 2015 Bastei Lübbe AG, Köln
Translation copyright © 2017 D. W. Lovett

Previously published as *Eine Hoffnung am Ende der Welt* by Bastei Lübbe AG, Köln in Germany in 2015. Translated from German by D. W. Lovett. First published in English by AmazonCrossing in 2017.

Published by AmazonCrossing, Seattle

www.apub.com

Amazon, the Amazon logo, and AmazonCrossing are trademarks of Amazon.com, Inc., or its affiliates.

ISBN-13: 9781503942677
ISBN-10: 1503942678

Cover design by Shasti O'Leary Soudant

Printed in the United States of America

Contents

Betrayal

TEHRAN, IRAN; BOMBAY, INDIA;
PAHIATUA, NEW ZEALAND (NORTH ISLAND)

JULY 1944–JANUARY 1945

1

Refugee camp near Tehran, Iran

Where's Luzyna?"

Adam, who lived on the west side of the refugee camp with his parents, stopped in front of Helena, panting. He must've run.

"I have no idea." She looked up reluctantly from her sewing. Until Adam interrupted, Helena had been sitting in the sun, happy to have escaped the cramped camp lodging. The day before had been rainy, so all the refugees had been cooped up inside. First Helena's sister, Luzyna, had complained about not being allowed to visit her boyfriend, Kaspar, in the men's barracks. Then she'd quarreled with the girl whose bed was beside hers, and then she'd worked herself up over the woman in the bed across the room constantly talking to herself. Helena had been relieved when Luzyna set out that morning for her work in the field kitchen. Now Adam was disturbing her peace. As usual, trouble seemed to follow her sister. "She's not in the kitchen?" Helena asked, resigned.

"She had to see the doctor," Adam told her, shaking his head. "Or at least that's what she told the cook." There was a small hospital adjoining the camp. "She was supposed to be back by midday. But she hasn't turned up yet—even though she's supposed to help me carry and serve the food. I can't do it alone, but I don't want to tell on her either. And if she's not at the doctor's . . ." Adam, a skinny blonde fifteen-year-old with a pimply face, shifted nervously from foot to foot.

No one ever wanted to make trouble for Luzyna. She always found someone willing to cover for her and take responsibility for her mistakes.

"She didn't have an appointment with the doctor," Helena said, and began to gather her sewing. The apron she'd made in her seamstress course hadn't been much of a success, and was already dirty since Helena was constantly pricking her finger while sewing. Her talents clearly did not lie in the area of handicrafts. "At least, she didn't say anything to me. But it's sweet of you not to want to tell. Let me put my sewing away and I'll come help you."

Helena stood up and entered the barracks, squinting in the half-light of the large room, which only had a few windows. She had to be careful to avoid stumbling over the residents' possessions piled along the narrow walkways and between the beds. The barracks were hopelessly overcrowded. The pallets were so close that you'd bump your neighbor just by turning over in bed.

Almost every night, Helena woke up because Luzyna slept poorly. Like many of the Polish refugees who found themselves in Iran after being in Siberia, her sister suffered from nightmares. Though they were finally safe, the past still haunted them. Before the Russians marched into their country in the fall of 1939, they'd been respectable Polish citizens. After signing a nonaggression pact, Hitler and Stalin had divided Poland between them, and to complete the annexation of eastern Poland, the Russian dictator had ordered much of the Polish population deported to Siberian labor camps. In June 1941, however, Germany reneged, and circumstances compelled Stalin to align with the Allied powers against Hitler, and the Allies forced Russia to free the Poles in Siberia. The Allies recruited former deportees into a newly formed Polish army, and sent them for training in Iran. Helena and Luzyna were free, and like many of the refugees followed in the wake of the Polish army to Iran. The country was under Allied occupation, and the Poles were welcomed there warmly by the local people. Although Helena and Luzyna's lives were no longer in danger, the young women were far from recovered from the previous few years.

When Helena reached the space she shared with her sister, she pulled back the improvised curtain and tossed her sewing on her bed. Then she hurried to the camp kitchen with Adam. The sun shone high above the snow-covered mountains. It was past noon, and the cook had the food ready. The refugees waited, a bit impatiently to be sure, though after being left to starve for years in Siberia, it was still a small miracle for them to receive three meals a day.

The field kitchen was several hundred yards from the barracks, and Adam and Helena reached it by way of a wide well-paved path. The refugee camp had originally been planned as a garrison for the Iranian air force, and its main brick buildings were more finished, surrounded by a neat yellow wall instead of the ugly barbed-wire fence that had been hurriedly erected around the lodgings. The four main buildings hadn't been enough to hold the flood of refugees. They had first lodged people in tents, then quickly built barracks. The main garrison was now used for public spaces like the hospital, the school, and workshops.

They also had two field kitchens and a mess tent, and in the warm Iranian summer the kitchen assistants sat happily in front of the tent to peel potatoes and chop vegetables for stew. After years in the Siberian cold, the refugees were grateful for every ray of sun. Of course, it would have been even more pleasant if there had been some trees or flowers, but there had been no time to beautify the grounds. Still, the distant peaks of the Alborz Mountains, at the foot of which the camp lay, were quite beautiful on their own.

"And little Luzyna?" asked one of the assistants as two young men loaded heavy kettles of canned goulash and macaroni onto handcarts for Helena and Adam and the other servers. "Isn't she supposed to be helping?"

Helena bristled. "My sister had to see the doctor," she claimed through pursed lips.

The other kitchen assistant laughed. "Doctor, my foot," he teased. "I saw her earlier behind the garage with Kaspar. Unless she's confused the mechanic for the doctor?"

Eighteen-year-old Kaspar helped repair the trucks that brought supplies and new refugees into the camp. He seemed to enjoy it, whereas Luzyna clearly despised her kitchen work. She hadn't really volunteered for it either; she'd simply given in to pressure from her older sister. Now Luzyna shirked work whenever possible, and Helena was already regretting having insisted. Helena thought that at sixteen Luzyna should be doing *something* if she wasn't going to school and had no interest in training as a seamstress. Luzyna didn't want to improve her English, or learn French or Persian. She seemed determined to do nothing but flit about and enjoy this idyllic place where they were stranded.

Helena looked around before starting to push the handcart while Adam pulled. She didn't think the refugee camp all that lovely herself, though it was certainly the best place they'd been since their deportation. The beauty of the imposing snowcapped peaks rising above green hills and date groves was eclipsed by the dismal barracks and camp roads full of downtrodden, uprooted people. And even though she enjoyed excursions into Tehran, just two and a half miles away, Helena felt like a stranger in the lively metropolis. The chaos in the streets, with drivers of cars, trucks, donkeys, and oxen yelling over each other, filled her with anxiety; the haggling in the bazaars, the blaring music, the calls of the muezzins from the mosques, and even the friendly people with their harem pants, long shirts, and headscarves unnerved her.

Helena admired the shah's glorious palace, but the fancy shops in the Western-oriented parts of the city, and the women in silk dresses and elegant makeup strolling there, didn't entrance her the way they did Luzyna. She was ashamed of her own simple cotton dress. The refugees had gotten new clothing after they'd been deloused in the transitional camp at Pahlavi, but most of the sweaters, dresses, and coats didn't fit well, or were too warm for the Persian summer. Compared to the women in Tehran, Helena felt like an ugly duckling—Luzyna, on the other hand, would've looked like a princess even in sackcloth. Her sister was already a beauty, and she knew it only too well. Luzyna was firmly convinced that the world would one day lie at her feet. She seemed nothing like the whimpering child who'd clung to Helena as Russian soldiers had ripped their family out of their spacious apartment in Lwów, striking their father and cursing their mother.

Helena still couldn't understand why Stalin had ordered them driven so brutally from eastern Poland after he and Hitler divided the country. They'd lived peacefully for years among Ukrainians and Belarusians, who were the majority of the population in that area. Helena's father, a dentist, had treated everyone equally, and her mother had taught English and French to Ukrainian and Russian children. But the Russians declared hundreds of thousands of Polish citizens "socially dangerous" and "enemies of the people." None of them really knew what was happening as they were pulled from their homes, loaded in carts, and shipped like animals to the north.

Helena's family had spent two years in the coal-mining town Vorkuta in Siberia. Helena, fourteen when they arrived, had worked with her parents in the forest, and sometimes even in the mine. Little Luzyna was too young to work, but managed to survive despite their meager food rations. Helena remembered Siberia only as an ice-cold hell, the family clinging to each other at night for warmth. They struggled through the cold, the vermin, and the hunger. Helena's father had died in a mining accident six months after they arrived. Her mother had stubbornly clung to life despite her persistent fever and cough; even though she could hardly grip an ax, she'd gone every day to cut wood in the forest. She had died a few months before their release. Helena still remembered how she and Luzyna had lain with her on the hard, narrow pallet to warm her. At some point, Luzyna had fallen asleep, exhausted, but Helena held her mother, listening to her labored breaths and, eventually, her last words. "Look after Luzyna, Helena. You must take care of your sister. Promise me you won't leave her alone. Luzyna deserves better. She must live . . . my little sun, my light . . ."

Helena promised, fighting back the familiar pain. Once again, there was only Luzyna—radiant Luzyna, the captivating golden-haired little angel with azure eyes, the whole family's favorite. Not that Helena could accuse her parents of neglecting her. On the contrary, Maria and Janek Grabowski had always been attentive to both daughters, encouraging Helena's interest in languages and literature as much as Luzyna's joy in music and dance. Helena remembered many times when she had been studying English or French with her mother, or reading her father's favorite books with him, and Luzyna had come whirling in to perform something. Helena could still see the pride in her mother's eyes when Luzyna played in the music school for the first time—at ten years old, she was already a talented pianist. Afterward, everyone had congratulated the Grabowskis on their beautiful and talented daughter, while Helena stood off to the side.

No one had ever congratulated her parents on Helena. Though she wasn't without her charms, she didn't stand out the way her sister did. Helena had straight brown hair, which became stringy immediately if she didn't wash it daily. Her face was symmetrical, with wide-set big eyes of a boring porcelain blue. And unlike her younger sister, Helena blended in and was well behaved.

After her mother's death, Helena had made every effort to keep her promise. She shared her meager food rations and worked harder to feed her sister. If they hadn't been freed, Helena would almost surely have perished. Iran had been their salvation. Luzyna still spoke enthusiastically of their transition camp on the beaches of Pahlavi, where there was finally enough food and the children could play in the warm sand and swim in the water of the Caspian Sea. Helena's own memories were not so rosy. She mourned the loss of the last of her parents' possessions— including photographs and letters—which had been burned on the beach as part of the quarantine measures. Helena watched, sobbing, as the wind blew ashes across the beach. For Luzyna, Iran might seem like paradise—but for her, the country was part of the nightmare that had begun with their expulsion from Lwów.

Now, as she pushed the handcart forward with all her might—she was still thin and weak—she tried not to think about the future. They said the war would be over soon. Perhaps then they could return to Poland and resume their old life.

In front of the barracks, the residents waited for their food—some impatient, most just apathetic. Though most of the refugees were barely middle aged, they looked old and worn. No one who wasn't young and resilient when they were sent to Siberia had survived their imprisonment. Many of them had been sick upon their arrival in Iran, and thousands died in the hospitals in Pahlavi and Tehran—no matter how hard the Iranian, Indian, and English doctors had tried to help them. Helena told herself that she owed thanks to heaven that she and Luzyna had survived, but she lacked the necessary humility. She couldn't bring herself to believe that God had really protected them from harm when he could've prevented the deportation from the start.

Adam had begun to serve the food, and Helena found a kind word for everyone whose tin container she ladled full of goulash and noodles. And there, near the end of the line, stood Luzyna. She flashed Helena her irresistible smile as she held out her plate.

"It's sooo nice of you to take my place," said Luzyna in her high, soft voice.

Helena made a face. "I didn't do it for you. I did it for the people who would've had to wait for their food otherwise," she said. "Where've you been? You weren't at the doctor's, were you? I won't put up with your lying much longer. Don't you ever think about what our parents would say to you? They'd be ashamed of your behavior."

Luzyna shrugged her shoulders gracefully. She had her hair tied at the nape of her neck. Though her dress was old and worn, it fit her well. All

Luzyna had to do was make a few stitches in her clothes, and they immediately looked better on her. Her feminine features were visible under her muslin dress—Helena observed with envy that her sister already had more of a bust than she did, although she was almost nineteen.

"Mother and father are dead," Luzyna retorted. "They can't be ashamed anymore. And if they were still alive, they'd have better things to do."

Helena nodded. "Undoubtedly," she said. "Our father would work in the camp as a dentist and our mother as a teacher. They certainly wouldn't lie around and—"

"Enjoy life?" Luzyna asked defiantly. "What's so bad about that? We've already had enough work and hunger. So why not enjoy today for once?"

"And tomorrow?" Helena asked. "We won't stay in this camp forever. People won't always be bringing you food. Someday—"

"Someday we might all be dead," said Luzyna, grabbing the ladle and filling her plate herself before turning to go. "There's still a war on, and who knows how it will end. The soldiers say the Americans are building a weapon they could use to incinerate the whole world. And the Germans are too. And if they ever finish, then: poof!"

Luzyna gestured dramatically before turning away with her plate. Probably headed back to the workshop or to Kaspar's quarters.

Helena looked after her unhappily. Luzyna wasn't alone in her thinking. Almost no one in the camp was planning for the future.

2

While everyone else was eating, Helena and Adam returned the handcart with the cauldron to the kitchen. They helped clean up and put away the dishes. Luzyna, whose job this actually was, didn't make so much as an appearance.

"She's sulking," Adam explained when Helena complained about it. "Normally, when she skips work in the morning, she comes back in the afternoon. For the extra meal if nothing else."

The kitchen personnel ate together in the tent before everyone else and usually managed to have a little something extra left over. That day they had managed to find some fruit for dessert.

"So this is common?" Helena asked, resigned.

Adam nodded. "She doesn't like this work," he said, defending her. "Besides, she—well, she's no kitchen girl. She says she wants to be a pianist. I'm sure she will be someday, pretty as she is."

"I'm no kitchen girl either," Sonia, a young woman who helped the cook, retorted. "I wanted to be a doctor. There's isn't much chance of that now. One could still start studying at my age, of course. I haven't completely given up hope. For a career as a pianist, though, you have to start young and practice, practice, practice. Every day, for hours on end. I can't imagine that much diligence in our little Luzyna."

"She did practice quite a lot before," explained Helena, annoyed with herself for defending her sister. In truth, she agreed with Sonia. Perhaps Luzyna dreamed of one day becoming a famous piano virtuoso, but she certainly wouldn't be willing to do the intensive work it would demand. "She was thrown off course."

The others laughed.

"We all were, dear," the cook answered, "and for most of us, starting again will be harder than for you young people. You still have possibilities. When the war is over, you could become anything."

Helena arched her brows. "Here?" she asked bitterly. "In Iran? Where we don't even speak the language? I'm trying to learn, yes, but it's terribly difficult. And I'm trying to train as a seamstress even though I haven't got the slightest talent for it. I doubt I'll ever be able to make a living with it. And Luzyna . . .'"

She quickly wiped a tear from her eye. The way things looked, Luzyna didn't intend to support herself. At least for the foreseeable future, Helena would have to continue being responsible for her.

"Luzyna wants to return to Poland," Adam, who seemed to know the girl best, announced. "As soon as the war is over."

"Yes, because she thinks everything there is the same as before," Helena confirmed despondently. "But if what they say is true, Europe has been destroyed. And even if our house still stands, Russians live there now. I don't think they'll let us just move back in."

"If I were younger, I'd go to New Zealand," said Sonia, still dreaming of her medical studies. Her voice was wistful.

"Where?" Helena and Adam asked it at the same time, but while the boy sounded as if he'd never heard of the country, excitement filled Helena's voice.

New Zealand? The name of the Polynesian island-state had never before come up in the context of war and flight.

"New Zealand. It's part of the British Empire," Sonia explained. "It's somewhere near Australia. Far, far away. And they're supposed to be taking in Polish refugees. My little sister is in the orphanage in Isfahan. She wrote me about it." The Polish exile government in Isfahan had organized a well-furnished orphanage for the children of deceased deportees. They had excellent schools and the best caretakers. Helena had been too old to be admitted, though, and Luzyna hadn't wanted to go alone. "There's an age limit, of course," Sonia continued. "But you two"—she pointed at Adam and Helena—"you'd likely be accepted. And Luzyna too. Just ask about it."

Helena was full of excitement on her way back to her barracks. New Zealand. Unlike Sonia and Adam, to her the country meant something. She could still recall packages covered with bright stamps, and letters in English, which her mother had translated with her. A friend of her father's, a German dentist, had fled to New Zealand right after Hitler seized power. As a Jew, he couldn't see a future for himself in Germany. In the years after his emigration, he'd shared his experiences in that new land with his European friends. The Grabowskis had read his letters with excitement. After the war started, when provisions ran low, they eagerly anticipated his packages filled with dried meat, fish, jars of preserves, and sweets for the children. Helena's mother had insisted that the girls thank him personally—a good opportunity to practice their English. Helena still had a rough idea of his address: Elizabeth Street, Wellington. The capital of his new country, according to Werner Neumann, was not unlike Lwów or Dusseldorf. He even mentioned theater and opera performances, warehouses, and a parliament building.

Naturally, contact was cut off when the Grabowskis were deported. But in Iran, where the refugees could listen to English radio broadcasts, Helena had always listened closely when the country was mentioned. She knew that, although New Zealand had sent troops to the war in Europe, there had been no bombing there. It sounded peaceful.

When Helena thought about New Zealand, she thought of shepherds in green pastures, brightly painted wooden houses, and kind people. Her "Uncle" Werner and his family had gotten their bearings there quickly. They had needed to learn English, but Helena already spoke the language quite well. It would be much simpler to find a job in New Zealand, or even to attend a university, than in Iran.

Helena's heart beat faster at the thought of perhaps even visiting the Neumanns if she could secure places for Luzyna and herself. She decided to ask the camp administration the next day—right after she had spoken with Luzyna.

✦

Helena steeled herself for a fight, only to be pleasantly surprised. Luzyna brought up the subject herself.

"Kaspar and I are going to New Zealand," she said as the sisters snuggled into their blankets that night. "Kaspar's going to open a car repair shop. There can't be that many there already. It's supposed to be all sheep and cows. Even Uncle Werner said so."

Helena furrowed her brow. She could hardly imagine that such a large and modern country as New Zealand wouldn't be motorized. And she didn't quite see Kaspar, who'd only been helping with camp vehicles for a few months, as the mechanic the country had been waiting for. She didn't particularly care about that, though. The main thing was that Luzyna was interested in going.

"You two already know how you're going to make this happen?" Helena asked cautiously.

Luzyna nodded enthusiastically. "Of course. Kaspar heard New Zealand wants to take in seven hundred refugees. They have to be orphans, but that's the only condition. Most of them will come from the orphanage in Isfahan, but we can also apply with Dr. Virchow. We just have to go see her. She's putting a list together."

❧❀ ❀❧

Dr. Virchow, a medical doctor employed by the Polish exile government, was responsible for the children in the camps around Tehran. She organized their health care as well as coordinating the schools and educational opportunities. Helena had already dealt with her on several occasions, when she'd registered for the sewing course and for Persian lessons. She had also applied to be an English teacher, though she was turned down because of her age. Dr. Virchow had decided kindly that Helena should concentrate on recovering from the strain of the journey and imprisonment in Siberia. After a year, they would discuss it again.

In any case, Helena didn't fear the doctor—although she could not believe that simply showing up would suffice to get a place on the list of the orphans bound for New Zealand. There would probably be a health exam, and English proficiency might play a role as well. Still, Helena had high hopes for both Luzyna's and her own prospects. True, her sister didn't speak English as well as she did, but she was still better than most of the people in the camp. And they were both healthy. The doctor herself had told them that repeatedly.

"You wouldn't mind my coming along, would you?" Helena finally asked after listening to her sister go on and on about her and Kaspar's rosy future at the other end of the world.

Luzyna smiled, leaned over, and hugged her. "I'm not going anywhere without you," she declared.

Her words warmed Helena's heart, whether Luzyna meant them or not.

❧❀ ❀❧

The next morning, the sisters met Kaspar in front of the camp administration offices. Luzyna was skipping kitchen work again—but this time with Helena's blessing. Kaspar hadn't just slipped away, either, having asked the manager of the camp's garage for the time off. The lanky, brown-haired young man greeted Luzyna as if they hadn't seen each other in months. Helena was embarrassed watching them hug and kiss in public. But none of the handful of other children waiting for Dr. Virchow paid any attention to them. There were three boys and two girls who Helena guessed were between fourteen and sixteen years old. One of the girls held a younger sister by the hand who stared at Luzyna and Kaspar with big eyes and giggled.

"What are you looking at?" Kaspar yelled at her.

He was short-tempered and unkind. Helena had experienced that herself. He was only different with Luzyna.

The little girl looked down, wounded. Her older sister seemed to want to say something, but just then her name was called. She pulled her sister along into Dr. Virchow's office, and ten minutes later they came back out. Luzyna was next. She walked in at ease and came back out after a short time.

"She wanted to know if I'd heard of New Zealand before and how I imagined the country. And if I'm in an English course. I told her I can already speak English and that we have relatives in New Zealand." Helena sucked in air sharply at the lie, but she had to admit that Luzyna's fibbing about the Neumanns must raise their chances. "And then she asked me if my parents were dead. I mean, did I know for sure? If the parents are just missing, they don't want to send the children so far away." Luzyna wiped a tear away. "Well, there's no doubt for us."

After the two boys, it was Helena's turn. Dr. Virchow smiled at her amiably.

"I believe we know each other, don't we?" the doctor greeted her. "You're taking a few different classes, and you, you're the girl who speaks fluent English, right?"

Helena nodded. "My mother was an English teacher," she explained. "I'm sure my sister already told you. Luzyna Grabowski. She was just here."

Dr. Virchow cast a glance at her files. "Oh yes, the blonde girl. I didn't realize she was your sister. Grabowski is a common name. Luzyna made a very good impression on me. And of course, you would be a good candidate for emigration. Only, I'm afraid . . . we can't recommend you."

Helena felt like she had stumbled and fallen in a dark hole.

"But, but why not?" she stammered. "There . . . I thought there were seven hundred places, aren't there?"

Dr. Virchow nodded. "For children and youths between six and seventeen years old. Your sister just makes it, Helena. And if you were still seventeen, I would try to recommend you, if only to not separate sisters. But you're almost nineteen. I'm so sorry, Helena."

Helena bit her lip. "But you will take Luzyna?" she asked with a choked voice.

"Yes, I'll be happy to recommend your sister," the doctor confirmed. "She seems like a good fit to me, and it would be a great opportunity for her. She'll have to agree. We won't force anyone. If you want what's best for her, tell her to go. A whole new life awaits these children there." Dr. Virchow played with her pen holder. "I almost envy them," she said softly. "They'll escape the war and the hard times afterward that await the rest of us. We'll have to build Europe up again from rubble, and I'm afraid Russia and the Western powers will carve it up between them. If they disagree about it, there might be another war right after. But in New Zealand, no destruction, no dangers, and fantastic possibilities, particularly for young women. Universities there are open to women. They've had the right to vote for fifty years. It's certainly not paradise, Helena, but it's the best thing that could happen to your sister."

Helena held back a sob. She heard her mother's voice again: *Luzyna deserves better.* It seemed Maria's dreams for her younger daughter would come true after all.

"I'll make sure she understands," Helen said woodenly. "Thank you, Dr. Virchow. Oh, and when Kaspar Jablonski presents himself . . . if you care about sending Luzyna, don't tell him that he's too old. Let them believe they can stay together. They're so in love, Luzyna would throw everything away for him."

Luzyna didn't learn of Helena's rejection until it was too late. Until then, Helena concealed her disappointment from her sister, crying silently on her pallet after Luzyna was asleep, or while she was sewing, spoiling her work with tear stains. At least, she told herself bitterly, she would only need to support herself. She would no longer be responsible for Luzyna. Helena felt guilty because it came as something of a relief.

When the list of the selected children was posted, although Helena had, deep down, hoped for a miracle, she found neither her nor Kaspar's name on it. Luzyna, however, was among the fifteen orphans from the Tehran camp who would be leaving ten days later. Luzyna's reaction was exactly what Helena expected.

"Admit it! You knew!" the girl screamed at her when Helena didn't look sufficiently surprised. "You knew that they wouldn't take Kaspar, but you didn't say anything because you want to get rid of me!"

Luzyna seemed less concerned that Helena wasn't on the list than her earlier assurances had suggested she would be. Helena was hurt but didn't let it show. She had to be careful to calm Luzyna so she wouldn't run straight to the administration and have herself removed from the list. That meant under no circumstances robbing her of the hope of being with Kaspar.

"Yes, I knew," Helena admitted. "But the age limit only applies to this trip, not for general emigration. Kaspar and I will come later. Dr. Virchow expressly encouraged us." Indeed, Kaspar had come from the doctor's office in high hopes. She had assured him that in New Zealand there were good opportunities for young, entrepreneurial immigrants. The country would be open to receiving him, whether he went with the group of émigré children or not. "And you couldn't just do whatever you wanted right away anyway, even if you traveled with Kaspar," Helena continued. "Dr. Virchow said you won't just be left on your own in Wellington Harbour. There's a transition camp and vocational school to attend first."

"I don't want to go to school." Luzyna had worked herself into a frenzy. "And Kaspar doesn't either."

Helena forced herself to be patient. "Of course!" she said. "But he can't simply open a mechanic's shop right away. And you two couldn't marry anyway; you're too young."

"You can marry at sixteen," Luzyna crowed—in Iran, she had heard, people sometimes married their girls off as children.

"Not in New Zealand." Helena had investigated this with the help of Dr. Virchow. "There you have to wait until you're seventeen, and then only with permission of your guardian. That will be someone from the camp administration, but they won't give it right away. They're not taking you to New Zealand as a bride but as part of the program for war orphans. Luzyna, you have to accept it: the way you two imagined it isn't going to happen. But he'll come soon after you, get set up first without a family, and then he'll get you from Pahiatua."

Luzyna sniffled. "Only if he promises me." She blew her nose, obviously soothed.

Helena took her in her arms. "Of course he will," she assured her sister. "If he loves you."

"Of course he loves me." Luzyna's sadness gave way to anger again. "You'll see. Kaspar will be there even before me."

Helena nodded, trying not to look skeptical. Kaspar would certainly promise, but Helena was convinced that the young man didn't even really know where New Zealand was. He didn't speak a word of English either, and had no savings. Without the program for war orphans, Kaspar Jablonski would never make it to New Zealand. She just had to make sure that neither he nor her sister realized that in the next ten days.

3

In the final days before Luzyna's departure, Helena hardly knew what to do with herself. Despite Helena's excitement, Luzyna was as calm as though she was merely going to Tehran. She made no effort to pack or prepare in any way, and she laughed when Helena told her to do so.

"Helena, I own precisely two dresses, two sets of underwear, one handkerchief, a bar of soap, a toothbrush, and a wool blanket. I can pack all that in five minutes."

"Maybe you should take one of my dresses," Helena offered. "My dark red dress is less worn than your blue one."

Luzyna rolled her eyes. "But that's a Sunday dress," she said. "You can't send that with me. They'll probably give us new clothes in the camp anyway."

"I don't need a Sunday dress," insisted Helena. "But you should be well dressed on the way too. Maybe we can trade something for a shawl too, so you won't freeze. You'll mostly be traveling by sea after all, and you remember how cold it was on the ship from Krasnovodsk to Pahlavi." Crossing the Caspian Sea had been a nightmare.

"We were coming from Siberia," said Luzyna with a laugh. "This time we're headed south, according to Dr. Virchow."

The busy doctor held a presentation every evening where she showed photographs of their future homeland. Luzyna's interest was lukewarm; Helena wasn't certain Luzyna would even have gone had Dr. Virchow not permitted her to bring her and Kaspar along. Kaspar enjoyed the presentations, although Helena suspected the slide projector the military had left behind interested him more than the information. Kaspar was excited by this little marvel and ingratiated himself on the second day by taking over the operation of the device.

What the doctor said seemed to go over his head—maybe for the best, Helena thought. Otherwise he might have realized how far away New Zealand was, and how hard it was to get there. One couldn't simply board a ship in Tehran and arrive in Wellington. The group would go overland first to India. The more Helena learned about it, the more her own hopes of someday following Luzyna faded. The journey would take them through several countries, and the bus and train tickets must have cost a fortune. At the same time, Helena's longing grew with every moment she spent listening to the doctor and with every slide cast on the wall. The natural wonders of Luzyna's new homeland amazed Helena: fern forests, volcanoes, hot springs, snow-capped mountains, palm groves, fish-filled streams and lakes, and seemingly endless farmland. And unblemished cities that looked clean and comfortable. The young immigrants might even be allowed to attend one of the excellent universities.

Helena could have lost herself in the dreaming about it all, but she forced herself to be realistic. She made Luzyna try on pieces of her clothing and, with a stitch here and a tuck there, tried to make them more attractive. With a guilty conscience she stole fabric from the tailor's shop and exchanged it for a shawl, which would keep Luzyna warm and, moreover, looked very pretty with the dark red dress. Helena constantly spoke English with her and was shocked by how much her younger sister had forgotten in Siberia. Helena did her best to help her regain her

English, and pressed her to memorize the Neumanns' address. She was fairly certain the city and street were right, but she couldn't recall the house number. Nevertheless, she decided to write to her father's friend. She told her "uncle" what had happened to her family and asked him to look after Luzyna. As she wrote, she allowed herself to dream that the Neumanns would be so moved by the Grabowskis' story that they would immediately send Helena the money for the journey, in order to reunite the sisters.

Meanwhile, Helena and the other refugees followed the developments in far-off Europe. The Allies had succeeded in penetrating the western German front, and they now hoped to push quickly through northern France. Their goal was Paris and, ultimately, Berlin. German defeat was now only a question of time.

Finally, the day of their departure arrived. The young refugees were told to be ready on the exercise grounds in the middle of camp by ten in the morning. A truck would take them to Isfahan, where they would spend a night in the orphanage. From there they would begin the journey properly the next day: first by truck, then by train to Bombay; and from Bombay by ship to Wellington.

At half past nine, Helena was already waiting with Luzyna's luggage, while her sister went to say her good-byes to Kaspar. The yard slowly filled, and the other children were impatient with excitement: like Helena, they'd come early. The sun was already peeking over the Alborz Mountains—it was warm, and the waiting was pleasant. The little ones played; the older children talked and kept an eye out so their younger siblings didn't wander off. Helena stood there on pins and needles. Where in heaven's name was Luzyna? Helena looked over and over again at the clock on the camp's main building and forced herself to be calm. It was still early—Luzyna had twenty-five minutes. Then twenty, then fifteen. At five to ten everyone else was there. A young woman Helena didn't know began crossing names off her list. At ten sharp the truck drove onto the grounds.

Helena thought feverishly. Kaspar and Luzyna were probably exchanging intimate kisses and embraces and assuring each other for the hundredth time that this was only a temporary separation. Luzyna must have forgotten to keep an eye on the time—or she was counting on Helena fetching her. That was exactly what Helena would have to do now. She knew very well where they were likely to be: there was a shed behind the mechanic shop, which gave them some privacy. But to get there and back she would need at least ten minutes. And the young woman with the list was already calling Luzyna's name, while the other young émigrés climbed into the back of the truck. Helena would have to ask both her and the driver to wait for Luzyna.

She grabbed her sister's bag and walked toward the truck. Her heart beat heavily. She loved Luzyna, but she hated always having to make excuses, to apologize, and even to lie for her.

And then reluctance and exhaustion gave way to anger. She was tired of always holding herself back, sacrificing for a girl who didn't appreciate it. Luzyna felt entitled to everything Helena did for her, and she certainly hadn't thanked her for helping her get this once-in-a-lifetime opportunity, which was now slipping away. Helena could picture her sullen face, could hear her whining: "I'm coming, I'm coming. Don't be so bossy." Luzyna would drag her feet and then put on an apologetic smile, wrapping the young administrator and driver around her little finger in no time.

Helena clenched her teeth. She had just reached the truck. The administrator gave her a quick glance.

"Grabowski, Luzyna?" she asked, and raised her pen to cross off the name. Helena opened her mouth, seeking the words to explain.

"Luzyna Grabowski?" the woman repeated impatiently and gestured for Helena to hurry up and get in the truck.

Helena swallowed. Her thoughts fought with one another.

"Yes," she said softly. The blood rushed in her ears. "Yes."

As though in a trance, Helena clambered into the back of the truck. A boy held out his hand to help her in; no one seemed to have any objections. Helena could hardly believe that none of these young people knew Luzyna. Or perhaps they hadn't been paying attention when her name was called. Or they had never taken an interest in Kaspar Jablonski's pretty girlfriend. Certainly, it was to Helena's benefit that her sister had never gone to school or taken any courses.

A girl smiled at Helena—they had seen each other before in the waiting room but hadn't introduced themselves. None of the other émigrés knew Helena by name: no one from her sewing class or Persian class was there.

"I'm Natalia," said the girl.

Helena cleared her throat. "Lu-Luzyna."

A shudder went through the heavy truck as the driver turned on the engine. Helena looked across the grounds. Her heart pounded against her chest. If Luzyna appeared now, Helena could still undo everything.

Luzyna didn't appear. Even as the truck began to move and the émigrés waved at those staying behind, Helena couldn't see her sister anywhere. The truck drove down the main street of the camp and past the garage—and then, at that moment, Luzyna and Kaspar ran out from behind the shed. Apparently they'd just noticed that the clock had long since struck ten.

Shocked, Luzyna stared at the back of the truck as it passed them. She and Kaspar waved, trying to stop the truck. But the driver took these for good-byes. He honked, pleased. The children cheered.

Luzyna's shouts were drowned out, but Helena could see that Luzyna was calling her name. She had seen her, had seen that Helena had taken her place. The expression on her face was indescribable: astonishment; outrage; incredulity at the betrayal, at the broken promises.

For one reckless moment, Helena felt a wild joy. She had taken her revenge. Luzyna finally knew what it felt like to be discarded. She recovered quickly, though, seized by cold horror at herself. What was she doing? Luzyna was her responsibility. It was her duty to withstand everything, and to sacrifice herself for her sister, who deserved something better. She couldn't leave her behind here. What would their mother have said?

Helena stood up, waved, tried to push herself forward.

"Stop! We have to stop. We—"

"Hey, are you crazy? Sit down. You're going to fall off the truck." Natalia pulled her back down beside her.

"No! I have to . . . we have to . . . my sister."

Helena pounded against the driver's compartment, but the young Iranian driver took no notice.

"Stop it. We're not going to stop now," said a boy, seizing her arm firmly. "If you forgot something, you'll have to tell them in Isfahan. They're supposed to be nice there. I'm sure they'll be able to help you."

Helena's helpless sobs were drowned out by the general joyful laughter.

As the truck struggled over the dusty, winding mountain roads and then along wider paths through date plantations and olive groves, Helena tried to relax. Of course the matter could still be handled. For the first few miles, she expected a car to appear behind the truck at any moment. She thoroughly trusted Luzyna to explain Helena's deceit to the camp administration and to organize a chase as well as the exchange of the sisters. Kaspar, too, could surely mobilize someone. Perhaps the garage manager would even give him a vehicle to drive himself.

But nothing happened that evening. They arrived at Isfahan tired and worn from the long journey over pitted roads, but the sight of the orphanage revived their spirits. It really was a little paradise. The dormitory and school buildings were surrounded by tropical gardens. Helena felt as though she had been transported into a story from the *Thousand and One Nights*. The buildings looked inviting and friendly; the children greeted the new arrivals with a happy song in Polish. They seemed well fed and wore clean school uniforms.

In the schoolyard, Polish and Iranian flags fluttered in the breeze. Caretakers welcomed the émigrés. A young man checked their names off a list without reacting at all when Helena once more presented herself as Luzyna. Helena was directed to a room with Natalia and her two younger siblings, and she settled in with a heavy heart. Luzyna hadn't betrayed her, so it was up to her to turn herself in.

Though she was hungry, she couldn't bring herself to eat much of the delicious food served in the dining hall. She had long since come to regret what she had done, but should she report herself? The thoughts that had already occupied her on the trip passed through her mind yet again. Would it help Luzyna if she told someone? The journey was already planned on a strict schedule. Would they delay that for a single girl's sake? And would Luzyna even want that? True, she had looked upset that Helena left her behind, but she had never really wanted anything more than to stay with her Kaspar.

Helena berated herself. What Luzyna wanted wasn't the issue. She had to do what was best for her younger sister. Helena had promised her mother that. And a young marriage to an idiot like Kaspar Jablonski was most certainly not the best thing for her.

Helena realized Natalia had been speaking to her, and apologized for not listening. She would have to start behaving normally if she didn't want to be discovered. Her head spun. On the one hand, she wanted to give herself up; on the other she wanted desperately to continue on the journey. On the one hand were her obligations to Luzyna; on the other was the irresistible desire to leave everything behind. A new country, a new life.

"I'm just so excited about New Zealand," Natalia repeated.

Helena forced herself to smile, and simply told the truth. "Me too."

4

The next day, though Helena's guilt hadn't abated, her fear of discovery vanished. During the night, more trucks of children from near Tehran had arrived. They must have departed later than the truck from Helena and Luzyna's camp. If Luzyna had spoken up, surely an exchange of the sisters could have been organized. Helena was now certain that Luzyna hadn't betrayed her, and the chance of being discovered during roll call had also lessened. Now that there were so many other refugees, as well as thirty guardians, packed into twenty buses in all, no one would compare their faces with their papers. At least no one would be particularly careful about it. Helena alone could end her journey now by coming forward, and despite all the guilt, she couldn't bring herself to do it.

She suppressed her dark thoughts and found a place beside Natalia on the bus. The two young women peered curiously out the window. First the buses crossed the Zayanderud river valley—a verdant, lush landscape. They could just make out the city of Isfahan at the foot of the Zagros Mountains. The orphanage lay a bit outside the city, and the children there had visited it often. By their accounts, it was a beautiful city, but Helena didn't mourn the missing out on the mosques and parks. She imagined she would have found Isfahan as strange and unsettling as Tehran. The villages they passed through that could be seen from the road also seemed strange to her. The buildings were mostly low and made of mud brick. Between the houses chickens, goats, cattle, and donkeys wandered freely. Everyone wore wide pants and long shirts that looked like pajamas, to which the women added veils and the men turbans. Helena supposed that not much had changed here in centuries. Iran was complex and beautiful, but it was not her world. When Helena thought of farming villages, she pictured gabled houses with stables and vegetable gardens.

Natalia nodded when she said this, and described how her family had been driven from just such a farm in Poland. As a child, she had helped care for the animals and hoped to be taken in on a farm in New Zealand. She didn't speak much English yet. She had only just started a class in the camp and was delighted to learn that Helena spoke the language fluently. During the rest of the journey, she insisted on practicing with Helena, and the time passed quickly. Everyone was happy that the route led mostly over level roads. The journeys over the mountains from Pahlavi to Tehran two years before and from Tehran to Isfahan the previous day had been horrible.

No one bothered to tell them where they were or how far they had yet to go. As they continued south over the following days, Natalia's little sister Katarina suffered from motion sickness, and the lodgings were bare and overcrowded, which didn't make things easier. And it grew hotter and hotter the farther south they went. At times, it was so hot in the bus that they could hardly breathe. Many children believed they would drive all the way to New Zealand, though Helena knew they would be taking a ship from Bombay.

Dr. Virchow had told her charges that they would be crossing many Indian provinces along the way, and Helena wondered if there would be border checkpoints at each. But the buses were only stopped briefly during their entrance into British India, and the mostly British border guards had no intention of examining seven hundred passports. They merely expressed their sympathies to the refugees, wished the children luck in New Zealand—which also belonged to the British Empire—and let the convoy through.

The fertile plains of Iran gave way to desert. Finally the emigrants' bus trip ended at a dusty train station in a large city, which to Katarina's delight was called Karachi, controlled by British troops.

"It sounds fun!" The little girl laughed, happy to leave the bus. Katarina did not get as sick in trains.

Helena, on the other hand, liked the bus better. The train compartments were dingy and crowded, the air was stuffy, and they never stopped, not even at night. The only food was the greasy sandwiches their caretakers had packed. They had to sleep in their seats or stretched out on the compartment floor or in the hall. It all reminded Helena of the cramped ship between Krasnovodsk and Bandar-e Pahlavi—except then they had been freezing, and now everyone was drenched in sweat. This did nothing for the air in the compartments. It reeked of unwashed bodies and human waste—the toilets were hopelessly dirty after the first day of the journey.

At some point they reached a provincial border and had to switch to a new train. It was night, and their papers were not checked there either. The young people from their camp were mostly left to their themselves during the journey. No young child was traveling alone, of course; most of the children were between thirteen and sixteen. A few exceptions, like Natalia's little siblings, were entrusted to the care of their older siblings. But orphanages had been attached to the other camps in Tehran and Isfahan, and many children between six and twelve had been chosen from them for the journey. They were assigned to adult supervisors, and these overworked men and women were constantly counting their little wards.

Helena was almost too exhausted to still feel anxious and guilty when the train finally entered the Bombay station. This massive city, too, was a British colony—the British military had sent the buses waiting for the children. Helena and the others were so tired and overwhelmed that they hardly noticed the big houses, the overflowing streets, and the new sounds and smells of the city. But everything here was colorful. Natalia admired the palm trees, and Katarina pointed excitedly at the bright oxcarts on the streets. Helena dimly recalled Dr. Virchow's stories about how in temples, many different gods were honored. In Iran she had found it all very enticing, but now she just wished she were in bed. Perhaps the ship to New Zealand wouldn't be so cramped.

To their surprise, the buses didn't take the young travelers directly to the harbor that evening, but to the British barracks instead. There they received stew, showers, and cots to stretch out on. Many of the children fell asleep immediately, so completely exhausted they didn't even manage to eat. Helena and Natalia, however, forced themselves to wash thoroughly before going to bed. When she finally pulled her covers over her, Helena felt better than she had in a long time. Luzyna, she thought as she fell asleep, wouldn't have enjoyed this journey at all. Perhaps it was all right that Helena had spared her. For the first time since leaving, Helena slept without nightmares.

⭒❧ ❧⭒

Well rested and happy, Helena awoke the next morning to breakfast porridge and drank tea with the others. First a bus ride through the exciting city, and then they would finally be on their way toward Polynesia. She didn't imagine that her past would finally catch up to her here.

As the refugees arrived at the pier, there were again men and women crossing out names from lists. A young man with a full head of brown hair and a round face seemed familiar to Helena. He of all people called her new name.

"Luzyna Grabowski?"

The young man let his gaze fall on the group of waiting emigrants.

"Here."

Helena announced herself firmly. It had become habit to listen for her sister's name. She stepped forward naturally and looked into alert brown eyes.

"You're not Luzyna," hissed the man.

Helena went pale. "I am. I am, of course I am. Who . . . who else would I be? I . . ."

The man leered at her. "Don't lie to me; you're not Luzyna. You're . . . oh yeah, I remember now, you're her sister. The hen who was always chasing her around the ship."

"On . . . on what ship?" Helena laughed nervously.

She looked around anxiously, but so far her conversation with the man hadn't attracted any attention. Natalia was busy with her siblings. The others were admiring the massive ship that was ready to receive them: the *General George M. Randall*, an American troop transport vessel.

"On the freighter, of course." The young man spoke quickly and quietly. That gave Helena hope. Maybe he wouldn't betray her. "You know, from Krasnovodsk to Pahlavi. You don't remember? We were together in Vorkuta. But then you didn't notice anyone but your sister. No eyes for anyone else. So? What's the story with Luzyna? Why are you traveling with her papers? Is she dead?"

Helena shook her head. "No, no, she's fine. She . . . she just didn't want to go to New Zealand. I did though, very much. I . . . I'm just a little too old. I . . . please, I don't know your name. Please, please don't turn me in. It would be too late for Luzyna now anyway."

She looked at him beseechingly, but saw in him neither sympathy nor understanding, just a glimmer of triumph.

"Witold," the man introduced himself. "Witold Oblonski. I'm one of the attendants. I'm a teacher. You'll see, on the ship." His voice was almost threatening. Or inviting?

Helena grew hopeful. "Then you won't report me, sir?" she whispered.

Oblonski grinned and looked Helena over from head to foot. "You can call me Witold, *Luzyna*." He emphasized the name sarcastically. "And no, I won't turn you in. As long as you show a little . . . gratitude."

Helena creased her brow.

"Gratitude? What . . . what do you mean by that?"

"Well, think about it, Luzy." Witold laughed cruelly. "I have to say, the real Luzyna wouldn't be so slow."

Helena bit her lip. She understood. "Was there something between you and Luzyna?" But that couldn't be. Luzyna had barely been fourteen on the crossing from Siberia to Iran.

Witold grinned. "Like I said, I'll be seeing you," he said, and ticked Luzyna's name off the list. "I'll find you, Luzy."

Helena sighed as she walked up the gangplank. At least she had made it on board, even if fear and doubt gnawed at her again.

She followed Natalia and the younger children through the halls of the ship looking for their quarters, but her mind was elsewhere. She tried to remember Siberia. True, she had rarely looked at the faces of the people who worked with her and her parents in the chain gang. Why would she? They were all wrapped up against the cold, and the prisoners, at least those who had family in the camp, hadn't been concerned with making friends. It was hard enough to watch your family die.

But it suddenly occurred to Helena how she knew Witold Oblonski. His name had come up in rare conversations among the camp workers—usually with a warning attached. The young man had lied and betrayed his way into being the overseer's favorite, often taking prisoners' minor infractions to the camp administration. He was a cruel, unpleasant man who now was in a position to reveal Helena's deception. Helena trembled to think what he would ask of her, but one thing was clear: she couldn't refuse.

The *General Randall* proved considerably more comfortable than the rust bucket they had taken to Iran. The American troop transport vessel had multiple decks, sufficient toilets, kitchens, and quarters to bring hundreds of soldiers to their deployments. Helena shared a cabin with Natalia, her two siblings, and two other girls. With six it was cramped, but they all had their own comfortable berths with clean bedding, and during the day they could go above deck whenever they wanted. They were even allowed to stand at the railing during departure and have a last look at Bombay. Only then did Helena realize how gigantic the city truly was, spread across the hills of Salsette Island. Bombay had been separated from the mainland by a bay, but they had built a dam and drained it, and Bombay now was home to millions of people.

Helena cursed her luck. Here, where there was so much anonymity, she had encountered the one cruel man who could recognize her. She noted bitterly that the *General Randall* was massive too. If Oblonski had not been specifically assigned to checking the lists, she would have been no more likely to encounter him than on the previous leg of the journey. As it happened, he didn't waste much time in demanding his reward.

The refugees got their food from the kitchen and ate it in their cabins. Helena felt safe from him for the day, seeing as it was almost bedtime. As Helena was bringing the dishes back to the kitchen, Witold stepped out from where he had lain in wait for her in the hallway between the kitchen and her cabin. She jumped.

"A very nice evening to you, Luzy."

Helena bit her lip. "What do you want?" she asked sharply. It was supposed to sound annoyed, at least. In truth, it just sounded anxious.

Witold didn't answer, but grinned and gestured for her to follow him above deck. At this time it was quiet there. The soldiers who served on the *General Randall* were eating, and the attendants did not allow the Polish children to leave their cabins after dark.

"You'll see in just a moment, my dear Luzyna," Witold said with a honeyed voice, pulling Helena into the shadow of a lifeboat.

"Helena," she corrected him, her voice catching. "My name is Helena. And, and I'm sorry. I, of course, I didn't mean to deceive anyone. I . . ."

Witold smirked. "Of course not. You're a good girl. I remember that from our last trip. I didn't try anything with you, but didn't Oleg ask?"

Helena frowned, but then recalled a scrawny, pimply, ferret-faced boy who had somehow managed to land a spot as a kitchen helper on the crossing from Siberia to Iran. He had indeed once offered to cut her a bigger slice of bread if she would be good to him. Helena hadn't really taken that seriously.

"Little Luzyna had fewer compunctions," Witold said.

Helena looked at him, horrified. "You mean . . . you took advantage of her? You . . . Luzyna gave herself to you for a piece of bread?"

Witold laughed. "Well, let's not exaggerate. Don't get so worked up. Your pretty little sister didn't lose her cherry to me, at least. She was still young back then. And we boys weren't in great shape after our time in the camp. Just a kiss, and a little game with skilled hands." He grabbed himself between the legs. "Little Luzy wasn't too good to do that."

Helena was disgusted. Luzyna had probably had no idea what she was doing.

"So then, you want me to kiss you?" she asked innocently.

Witold snorted. "Kiss? No, Helena, you won't get off that easily. After all, you're grown, aren't you? A woman, not a little girl. And I am a man."

"How did you even get this position?" asked Helena, hoping to distract him. "A man like you, why are you an attendant here?"

Witold sneered. "I'm a teacher, my little Helena, taught at the middle school in Białystok, mathematics and geography. I had just finished studying to teach high school when the Russians came. Too bad; the high school was full of cute girls too, who would gladly have shown gratitude for a better math grade."

"You . . . you're . . ." Helena wanted to curse him, but couldn't find the words.

"A pig, is that it?" Witold offered, laughing. "I've heard that before. You girls aren't very imaginative. But thanks, I take it as a compliment. A wild boar. Who wouldn't take that as a compliment? And now, Helena my sweet, take off your clothes. Quickly." His voice had become hard.

Helena stared at him in shock. "I'm supposed to take off my clothes? Here?"

Witold nodded. "I picked this spot especially," he explained, completely at ease. "I like to see what I'm getting. Doing things fast, with the skirt pulled up in the school hall, that's no fun. I like it better slow, and it's better for you that way too. We'll get in one of the lifeboats; no one will see us there. Hurry up, Helena. Before your little friends miss you and start looking."

Helena felt as though she had turned to stone, but she let Witold push her into one of the boats. He quickly opened his fly, breathing faster and faster. She had to hastily take off her dress before he could yank it down. She hoped he would be satisfied to see her standing in front of him in her underwear and stockings, but he insisted on seeing her completely naked. As Helena pulled her undershirt over her head, tears streaked her cheeks. She was afraid, and felt dirty already, and in spite of everything could not stop feeling that she deserved everything that was happening to her. She thought of Luzyna's disappointed, shocked last look, and the memory was almost worse than the look in Witold's glassy eyes as he examined her naked body carefully.

"A little thin," he said. "Lie down."

Helena lowered herself down, trying hopelessly to find a position between the benches that didn't hurt. The planks were hard, and when Witold threw himself on her, her back slammed against them. He wasn't fully undressed, had just pulled down his pants. Helena saw his erect member in the moonlight. It seemed monstrous: a disgusting, quivering club. She felt like vomiting, but her disgust was replaced by pain. She almost screamed when he pushed into her without a word, but Witold covered her mouth with a brutal kiss. The pain in her abdomen was as hellish as the violation. Witold wore himself out on her, and Helena felt something wet between her legs. Was she bleeding? Once more, Helena was overcome by nausea, as Witold finished with her and warm liquid rushed into her and trickled out when Witold finally withdrew himself. Her naked back hurt. The next day it would be bruised blue and green. Helena could hardly get up when Witold finally got off of her, after what felt like an eternity. Her whole body burned with horror and pain.

Witold looked at her bruised back while she slowly pulled her shirt back on.

"Bring a blanket with you next time," he said.

With that, he turned, zipped up his pants, and disappeared into the darkness.

5

T he passage from Bombay to Wellington became a private hell for Helena. Every single day Witold demanded his payment, and Helena couldn't escape him. She tried, of course, to avoid the public rooms after dark, but it would draw attention if she always refused to take the dishes back. Besides, Witold liked to find her during the day, adding the fear of being seen to her shame and humiliation. This didn't seem to concern Witold, though; he was shameless. Once, Helena did manage to escape him for a whole day, but he had her summoned to him in the evening. Then she had to come up with a believable story about what the attendant wanted. She managed a halfway plausible story, but she didn't want to risk her reputation again.

Still, there were moments, particularly in the bright light of day, when everything seemed peaceful: children playing on deck, Natalia entranced by the dolphins frolicking around the ship. In these moments, logistical concerns took the place of the panic that dominated Helena's nights. She asked herself if Witold really posed enough of a threat to make this suffering worthwhile. After all, she was already on the way to New Zealand. They wouldn't send a young woman back by herself, and it would be just his word against hers. Witold's claim would be extremely difficult to investigate. Would anyone really bother to find out whether this girl was named Luzyna or Helena and was sixteen or eighteen?

Witold laughed mockingly when she finally summoned all her courage and flung these considerations at him.

"You are still far from being in New Zealand, my dear *Luzy*," he mocked. "Entry won't happen until Wellington, with strict passport control. Think about it, sweetheart. Do you really look so much like your sister that a border guard wouldn't notice if he looked closely? And then, dear *Luzy*, then you'll land in a New Zealand prison. Until the next ship leaves. They call it deportation custody. And where is the ship going? To China, maybe? Or do they ask for papers there too? Wake up, Helena. No country in the world will let you in with fake papers. So enough back talk. It's getting late. Take off your clothes."

Helena complied. That evening Witold thrust into her especially brutally, and she wept silently as she thought about her future. If it really was as Witold said, then he would be able to force her in the new camp in New Zealand too. He had her completely in his hands. Her only chance was to flee the camp as soon as possible and try to make her way in her new country.

The next day this thought, too, was put into perspective in the steady sunshine. Theoretically the threat might persist after entry, but in reality Witold would have to explain himself if he waited any longer to turn her in. Officials and the camp administration would ask questions, and while Helena would have to admit her deception, she would no longer need to remain silent about Witold's abuse. She decided she would be completely safe as soon as the entry formalities in New Zealand were behind her. Until then, she bore the daily rape in silence. She didn't dare to anger Witold further.

On November 1, 1944, the *General Randall* entered Wellington Harbour. It was a clear spring day. Helena already knew from the Neumann family's letters that seasons on this side of the world were exactly opposite—when it was summer in New Zealand, winter covered Poland. Still, it seemed unbelievable to her, almost miraculous, how green the hills were around the city and how the trees along the coastal promenade bloomed. Wellington, a rather small settlement for the capital of a country, spread out from the bay in a semicircle. The water was azure blue. Its color competed with that of the sky.

"A natural harbor," said one of the American matrons with whom Helena had practiced her English during the voyage.

Helena found the scene hopeful. The wind blew gently, the air was remarkably clear, and you could see all the way to the distant mountains. Although the entry formalities still lay before her, all her sorrows seemed to fall away at the sight of this new land. It did not seem to her that strict border guards awaited them. On the contrary, the other ships in the harbor greeted the *General Randall* with cheerful tooting, and Polish cries even drifted over from one of the steamers. The *Narvik*, a Polish ship, was anchored here, and the captain must have heard of their arrival.

The welcome committee at the pier, too, included Polish landsmen, alongside a group of New Zealand school children who sang while waving the New Zealand and Polish flags. The Polish envoy, Kazimierz Wodzicki, and his wife, Maria, waited on the docks. Even Peter Fraser, the prime minister of New Zealand himself, made an appearance and boarded the ship to greet the children. He greeted them in English, and then Wodzicki spoke a few moving words in their mother tongue. Wodzicki's wife didn't speak, but she took the first children who set foot on land comfortingly in her arms.

"I know you've suffered terrible things," she said, "but nothing more can happen to you here. This is a beautiful, peaceful country. You'll see. Everything will be good from now on."

Natalia smiled at Helena, and Helena returned the smile brightly. She was on the verge of happiness as she walked down the gangway into her new life. If only Luzyna were with her. Her guilt once again darkened her joy at having finally made it.

Because of course no one had thought of strict passport control. True, lists were once more crossed off, but this time it was a young woman who was responsible for Helena's group. She wasn't one of the Polish attendants but a New Zealander, and she spoke English. Helena immediately liked her. She was short and delicate and had freckles on her mischievous little nose. Her red hair fell over her back in countless frizzy strands. She had carelessly tied it at her nape and wore in place of a hat a sort of cap, a brash little beret, which seemed to dance on her locks. It suited her sailor-style dress.

"I'm Miranda," she introduced herself cheerfully and openly looked at the young émigrés. Helena thought she had never seen such shining green eyes before. "Miranda Biller. Does any one of you speak English? Or French? I, uh, can speak that too. Just not as well." She winked at them, embarrassed. She had probably received this position primarily because of her supposed French abilities. In Poland many more people spoke French than English.

Helena didn't want to draw attention to herself, but Natalia shoved her forward energetically. "Go," she whispered.

Helena curtsied shyly. "I have a rather good command of the English language," she said formally, adding, "Miss Biller."

Miranda Biller beamed at her. She seemed to be about Helena's age. "Call me Miranda," she corrected her. "We usually call each other by our first names here. At least among peers. Naturally, I wouldn't call Major Foxley by his given name . . . hmm, whatever it is. Well, or Mr. Sledzinski."

Miranda spoke very quickly. Helena had to strain to follow her English, and of course she had no idea who Major Foxley was, or

Mr. Sledzinski, whose name Miranda had completely mispronounced. Major Foxley turned out to be the commander of her refugee camp, and Mr. Sledzinski the delegate of the Polish exile government, the senior camp administration officials.

"Miranda." Helena repeated her young caretaker's name slowly, trying to pronounce it correctly.

Miranda corrected her amiably. "It's not simple, I know." She was understanding. "It's a strange name. But my brother's got it even worse. His name's Galahad. And you? What's your name?" She looked with interest at Helena.

"He—Luzyna." Helena blushed. Her real name had almost tumbled out at the friendly greeting.

"Luzyna, lovely! Not easy either though. Oh well, please tell the children, Luzyna, that we welcome them very, very cordially here. You'll be traveling by train to Pahiatua. The train station is nearby; we'll be walking there. As for the luggage, you don't have much, do you? Only what you're carrying? Good, then you can take it yourselves. And once again, we're happy you're here!"

Helena translated, and Miranda went ahead of them in the direction of the train platform. They could already see the two waiting trains. The path was lined with singing and flag-waving Wellingtonian school children, arranged by grade. Laughing and waving teachers supervised their charges. On the train platform, lunch bags were distributed. Little Katarina tried her first bubbly soda.

"No one will check our papers?" Helena asked Miranda anxiously after the young woman had come to some agreement with the other caretakers and directed her group to a train car.

She looked around the train station nervously for Witold, but did not see him anywhere. That was no surprise in all the chaos, but it frightened Helena a bit. If it became clear to him that he had no power over her anymore, would he betray her out of sheer cruelty?

Miranda shrugged her shoulders, uninterested. "No idea. They'll probably stamp something. Do you even have your passports on you, or were they already collected?"

"They were collected," Helena said. Indeed, they had turned in their passports in Iran.

"Then you don't need to worry any further," the New Zealander explained. "You'll get them back again sometime. Or new ones. Why is it so important to you? Do you mean to marry?" She giggled. "My mother eloped with my father when she was seventeen, and the story with his pass was really rather dramatic. I'll have to tell you sometime." Miranda seemed already to have chosen Helena for her friend. And apparently she had no idea how vital possessing a proper passport was in war-torn Europe.

With a charming mix of English, French, and gestures, Miranda organized her group of refugees into their compartments. "Your camp is in Pahiatua, just about a hundred miles from here," she informed Helena, and asked her to translate for the others. "Pahiatua is Maori and means 'gods' resting place.' But it's not like the spirits lie down to sleep there. It goes back to a Maori chief who was fleeing from enemies. His war god showed him the way there, where he was able to find refuge."

"And now God is sending us too," said Natalia devoutly.

Helena had noticed earlier that she was very religious. She repeated Natalia's remark for Miranda in English.

Miranda smiled. "What a nice thought. You could even talk about that with the Polish priest. There's one in the camp. And a church or chapel or whatever you call it. You're all Catholic, right? There're hardly any around here, just farther north where the French settled." Miranda seemed determined to impart the whole history of New Zealand to her charges as quickly as possible. Words just seemed to spill out of her, and as the train departed, she told Helena about Wellington. "It's one of the oldest settlements in New Zealand. The first Englishmen came in 1840, and they named the city after the Duke of Wellington. At first it was rather small, much smaller than Auckland. But twenty years later it became the capital. It's just more central than the other cities."

The train left the city, pulling them through a sweeping landscape, first just hilly, then becoming mountainous. Miranda spoke eagerly about the railroad construction: the Rimutaka Incline Railway, on which they were traveling, was a wonder of modern engineering. As they ascended, the view became more and more spectacular, while the bridges seemed more and more precipitous and the tunnels longer and longer. The train stopped in towns along the way, and each time there were children cheering on the platform.

"We've seen those children before!" Helena exclaimed.

"It's true, they're the same ones," Miranda said. "At least so far. But they won't let them come as far as Masterton. They're busing them from one train station to the next, to sing for you. It's all a little peculiar, but sweet, too, don't you think?"

"How nice!"

But Helena was too exhausted to feel glad, and even Miranda's friendly conversation was wearing her out. As the train left the mountains behind and continued through farmland, she nodded off, and when she woke, it was already afternoon.

"We're almost there," Miranda declared. "Pahiatua is the next station. I'm excited to see the camp. I've never been there." Natalia looked out the window, contentedly counting the sheep grazing on either side of the tracks. They passed neat little wooden farmhouses, complete with a horse in their pasture and a truck in the drive. "We live in Wellington," Miranda explained. "My dad's a professor at the university, and my mom writes books. Romance novels. My dad and brother think they're terrible, of course. But actually they're quite good. So sweet! People seem to like them, anyway."

"And is your brother in the army?" Helena asked. In Europe, every healthy young man was in the army.

Miranda shook her head. "No, he's in Greymouth, on the South Island. Our grandparents have coal mines there, and Gal studied mine engineering. Since coal mining is important to the war effort, he didn't get conscripted. I don't know what Gal thinks about it exactly, but my grandpa says that you can't put someone named Galahad in the army. Of course, my mother says that doesn't make any sense, because Galahad was a knight in King Arthur's court. Anyway, she's happy that he doesn't have to go. My cousin James is in the war, though. He didn't actually have to go either. His parents have a huge farm in the Canterbury Plains, which is just as important for the war effort. And his father didn't want him to join up. He was at Gallipoli, you see?"

Helena did not. She hadn't heard of World War I's Gallipoli; she'd been concerned with surviving this war.

But Miranda kept right on talking. "And he thinks there's no reason whatsoever to go to war. He thinks under any circumstances, war is wrong. James sees it differently. Because of Hitler, you know—you can't just let him do whatever he wants. Although I think for James it's more about flying. James is crazy about planes. We guess he's with the air force now."

"Guess?" asked Helena.

"James ran away a few months ago. In the middle of the night, as soon as he turned nineteen. He volunteered. And we haven't heard from him, probably because he's afraid his father could have him sent back. And he's not wrong. Uncle Jack's already called in some favors and sent men looking for him."

"Final stop: Pahiatua," the announcement interrupted, and Miranda sprang up.

"Did you hear? We're there," she announced. "Gather your things, and don't forget anything. We'll go the rest of the way by truck. It's not much farther, just a mile south of the city. And no need to rush, there's room for everyone!"

There was not only a new group of singing children but a convoy of trucks waiting for the refugees at the station. Miranda, with Helena translating for her, made sure everyone found a seat. It was then that she saw Witold again—and fear cut her to the quick. Her torturer sneered at her as he rode past in a truck full of children.

"See you around, Luzy," he mouthed.

Helena felt the words more than she heard them.

6

Helena and Natalia climbed into the last truck while Miranda chatted with some other girls. They were discussing female students who had volunteered for war duty to support the nation.

"I actually wanted to drive a streetcar," said Miranda. "I heard in Europe it's all women doing that now. One of the cable cars in Auckland, that's what I wanted. But apparently none of the conductors joined the army."

In New Zealand, the Polish girls learned, military service was voluntary: people here could choose whether to take part in the war. And Miranda and her friends didn't seem to be taking their part all that seriously. Helena thought she should be outraged. The horror and suffering of so many people were no more than distant stories for these protected young women. But in truth, she felt relief. If it hadn't been for her betrayal of Luzyna, Helena might have even hoped to forget her past in this peaceful land.

After passing through green, hilly country, the trucks drove through a gate reading "Polish Children's Camp." It felt as though they had been taken back to Poland before the war. Helena smiled to see streets with Polish names between inviting wooden houses. It looked nothing like the barracks they had spent the past few years in. There seemed to be no common sleeping rooms, there were lawns and playgrounds, and the fence around the camp was low and charming. The wooden gates had simple closing mechanisms, and Helena couldn't imagine anyone guarding them.

"Before this, it was an internment camp," Miranda said, without specifying who was kept there, or why, "and before that, a racing track."

Natalia was overjoyed. "It looks more like a village than a camp."

Helena nodded, astonished at the friendly reception. Inside the houses they found rooms with four beds, already freshly made, and each room had a vase full of colorful flowers.

"The women of Pahiatua did that," said Miranda. Like the other volunteers, she was housed in a similar room. "They formed a special committee to get everything ready for you. Well, first things first, settle in. There'll be food in the dining hall when you're done."

It turned out there were several dining halls, to accommodate all seven hundred of them, and Helena noted that Witold's group was assigned to a different one. That would make it harder for him to find excuses to see her. She sighed, relieved, feeling another weight lift from her. But as she got ready for bed she thought of Luzyna, and the weight of her guilt settled on her again. True, her sister would have complained about the trip, but she would have liked it here.

Pahiatua was a small country community. The farmhouses were scattered about, and the town held only a general store, a café, and a gas station. The refugees were allowed to go into town in their free time, but most preferred to wander the countryside. The area around the camp was a lovely place for the children to play. They explored the meadows and groves, waded through streams, and tried fishing. As long as they attended school, no one minded. Pahiatua was peaceful; there was no danger, and the children could hardly get lost. Natalia was fascinated by the landscape, learning the names of the strange bushes, trees, and birds. She still dreamed of life on a farm. For Helena, the school was a greater wonder than this new country's wildlife. There were an elementary, a middle, and a high school in the camp, and classes were held in Polish. After a short test, Helena found herself back in eighth grade. Very few of the other children had made it past that, since their education had ended abruptly with the war. Some had been in family camps in Russia with something like a school, but they had hardly learned anything there. And though Helena didn't stand out in general, she shone in class. She threw herself into natural sciences, which was her weakest subject. Her English, on the other hand, was very good, and her French was better than Miranda's. Miranda, Helena learned, had finished high school in Wellington and wanted to go to college but didn't know what she would study.

"Do you know what you want to do?" she asked Helena.

Helena could only shake her head. Before this her only goal had been to survive. Now, though, she thought about becoming a teacher like her mother. She even asked the camp administration if they could use her assistance with the younger children.

Mr. Sledzinski, though, declined just as kindly as Dr. Virchow had in Iran. "That's good of you, Luzyna, but you don't need to work here. Just go to school, and try to recover a bit. You're so thin and pale . . . maybe you should see the doctor. Why don't you stop by the nurse's office tomorrow?"

Helena was surprised. She thought she'd gained weight in the four weeks she'd been at the camp. Her dress seemed tight over her bust, anyway. And though she did often feel tired, she had thought it was because of all the new experiences, and the nightmares that had grown worse. Almost every night now in her dreams she saw Luzyna staring in shock at her in at the truck, and then felt Witold on her and heard his hideous laugh. She thought she had ended that horror.

Witold only approached Helena once in New Zealand—in a corner of the schoolyard. "I'd really like to see you again, Luzy." He grinned. "What d'you think? Want to take a walk with me this evening in the woods? It would be romantic, don't you think?" Helena's heart raced, but she thought of Miranda's confidence and fearlessness. Miranda wouldn't have let anyone get away with that. She would put Witold in his place. Helena inhaled sharply. "No, it wouldn't be romantic. It would be disgusting, like every other time," she replied. "Get lost, Witold. I've paid my debt. And don't threaten me again. Nobody here would buy some crazy story about mixed-up sisters. And don't touch me." She recoiled as he reached for her. And then she was struck with an idea worthy of Miranda Biller. To be rid of Witold once and for all, she would have to scare him. "I'll scream and say you reached under my skirt. Who do you think they'll believe, *sir*?"

From then on he left her alone. He'd started courting one of the New Zealanders, an English teacher. It surprised Helena, since she and Witold didn't even speak the same language. Miss Sherman was stocky and wore glasses, which accented the roundness of her face. She was kind, but Helena didn't think that he'd fallen in love with her because of her looks or personality.

She finally understood when Miranda gave back their passports one day after dinner.

"The camp administration apologizes for how long it took," Miranda explained. "At least now you all have your visas."

Natalia looked at her Polish passport, disappointed. "Not New . . ." Her English was still shaky. "Not New Zealand?"

Miranda frowned. "Well, you wouldn't be naturalized straight away," she said. "At least, that's not the plan, as far as I know. Why would they have made all the effort with the Polish caretakers and schools? If you were to become citizens, the emphasis would have been on learning English."

"So they'll send us back at some point?" Helena asked, in a choked voice. Dr. Virchow had led them to believe they could stay in New Zealand permanently.

"No one will simply throw you out," Major Foxley, the camp director, interjected into the conversation, kindly. He often stopped by during a meal to talk with the children and make sure everyone was happy. "When you're an adult, if you want to stay, to work, or to marry a New Zealander"—he winked at Helena—"then you'll be naturalized. But you should at least have the chance to return home after the war. You might have family there who misses you. We don't want to limit your options. For now, though, you are comfortable and safe. So don't you worry."

Helena finally understood what Witold was up to. He was here as a caretaker, not as part of the refugee contingent. The Polish exile government was probably paying his salary as a teacher and would bring him back to Poland when he wasn't needed here any longer. That might happen soon. The children were learning English quickly. Miranda and the other New Zealand helpers supervised English play groups after school. They wouldn't need a Polish math and geography teacher much longer. If Witold wanted to stay in New Zealand, his best path was marriage to a local—and Miss Sherman didn't seem opposed. Helena pitied the young woman, but was relieved that her torturer was otherwise occupied.

Helena took Mr. Sledzinski's concern about her pallor to heart. Summer had begun, so she tried to spend as much time outside as possible. The children played soccer and rugby, and Miranda and her friends taught groups about local nature and culture. The older boys and girls helped with vegetable gardens to grow food for the camp. Natalia was completely in her element planting beans, peas, and potatoes and experimenting joyfully with new vegetables like *kumara*.

"Sweet potatoes aren't unusual at all, here," Miranda teased her. "They've been grown here since long before the British. The Maori brought them with other crops from Polynesia, but the *kumara* was the only vegetable that really grew here. It was too cold for all the other plants, so they had to hunt in order to feed themselves. The first few hundred years, they hunted several species to extinction, and ruined a lot of the land by clearing it for crops. But now they're very careful with the land. They sing *karakia*—a mix of prayer and magic spell—during the harvest to apologize for taking from the earth. My father could tell you about it for hours." Miranda's father taught Maori history and culture at the university, and Miranda talked about the Maori as if they were part of her family. None of the refugees had met any Maori, though. "The kids are practicing their *karakia* already."

Miranda laughed and pointed to the rugby team as the players jumped around, stomping and singing while making faces.

"What are they doing?" asked Helena.

"They're dancing a *haka*," Miranda explained. "That's how Maori prepared for battle. And we're also practicing Maori hunting techniques. I'm showing my group how to make fire, and weirs for fishing."

Helena had heard bad things about other colonies, but here it seemed the natives and the colonizers lived in peace. She and Natalia wanted to know more about the Maori, and Miranda was able to organize a trip to a Maori village.

"We won't be able to find a traditional *marae* anymore," she mused regretfully. "That's what their community buildings are called. My father says they're mostly gone, thanks to the *pakeha*—that's what they call the Europeans. The live near towns because Maori children have to attend English schools. My father condemns it."

Helena was fascinated, and one of the first to sign up for the trip—a drive to Palmerston, where they would visit the Rangitane tribe. When the day arrived, though, she had to force herself to go. Things that used to be easy had become more and more difficult for her. After school and her daily chores in the house and garden, she was usually too tired to do anything else. And she felt sick more and more. She decided to go to the doctor after the trip to Palmerston. She probably just needed some vitamins.

7

Palmerston was just a few miles from Pahiatua, but a lot bigger. The teacher who led the trip explained that the first Europeans there had bought their land from the Ngati Rangitane.

"There was conflict, though, because it wasn't clear whether the land was theirs to sell or belonged to the Ngati Raukawa," he added. "Fortunately, they came to terms peacefully. This region was spared from most fighting, even during the land wars. Still, there aren't many Maori left in the area."

"Miranda told us most of the tribes' descendants live in white men's cities and no longer in their *marae*," said Helena, between deep breaths.

Although the road was well paved and not especially winding, Helena felt sick, again. Maybe she was getting a cold. There was one going around Little Poland, as the children's camp was jokingly called. Miranda and Katarina were two of the first to catch it, which was why she and Natalia were missing the trip. In Miranda's place they had Mr. Tucker, a lanky young man who'd been spared the war by a heart condition he complained about regularly. He nodded.

"Right. Some of their houses are really beautiful—or were, anyway. Colorful, decorated with carvings and statues of gods. Over the last few years things haven't been as well cared for. It's just the elderly left in the *marae*. The younger people are all moving to the cities for jobs at the factories. Today we're going to a *marae* on the Manawatu—that's a river that gave the region its name. It's near enough to Palmerston that people can work in the city and still live there. They allow visitors to come to earn extra money. They perform traditional songs and dances, even their *haka*."

Helena nodded. Miranda had told her the songs and dances bore only a passing resemblance to their traditions. "My dad thinks they're missing the spiritual element," Miranda had explained, wrinkling her forehead in mock seriousness. "Before, when a *powhiri* was held, it bound the souls of visitors with those of the tribe. The gods and spirits were invoked. Now when the greeting ceremony is performed it's less powerful. My dad's worried about the lack of spirituality."

The bus passed beneath a gate decorated with carvings.

"These are called *tiki*." Mr. Tucker gestured to the carved figures. "They're the guardian gods. They watch over the *marae*."

The reed fence surrounding the village looked to be badly in need of repair. Trampled down in some parts, it definitely wouldn't keep anyone out. Not that the tribe seemed to have any enemies, or much to steal. Facing the gate was a gabled building with carvings that seemed to be relatively well maintained. The rest of the houses were wood, with porches and shutters, just like the ones in Pahiatua but more run down. Though children played between the houses, and old people watched from their porches, the furniture all looked shabby, as did their clothes.

The people didn't look particularly exotic—their skin wasn't much darker than many *pakeha*. Most of them had black hair, and a few were stocky, but there were people of all sizes. Only a few faces were tattooed. Miranda had told her that every tribe had its own *moko*, which was painted and tattooed onto the warriors. This, and the patterns woven into their traditional clothing, indicated one's tribe—but none of that was on display here. The residents of the *marae* for the most part looked no different from anyone else in the city.

As the bus stopped in front of the colorful gabled house, a woman began to sing, and a few younger people who looked quite exotic appeared from within the building. The men's hair was tied into knots, they had bright blue *moko* painted on their faces, and they wore only knee-length skirts of hardened flax leaves. They carried spears, and other weapons hung from belts. The young women wore black, yellow, and red shirts over their flax skirts, and their long, loose hair was held back by wide headbands. As they sang and danced in greeting, they spun small flax balls around them on long strings, which made a strange buzzing sound to accompany the melody.

During this greeting dance, the Polish children climbed out of the bus. The Maori smiled at them, and as the song ended, a woman stepped forward. Helena guessed she was around twenty.

"*Haere mai!*" she greeted them. "That means 'welcome.' My name is Kaewa, and I'm happy to get to share my culture with you today. You'll sing and dance, eat, and work with us—and perhaps you will come to know our spirits as well."

A few boys hooted, but they were quickly distracted by the men, who performed their war *haka*. It was similar to what Helena had seen the rugby players practicing earlier, but she didn't really enjoy it. The men's grimaces weren't exactly frightening, but they did rouse a vague feeling of anxiety. And the stomping to the music was giving her a headache. She was definitely going to be sick.

When the dance finished, Kaewa taught them a few Maori phrases. *Kia ora* meant "hello"; *haere ra*, "good-bye"; and *aroha mai*, "excuse me." She told them that the flutes the musicians had played during the dances were played with both the mouth and nose. She passed some around, and the children tried to make sounds with them, and soon everyone was laughing and giggling. The younger girls whirled *poi-poi*, the flax balls on strings, and tried some dance steps. The boys were interested in the weapons. And then someone pointed out with a laugh that the Maori tattoos were only painted on.

"These days very few Maori are tattooed," Kaewa explained. She had a real *moko*, though, a few delicate blue loops around her mouth.

"It is easier for us with the *pakeha* when we don't look so different. When a man has a lot of *moko*, he has trouble finding a job in the city too. He frightens the *pakeha*. But to us a lot of *moko* means a lot of *mana*, that is, respect. We would be more likely to trust a heavily tattooed man than one who isn't."

Kaewa owed her tattoos to her grandmother, it turned out. Old Akona was a *tohunga*, an expert healer. She had insisted on raising her granddaughter in the traditions of her people.

"Are women usually only tattooed around their mouths?" Helena asked.

"Yes," answered Kaewa, "as a sign that the gods breathed the breath of life into us. The *pakeha* say it happened the other way around, that God woke Adam to life with his breath, not Eve." She winked. "We Maori believe the opposite. The divine Papatuanuku, Mother Earth, was the first female being. And Tane, her son, formed the first human woman from clay. Later he bore a daughter with her. Sons too, of course. Still, the first person was a woman. We Maori are sure of that." She smiled again. "If you're curious about other legends of our people, you can come listen to my grandmother. She likes to speak with our visitors, but only those who are truly interested. She won't have anyone coming in and getting bored and playing around while she tells stories. So now we will split into groups."

"Anyone who wants to learn more about our traditional food and farming, come with me," said the young woman who had played the nose flute. "My name is Emere. I'll take you across our fields, and you'll learn how to lay a *hangi*. We use the earth for an oven, heating stones in a pit and burying the food in it. Everyone will get to try the meal later, when we eat together at the end."

"Anyone interested in how we work the flax," Kaewa resumed, "like for the *piupiu*, the skirts, or *poi-poi*, go with Aku." Another young woman stepped forward. "Aku will also show you our traditional weaving." Kaewa smiled, seeing disappointed faces among the boys. "And anyone who wants to know what it's like to be a Maori warrior should join Hoani." One of the young men stepped forward and grinned. "Hoani and his friends will show you all how to use a spear and war club, and will paint *moko* on you. Only once you have earned it through bravery in battle, of course." Kaewa laughed.

"Can I go with the warriors?" asked a slight girl of about twelve with curly black hair.

Kaewa said yes at once. "Our women often fought alongside the men. There are special weapons made for their hands. Hoani will show them to you. Before the *pakeha* came, many tribes had female chieftains. The British wouldn't recognize them, though, and they sent the women away when they came to sign the Treaty of Waitangi. Strange, seeing they had a queen themselves at that time. Victoria, I believe?" She turned questioningly to Mr. Tucker. "They didn't take our women seriously, anyway, and our men took the opportunity to depose the female *ariki*." She made a face. "Later our men even took land ownership away from our women, because the *pakeha* didn't recognize female landowners. When it came to women, the Maori and British quickly saw eye to eye," she concluded bitterly.

"Well, I'm going to learn how to fight them," the little black-haired girl announced determinedly, and went off with the warriors.

Helena couldn't quite decide which group to join. Other than the warriors, everything interested her. But she thought she might vomit if she smelled food cooking, and she felt too tired to weave or braid. She had always liked to hear stories, and so she found herself alone with Kaewa and an ancient little woman by a fire. Akona had lit the fire in front of her hut, which was small and looked different from the other houses. There were no chairs or benches like the other houses, and she invited Helena simply to sit on the ground under a wide-branching tree. Kaewa sat down beside her, and Helena suddenly had the feeling she was slipping into the life of the Maori. Akona's appearance was different too. She didn't wear a *pakeha* dress but a long woven skirt and shirt in the tribe's colors. Though it was warm, she had a blanket around her shoulders.

"You brought one guest only?" Akona asked her granddaughter, disappointed. She spoke broken English.

Kaewa answered in Maori, and then turned to Helena. "I told her that you Poles are new to Aotearoa—Aotearoa means "long white cloud" and is the Maori word for New Zealand—and that you might not even stay here. So it's normal that you're not all that interested in our history. Still, it's not any different when others visit us. They're interested in the weapons or the food, but to listen to us for a long time, to really understand us—only a few ever want that."

Helena was excited to hear what Akona had to say, but the smell of the herbs Akona threw in the fire to soothe the spirits intensified her headache. And it wasn't easy to follow the stories in Akona's quiet voice. And occasionally the old woman would slip into Maori, and then Kaewa would have to interrupt her to translate.

Despite all that, Helena learned a lot about the Maori. They, too, were immigrants to the country, but they had come seven hundred years earlier than the first *pakeha*—from a legendary island paradise called Hawaiki. Akona told the story of Kupe, the first person to set foot on New Zealand, who had fled his homeland because he'd left his brother to drown and ran off with his brother's wife. She told of the creation of the world when Father Sky and Mother Earth were forced apart by their children. She spoke of Maui, a demigod who captured the moon and wanted to outsmart death. Finally, Helena learned legends of the region of the Ngati Rangitane's *marae*.

"Hau was a warrior. His wife left him for another, and he followed them over mountains and across rivers. But when he saw our river, so wide, he thought his heart would stop. So he named it Manawatu—*manawa* means heart; *tu* means to stop."

"Did he find his wife again?" asked Helena.

Kaewa nodded. "Yes, at Paekakariki. He wanted to throw her into the sea, but couldn't bring himself to do it. So instead he turned her into a rock. She watches over Pukerua Bay to this day."

"A sad story," said Helena. "Aren't there any that end well? Of people who love each other until the end of their days?"

Helena stood up, and everything seemed to spin around her. She leaned against the tree they'd been sitting beneath: a manuka myrtle, Akona had called it, a tea tree. Its oil was supposed to help with every imaginable condition. Akona said the tree was strong, resisting wind and cold and fire and offering protection to other plants. Manukas, she explained, had been guarding their *marae* for many generations. When an old trees dies, a new one grows from its ashes.

Helena imagined she felt the comforting embrace of the tree's spirit, and then succumbed to the blackness spreading before her eyes.

"Here, drink this."

Helena blinked and swallowed the bitter brew. Everything still seemed dark, and for a moment she feared she'd gone blind. Slowly she realized that she was lying in Akona's hut. Kaewa leaned over her, concerned, and poured the tea into her mouth. Akona was sitting outside at the fire, stirring a pot. The old woman sang *karakia*—it looked as if she were preparing a potion.

Helena swallowed obediently, although the tea tasted horrible. "What is this?" she asked with a weak voice. "And what happened to me?"

"You fainted," Kaewa informed her. "Maybe you got too much sun. Akona made you some tea. You'll feel better, don't worry. She's a master healer; she won't poison you."

Helena hadn't been worried about that—something else concerned her.

"I've never fainted before," she said quietly. "Never. Not even in Siberia with all the hard work and cold and hunger. I . . . I must have caught something."

Akona came in and handed Helena a porcelain cup with another strange-smelling brew, shaking her head. She said something in Maori, and Kaewa looked at Helena questioningly.

"You're not sick," the young Maori translated. "Akona says you're pregnant. Is that possible?"

Everything around Helena began to spin again. "No!"

Her first reaction was absolute denial. But of course it could be, she realized. Helena hadn't even thought about it—her period was always irregular, and hadn't come for months at a time in Siberia when the work was too hard and the food too scarce. Not a single woman became pregnant in Siberia, though Helena knew young girls who had been raped by guards. She'd never even thought of herself as a woman who could have children. And she had only ever thought about Witold with fear, disgust, and pain. Never once had she thought about conceiving.

But everything had changed since Siberia. Helena had long since been well fed. For a few months her period had also been regular. And then Witold—time after time, for weeks. It was very possible that she had become pregnant.

"Akona says there's no doubt," Kaewa translated, softly stroking Helena's forehead. "I can see you're not happy about it."

"Happy?" Helena cried. "How could I be? If I am pregnant, then it's all over. I thought I'd made it. New country, school—I wanted to study, and now . . . It can't be true. It just can't."

"You don't love him?" Kaewa asked quietly.

Helena shook her head wildly. "I loathe him," she whispered. "I hate him." She repeated, "I hate him, I hate him, I hate him."

Then she wept. For the first time since Witold had forced her, she sobbed, loudly and desperately. She let the fear and pain out of her—in the house of these two strange women, who might not even understand her grief. Kaewa said that among the Maori, children belonged to the whole tribe and were always welcome. How could they understand that in Poland, to become pregnant without a husband . . .

Helena's countrymen were strict Catholics. In the camp, they kept the girls' and boys' sections separated, and as friendly as they were to the children otherwise, romances were not allowed. If a girl from Little Poland got pregnant, Helena was sure they would throw her out. No one would believe she had been raped. Witold would deny it, and there were no witnesses. How was she supposed to survive here, in this strange land, without friends or family, and with a baby?

Kaewa laid her arms around her and stroked her hair over and over. "There, there."

"He wrecked everything," whimpered Helena. "Everything I've fought for. But maybe it serves me right. It was all a lie from the start. I shouldn't be here. My sister, Luzyna, is supposed to be here. I . . . I don't . . . I don't want to live."

Akona pointed at the porcelain cup. "Drink," she ordered, firmly but kindly. "And don't talk of death. Your baby will be afraid. You are young, and you will live. You both will live." She laid her hands gently on Helena's stomach as if she could already feel the life coming into being. "I will sing *karakia* for you and your baby."

With that she left the hut, and Helena and Kaewa listened to her high-pitched, elderly voice weave into the crackling of the fire.

Helena drank the tea.

"Feel better?" Kaewa finally asked once Helena had emptied the cup. "We should get back to the group. There'll be a meal, and then you'll drive back to Pahiatua."

Helena nodded. She was feeling more calm. The pounding in her head had stopped, but now it felt like it was filled with cotton. That was fine; she didn't want to think anymore.

"Maybe I should wash my face first," she murmured.

Kaewa pointed. "The river is there," she said.

Helena washed her face in the water of the river that had frightened the warrior Hau so much he thought his heart would stop. She wished someone would turn her into a rock as Hau had done to his unfaithful wife. Of course nothing happened.

As she followed Kaewa to the gathering place, Helena started to feel a bit hungry. The others were already busy serving food from the cooking pit. Everyone seemed happy; some girls swung *poi-poi* they had made of braided flax, and the boys proudly showed off their *moko*.

The girl with black hair—Karolina was her name—held a hardwood war club in her hands. Her face was painted with martial tattoos, just like the boys'. Karolina must have insisted they give her the *moko* of warriors.

"That is a *mere rakau*." She showed Helena the club excitedly. "You can kill someone with it!"

Helena attempted a smile. "You'll lend it to me if I ever need it, won't you?" she asked quietly.

Karolina remained serious. "Do you want to become a warrior like me?" she asked skeptically, turning her blue-painted face up at Helena.

"She already is," Kaewa intervened, bringing Helena a bowl filled with meat and vegetables. She looked happy as Helena took a spoonful and chewed it bravely. It tasted surprisingly good; Akona's herbs seemed to have restored her appetite.

Kaewa pressed a small bundle into her hands. "Here, my grandmother says you're to make a tea with these herbs if you feel sick again. And here." She pulled a small figure on a leather band out of her pocket. "Akona made it. It's to protect you." Helena looked, bewildered, at the manuka wood carving. "It's Hineahuone, the fertility goddess. She was the first woman formed from the loam. Do you remember? Tane, the god of the forest, brought her to life."

Helena suddenly thought she could feel the spirit of the manuka myrtle again. Perhaps this new country really would protect her. She exchanged the *hongi*, the Maori traditional greeting, with Kaewa before she climbed on the bus, comforted as her nose and forehead gently touched Kaewa's.

"*Haere ra, taina*," Kaewa said. "Take care, little sister. I wish you luck."

And Helena couldn't help thinking about Luzyna again.

8

Helena needed a few days to come to terms with her pregnancy. At first she hoped the old Maori might have been mistaken, but eventually she realized that the evidence was against her. She definitely didn't have a cold—while everyone else in her residence suffered with sore throats and runny noses, Helena felt better and better each day. Akona's tea rid her of the nausea and fatigue, and freed of those, she now noticed all the changes in her body. Her breasts had grown, her stomach felt harder, and she was certainly gaining weight. There could be no doubt, she was pregnant, and she wouldn't be able to hide it much longer either. Helena estimated she was in her third month.

She didn't really know when one started showing, but she probably didn't have much time. Even now, it was hard not to draw attention. The cold going around was a bit of a blessing, since all of her housemates were busy taking care of themselves or their younger siblings. Soon enough, though, Natalia would recover and start to ask questions. And so would Miranda.

Helena thought feverishly. Her first impulse was to tell Miranda. She trusted her not to react badly, and maybe Miranda could even think of a solution. But she could hardly ask Miranda to keep the knowledge to herself. As a caretaker she would have to report the pregnancy to the camp administration, and then they would probably throw Helena out. Helena's survival instinct told her to keep the safety of the camp, the food, and the shelter as long as absolutely possible. Maybe she could even hide the pregnancy until the birth. It was worth a try.

It was also worth trying to talk to Witold. The thought alone disgusted Helena, but she knew the baby growing in her had only one chance at a happy life: Witold would have to recognize it and marry Helena. She owed the child this sacrifice. The alternative would be life on the street. They might even send Helena and her bastard back to Poland as soon as the country was liberated.

Helena couldn't sleep, imagining one terrible scenario after another. She pictured herself begging on the snow-covered streets of Lwów or Warsaw, listening to a big-eyed baby crying with hunger. She imagined herself desperately begging Polish housewives for sewing work, although they themselves would have nothing after the war. And what if she didn't find honest work? She would have to sell her body, would have to do willingly what Witold had forced her to do. A marriage to Witold was better than any of that. With him she could at least try to attain citizenship in New Zealand.

⁕⁜⁙ ⁙⁜⁕

Reluctantly, she found the baby's father a week after the excursion to Palmerston. Witold was alone in the school's library, a place well suited for a private talk. Helena took that as a good sign and forced herself to greet her rapist as pleasantly as possible, although she was disgusted by just the sight of him. Witold didn't seem happy to see her either. He looked at her suspiciously.

"What do you want?" he asked. "To beg forgiveness? So you miss our little meetings. A shame, but I can't do that anymore." He straightened up proudly. "I'm engaged, my sweet Luzyna, and will soon be an upright citizen of this beautiful country. I'm not about to risk that for your pleasure."

Helena froze. "It . . . it was never pleasure for me," she said stiffly. "And I don't want to repeat it either. But you won't be able to marry

Miss Sherman because you have to marry me. I'm pregnant, Witold. You got me pregnant." Witold looked disbelievingly over her pale face and her still-slender figure. "It's true," Helena added.

Witold got ahold of himself, and his initial look of fear gave way to his usual apathetic gaze, and then to an ugly grin.

"I'm supposed to marry you?" he hissed. "You don't really believe that. I won't let you pin that baby on me. Who knows how many others you did it with? I'm warning you, Lu-zy-na. Don't try to ruin my name. I can still tell everyone how you sneaked over here. I can tell them how I sympathized with you, thought you were a good girl, until you claimed I'd touched you. And when your belly gets big, everyone'll see what kind of girl you really are."

Helena bit her lip. Would the camp administration see it that way? Could Witold turn things around so that the obvious proof of abuse spoke against her too? She didn't know what to say.

"So get going, Luzy, and look for another idiot for that bastard. Better yet, get rid of it. If you can find the money for that."

"M-money?" stammered Helena.

"You won't get it from me," Witold clarified. "I don't want to hear from you again, and if you throw yourself at me again, I'll report you."

He tossed the book he had been holding on the table, turned, and left the room. Helena remembered little Karolina's war club and her joyful insight: *You could kill someone with this.* She did not know what horrible things had been done to that girl, but Helena would no longer have any scruples about using it either. Just then, she would have gladly smashed Witold's skull in.

Full of rage, Helena let dark fantasies fill her mind as she walked back to her residence, but hopelessness once again took over. As if Witold's cruelty hadn't been enough, the mail held a new blow. During the first days in Little Poland, out of a combination of guilt, a desire to share, and a need for forgiveness, Helena had written to Luzyna. Her sister was surely furious and would answer with a flood of anger, but she should at least know that Helena was all right. Helena had still been full of optimism then, and believed that if she studied and worked hard, she might earn enough to send for Luzyna. So she had asked her sister for forgiveness, assured her of her love, and hoped for an answer.

That day the letter came back unopened, along with a note from the camp in Tehran: *UNABLE TO DELIVER. HELENA GRABOWSKI LEFT CAMP 3 OF HER OWN VOLITION.*

Helena felt tears welling up. Luzyna probably hadn't even waited a day. With her older sister's papers, she was eighteen, and when she turned nineteen she could legally marry. Helena imagined she'd run off with Kaspar—into a future her parents would never have wished for her.

Helena cried herself to sleep that night, too, but at least she didn't need to hide it. She told Natalia about the letter and her sister's disappearance.

Natalia became angry. "This Helena doesn't seem to care much about you," she said. "She could have left you an address. Or asked for your address before leaving. The camp administration would know where you are, after all."

After that, Helena couldn't stop weeping. She knew well why Luzyna hadn't asked after her. She would have run the risk of running into Dr. Virchow, who would have recognized her. There were other ways of finding Helena in New Zealand, though. Natalia was right. Helena wasn't sure she was even angry, though she was now all alone in the world. The only family she had now was the unwanted baby in her womb.

At some point Helena fell asleep, exhausted, only to wake again with a start in the early morning, trembling with fear, to brood further—and suddenly she had a new idea. Perhaps she wasn't so alone here in New Zealand. There were still the Neumanns, Uncle Werner and his family, in Wellington. She hadn't yet tried to contact them. Life in Little Poland had been so exciting and fulfilling that she hadn't had the time or inclination to write to her parents' old friends, let alone plan a visit. Now things were different. Helena's heart felt heavy with hope and with shame. Could she go to the Neumanns, pregnant and without anything to her name? Should she try even try? Uncle Werner wouldn't have to take her in forever, of course. Perhaps he could help just until she found work.

Witold's words sounded in her mind. *Better yet, get rid of it.* Was there really a way to end this pregnancy? And if so, wasn't it wrong? But Helena couldn't imagine how she could care for a baby in her situation. Maybe she could induce a miscarriage? That way it wouldn't be as wrong.

Helena tried first by running as fast as she could around the perimeter of Little Poland, but aside from cramps in her legs, the exercise did nothing. She didn't know what else to try. Witold had said she could "get rid of it" with money. Helena wondered where she could even ask about something like this, and then she rejected that too. She didn't have any money. All she had was Werner Neumann's address.

The next afternoon she went to the train station to ask the cost of a ticket to Wellington. The young émigrés received a small allowance for sweets or ice cream during their trips to town. Helena hadn't spent any of it, and so managed to save a few pounds. It might be enough for a third-class ticket.

"Only one way," a lazy-looking woman at the ticket counter informed her. Helena had simply put all her money on the counter for the woman to count. "For a round-trip ticket you need another pound."

Helena bit her lip. Should she take the risk? She nodded.

"Then a one-way ticket to Wellington. For next Sunday."

The Neumanns would surely give her a pound, even if they refused her any more help.

A Way Out

High Wycombe, England; Lower Hutt and
Wellington, New Zealand (North Island); Canterbury Plains,
New Zealand (South Island)

January 1945

1

Anything else?"
Arthur Harris, commander-in-chief of the Royal Air Force Bomber Command, was clearly ready to leave. He had just finished a briefing, and his officers had their orders. That night more German cities would be carpet bombed. Entire streets would go up in flames. Thousands of people would die. Harris defended these carpet bombings every time: they demoralized German civilians, who would then stop supporting the army. Since the Americans and British had landed in Normandy the previous summer, the Allies had only met halfhearted resistance from the German Wehrmacht. The Allied military commanders believed that was due to the bombing of the cities. The people, civilians and soldiers alike, had simply had enough of war. At some point Hitler and his advisors would have to see that, and until then, the British and Americans would continue their bombings.

Despite all his justifications, it was hard on Harris and his men to be responsible for the deaths of thousands of people in the cities of the Ruhr region night after night. After curtly announcing the targets for that night—usually he just named the cities—he wanted to be alone. And there was always, after all, paperwork to be done.

Harris entered his office and would have shut the door right away, but his adjutant was poking nervously around his desk. Wilson seemed to have something on his mind but had trouble speaking it.

"There's something else, sir," he began. "We have a . . . hmm . . . problem. A young man, a pilot. One of the New Zealanders . . ."

Harris—a strong man with sandy hair and clear eyes in an oval face with a carefully groomed mustache—nodded, understanding. "Brave boys, the lot of them. Nearly mad, the way they fly."

"Indeed," Wilson sighed. He looked almost unhappy. "That's just it. What the boy does, it's crazy. He flies a Mosquito."

Harris nodded. The de Havilland Mosquito was among the most versatile fighter planes the Royal Air Force had. One or two of them were assigned to every bomber unit Harris sent to Germany. In the previous few months, they had primarily been used as fighter planes, carrying bombs and machine guns. They generally targeted German trains, stations, and supply convoys. In Belgium, the small, sleek machines had targeted the Gestapo headquarters as well. It required considerable flying skill. Only the best piloted a de Havilland Mosquito.

"And he flies like the devil." Wilson continued his description of the problem pilot. "Every machine we give him. He did his training here, but it seems he could fly beforehand. His instructors had nothing but praise."

"And?" Harris interrupted him impatiently. Sometimes his adjutant's digressions got on his nerves. "Come to the point, Wilson."

"The man has now flown three bombing missions. Twice he was to target train stations and once a military convoy. But he didn't drop the bombs. At least not over the target areas. He dropped the first two over fields, the third in a canal."

"What?" Harris roared. "Refusal to obey orders. Cowardice before the enemy. His superior officer should have him arrested and threatened with the firing squad."

Wilson bit his lip. "That's not quite it, sir. He's no coward. On these three missions, he took out eight enemy fighters. As soon as he's attacked, he throws himself into the fight, chases the Germans, fires from all barrels. Just like the other Kiwis. They don't shy away from battle."

Harris paused and furrowed his brow. "Eight kills in three sorties? That's worth a Victoria Cross."

"Exactly," said Wilson. "The boy stands between a Victoria Cross and a court martial. Do you want to speak with him, sir? Wing Commander Beasley has brought him along. He's waiting outside."

Harris stood up, imposing in his dark-blue uniform. On his left lapel his rank insignia gleamed.

"Then for God's sake call him in."

❧❧❧

The young man was tall and lanky. He had curly red-brown hair and expressive brown eyes that betrayed his concern. He walked in and saluted.

"Flight Sergeant James McKenzie, Number Five Group," he introduced himself.

"At ease, Sergeant," Harris commanded him. "Do you know why you're here?"

McKenzie nodded. "Yes, sir. I . . . I dropped my bombs off target." He sounded sheepish.

"And?" Harris asked. "What do you say about it? What were you thinking?"

The young man bit his lower lip. "I wasn't thinking anything, sir," he admitted. "Well . . . I didn't plan it, anyway. I meant to drop the bombs on the targets. I . . . I just couldn't."

Harris grimaced. "Couldn't find the switch?" he asked sarcastically.

McKenzie ran his hand through his hair. "Sir," he said, pained. "I was supposed to drop my bombs on a train station, in the middle of a city full of people. There were children below, women, and elderly. And the . . . what was supposed to be a military convoy . . . well, there were a few tanks. But it was mostly horse-drawn carts and trucks with refugees."

Harris rolled his eyes. "Even if that were the case," he allowed—since the Mosquitos were supposed to be used for military targets alone—"what's the problem? Our strategy is to demoralize the German civilian population. The point is to wear down their morale. If the population denies Hitler their support, he won't be able to go on."

James ran his fingers through his hair again. "I thought . . ." he muttered. "I mean, I'd hear that Hitler had people shot. I mean, people who don't support him."

Harris glared at him. "Are you saying that carpet bombing won't work? Are you questioning our strategy? You think you're smarter than all of our generals?"

McKenzie shook his head. "I wouldn't dare to judge it, sir," he said quickly. "It's just . . . I can't. I can't do it. When I try to drop the bombs, it's like I go limp. I see the children and the . . ." At the last moment, he managed not to mention the animals as well. It was too embarrassing, and Harris would probably think it degrading if he admitted that he saw more than children, pregnant women, and the elderly below him when he tried to drop the bombs. But he couldn't help but think about the friendly faces of the sheepdogs at Kiward Station, the cats sleeping in the hay, and the horses pulling the refugees' carts. Neither children nor animals would understand why their homes had turned into an inferno of fire and death, and many adults wouldn't either. And even if the people below should feel guilty about the bombing of London and Coventry, they couldn't change it. James had come to understand why his father, a veteran of the First World War, had become a pacifist. He imagined he knew what Jack McKenzie had felt on that beach on the other end of the world, killing people who had done nothing to him. And who had probably wanted to fight just as little as he. "I just can't . . ." James repeated, despondently.

Harris frowned. "And what about the crews of the eight fighters you've shot down?" he asked. "You must know that those people didn't survive?"

James bit his lip. "I'm no pacifist, sir," he said. "I volunteered. I'll fight for the British Empire. Just not against . . . against women and children."

"You understand that in shooting down these German fighters, you made it possible for your English comrades to drop their bombs on the aforementioned women and children?" Harris continued his examination without pausing.

The young man swallowed. "Yes, sir. And I . . . as I said, I don't have a plan. There's no logic to it, and I . . . I'm not questioning your strategy. If the bombings must happen, then . . . then . . . I just can't." He lowered his gaze.

Harris sighed. "Then for now: dismissed," he ordered. "Wilson!"

The adjutant appeared at once. He must have been waiting just behind the door, probably listening.

Harris waited until James McKenzie had left. "Transfer the man to the fighter pilots," he directed his adjutant. "They're to give him a Spitfire and to employ him in support of infantry and tank divisions. If he requires retraining, he's to get it. We won't say a word about this bombing fiasco—the boy's a bit odd, but honest, and he can fly. He's of more use to us in a cockpit than a cell."

Wilson nodded but still looked anxious. "There's just one more thing, sir," he said, pulling a letter from his folder. "It's also in regard to Sergeant McKenzie. Here."

He handed his superior the paper. Harris recognized the letterhead.

"The Prime Minister of New Zealand? What interest does Mr. Fraser have in our pilot?" Harris pursed his lips.

"Well, this young man . . . hmm . . . his family seems to have some influence. At any rate, Mr. Fraser suggests, as politely as possible, that you release Sergeant McKenzie from combat duty. It seems responsibilities of the utmost strategic importance await the young man at his family's coal and steel works. Sergeant McKenzie evaded them by volunteering. He's not cowardly, as I said. But apparently nothing in Greymouth will run without him."

Harris furrowed his brow. "You mean that the coal and steel industry of an entire country depends on whether this young stick of a boy sits in an office in Greymouth or flies for us? He doesn't seem like a pencil pusher to me. I thought he'd come from a farm."

Wilson shrugged his shoulders. "I'm not saying anything, sir," he said stiffly. "I'm telling you what the letter says. It seems clear that the McKenzie and Lambert families—the letter came at the behest of one Ruben Lambert of Lambert Coal and Steel—are quite important in New Zealand. Mr. Fraser clearly does not want to irritate them. Your orders, sir?"

Harris raised his hands resignedly and paced the length of his office once. "Send the boy back to them," he decided. "He's more trouble than he's worth. But do break it to him gently. It sounds like he ran away from home to volunteer, and he won't be happy to learn about this letter."

❀❖❀

James McKenzie awaited his sentence in the officers' mess, which felt surprisingly civilian. The Royal Air Force headquarters in High Wycombe was well disguised to look like typical village buildings. The officers' mess seemed from the outside to be a quaint farmhouse, the fire station looked like a village church, and most of the briefing rooms and command centers lay in underground bunkers.

James was nervously stirring a cup of tea—he found the English coffee atrocious—when Wing Commander Beasley joined him. The officer gestured for him to stay seated when he moved to salute.

"As you are, McKenzie. It doesn't matter now."

McKenzie frowned. "What doesn't matter, sir? Does that mean I'm being demoted? Or . . . or am I facing a court martial? I know I've made mistakes—"

"Don't start that again," Beasley said, tired. "You've already explained yourself to me, and to Marshal Harris. He was going to transfer you, but there was an intervention from higher up."

James McKenzie was furious when Beasley told him of his strategically vital recall to New Zealand.

"Excuse me sir, but that is utter nonsense. Nothing more than a dirty trick. Not even a new one: they used it during the Great War to have my great-uncle's servant recalled from the front. My father still talks about that feat. And now he's trying it with me? I have nothing at all to do with the mining; I'm not even from Greymouth. I'm from the Canterbury Plains. We have a sheep farm." James's brown eyes blazed.

Beasley shrugged. "A big one, I'd wager," he remarked, "or your parents wouldn't have so much influence. What does your father have against you serving? I mean, he must have moved heaven and earth to get the prime minister involved."

"My father's a pacifist." James steamed. "He doesn't think there should be war under any circumstances. He doesn't know what we should do in the case of Hitler, but he won't get hung up on that. He's a farmer, he says, not a politician. War, in any case, is never the answer."

Wing Commander Beasley rubbed his forehead. "Is he religious or something?" he asked.

James shook his head. "No. Not particularly. But he wasn't always like this. He fought in the Great War. Bravely. He even received a medal, but I don't know which. He gave it away, and never talks about it."

Beasley raised his eyebrows in surprise. He'd never heard of anyone giving away a medal of bravery.

"Maybe it was a medal for wounded soldiers," James speculated. "My father was heavily wounded. During the last offensive in Gallipoli."

"Oh." Beasley understood. The siege at Gallipoli was one of the great disasters of the war. The ANZAC, a collection of forces from New Zealand and Australia, had attempted to occupy the Turkish peninsula of Gallipoli to use it to stage the taking of Constantinople. ANZAC and Turkish soldiers faced off for months in intense trenched battle, and more than a hundred thousand shed blood on that idyllic beach. Nothing was accomplished. The Turks' position proved impregnable, and in the end, the last fourteen divisions of ANZAC were evacuated under cover of darkness. If McKenzie's father had been there from beginning to end, that explained his attitude toward war. "I'm sorry to hear it, son," Beasley said. "I've read about Gallipoli. It must've been horrible—and so senseless. Heaven knows who ordered that; one look at the beach and anyone could see it was impossible."

James nodded. "That's what my father always says. No one could've taken Gallipoli. It was too easy to defend. As long as the Turks didn't run out of ammo, they could've sent millions of men and it would've been useless. But now . . . it's completely different. I mean, we have better people making decisions. Our strategies—" He broke off and bit his lip. In a few decades, would people think the carpet bombing as senseless and preventable as they did Gallipoli? "We're going to win the war, aren't we, sir?" he asked quietly. "Even if I go back to New Zealand?"

Beasley clapped him on the shoulder. "Son, we've already won the war," he said. "That madman in Berlin just hasn't realized it yet. It may drag out a few more months, but it'll be over soon. With or without you. I promise, McKenzie. So, give your father my regards. He's right, you know. When this is finally over, no one will ever want war again."

2

Helena didn't notice the beauty of the landscape as it rushed by, nor fear crossing the bridges on the Rimutaka Incline, as she had on the trip from Wellington to Little Poland. She was preoccupied trying to fight her anxiety and her worry. So far everything had gone remarkably smoothly. In the morning she'd told the camp administration she wanted to spend the day in Palmerston with acquaintances. No one questioned her—otherwise she would've claimed to want to visit Kaewa. She had told Natalia her true destination—she didn't want to disappear without a trace, and in case something happened to her along the way, someone needed to know where she had really gone. Her friend was delighted that she had acquaintances in Wellington, and asked why she hadn't written to them first. Helena had tried, but the letters were returned.

"I probably have the house number wrong." She tried to sound unconcerned. "But Uncle Werner's a dentist. Someone will know him."

Fortunately it didn't occur to Natalia that the postman would also have known where to find his practice. She wished Helena luck.

Miranda would've asked a lot more questions, but she'd taken the day off to spend the weekend with her family and pick up a relative returning from the war. Helena wondered again if she should've shared her secret with Miranda, or at least told her about the Neumanns.

Miranda would've lent her the money for the return trip, at least. But it was too late to change things now, and Helena had to make the best of it. She hoped that Elizabeth Street wasn't too far from the train station, or too long a walk.

She was in luck. She asked for directions at a newsstand, and the shopkeeper showed her a map.

"It's not very near, but you can get there on foot," he said. "About two miles, and impossible to miss. Walk along the harbor to Kent Terrace, then take a right, then a left."

Helena thanked him and set off. She wrapped herself in her shawl against the mist, feeling the unexpected cold snap well suited to her mood. She didn't have an umbrella or rain jacket, and by the time she reached Elizabeth Street, she would be chilled to the bone.

She noticed a troop transport had arrived in Wellington that day, carrying not refugees but wounded soldiers. They, too, had escaped the war—and probably with brighter hopes for the future than hers. She put it out of her mind, focused on her search.

***

Elizabeth Street was a quiet residential street, not quite at the center of town but easily reached, ideal for a dental practice. The street was only five blocks, and Helena was fairly sure that the Neumanns' house number had two digits, so she began with number ten and worked her way up, reading the names by the doorbells or mailboxes. She attracted attention quickly, and an older woman opened the door as Helena was looking at her mailbox.

"Can I help you?" she asked, with friendly caution.

Helena smiled, embarrassed. "Yes . . . I . . . I'm looking for the Neumanns. Dr. Werner Neumann is a dentist. He lives on this street, but I can't remember the house number."

The woman nodded. "The Neumanns used to live just there." She pointed to a quaint wooden colonial house on the other side of the street. "Very nice people."

Helena bit her lip. That didn't sound good.

"They . . . they've moved?" she asked, disappointed. "Do you happen to know where they live now?"

The woman nodded again, making a sad face. "They're on Somes Island, dear, in the internment camp. They are German, after all. At least, that's how they're being treated. An outrage if you ask me. Mrs. Neumann cried so bitterly. She was so terribly afraid, because they're Jews, you know, and now they're locked up with the Germans."

"Locked up?"

Helena felt the world start to spin around her again. She hoped she wouldn't faint. She should've brought something to eat, at least to keep her energy up.

The woman seemed to notice that something was wrong. "Why don't you come in for a moment, dear?" She opened the door. "You look pale. Are you family? Are you German? No, no, then you'd be at Somes Island, too, of course. Let me make you some tea." In a flash, Helena was sitting in Mrs. Deavers's warm kitchen, sipping tea and listening to the story of the Neumanns in New Zealand. "The family fled Germany right after the Nazis came to power. Dr. Neumann bought the house across the street and opened his practice there. At the time there was, of course, blustering in the papers about immigrants from Germany—they said we'd be overrun with doctors and dentists if we took in the Jews—utter nonsense. Still, the Neumanns settled nicely. Mrs. Neumann is kind, and their children went to school with ours. Children learn so quickly; they picked up English right away, and soon you couldn't tell they hadn't grown up here. Everything was fine until the war started. The government decided that Germans in the country could be spies, assassins, traitors, or whatever else, so they interned them. Dr. Neumann protested—he'd long since become a citizen, and a Jew spying for the Germans didn't make any sense. But it made no difference. The Neumanns were sent to Palmerston and then to Somes Island. One hears such terrible things about how the Jews are treated in Germany. Why would a Jew spy for them? And what would Dr. Neumann even learn, as a dentist? I doubt Adolf Hitler is interested in the teeth of New Zealand's citizens." Mrs. Deavers paused for a moment and noted Helena's distraught gaze. "Now, don't look so hopeless, Miss Grabowski. They're doing all right there. Mrs. Nails next door is friends with Irene Neumann, and they've stayed in touch. She can give you their address. And we all keep an eye on the house. The Neumanns will be able to move right back in when this is all over."

❦

Helena rubbed her head, which had started hurting. She hoped the Neumanns really were all right, but it wouldn't help her any. She talked with the Neumanns' inquisitive neighbor for a bit longer, telling her about her own journey and Little Poland. She thought briefly of asking Mrs. Deavers to borrow money for a train ticket, but was too shy. She was able to force herself to eat a few cookies Mrs. Deavers served. She had no idea how she was going to get back, but fainting in the street wouldn't help.

After thanking Mrs. Deavers and saying good-bye, she counted her remaining money. She could try to get as close to Palmerston as possible. Or she could just stay in Wellington. As long as she wasn't showing, she was likely to find a job quickly in Wellington. It might be better to leave Little Poland before she was found out. Helena had seen job advertisements in Pahiatua's newspaper—a big paper in Wellington would certainly have more.

So she made her way back to the train station, hoping the shopkeeper she'd asked for directions might let her look at the advertisements for free. But it was already afternoon, and she wouldn't be able to apply anywhere before the next day. Did she have enough money for a night in a cheap hotel? Surely not. Or in a hostel? She suddenly realized that she didn't have her papers on her: her passport was safe in her dresser in Pahiatua. Nausea rose within her anew. She might have been able to survive alone in Wellington, but certainly not illegally.

At the train station, it was more bad news: a one-way ticket was more expensive than round trip. She didn't have enough to get to Greytown or farther, as she had hoped; just to Upper Hutt, a small town about twenty minutes outside of Wellington. Not even a quarter of the way to Pahiatua. Helena bought the ticket anyway, just to get out of Wellington. She might be able to hitchhike in the more rural Upper Hutt area.

She didn't want to think about it anymore; she didn't want to think about anything anymore. She didn't want to admit that all her plans had failed and there was no more hope for her. The only thing she could do now was try to hide her pregnancy until the end, give birth to the baby somewhere alone, and then leave it in front of a clinic. Was it even possible?

Helena curled up in a corner of a compartment and stared out the window. She didn't want to plan anymore. Mostly she just wanted to die.

"This is your stop, miss: Upper Hutt."

The conductor pulled her from her thoughts, and Helena nodded unhappily.

It was five in the afternoon, and the sleepy town of Upper Hutt was desolate and gray beneath a veil of cold mist. Helena left the train listlessly and forced herself to hurry toward Main Street. It was deserted—no pedestrians, no cars, and certainly no trucks bound for Palmerston or Pahiatua. Helena sighed, drew her shawl tighter as the mist turned to rain, and started walking north. She hadn't felt so alone or hopeless since her mother died.

Forcing one foot in front of the other, Helena thought seriously about ending her life. She remembered that in the novels she used to enjoy, women with unwanted pregnancies threw themselves in front of trains or in the water. Helena didn't want to drown—the water falling from above was enough for her. And she was already too far from the train tracks. She laughed bitterly. Another opportunity missed.

Guilt welled up fiercely within her. She hadn't survived internment just to kill herself later. In the camp she had clung to life to protect Luzyna. That had been her duty, it was what her mother and perhaps God, too, had expected of her. The moment she betrayed her sister, she had forsaken her chances at life.

Helena splashed through another puddle. Her shoes were soaked through, her feet slowly turning into blocks of ice. Maybe this forced march was the solution she was searching for. If she walked to the point of exhaustion and froze, she would surely lose the baby. Or if she fasted once she got back to the camp. Surely her body would end the pregnancy before the mother starved. A miscarriage, as soon as possible while it could still be disguised, was her absolute last chance.

Suddenly she remembered a neighbor in Lwów, Dora Chombski, had lost her baby after being hit by a car. An accident, easily created. Of course, there was a risk of dying, but either way would be a way out.

Helena dragged herself forward. It would soon be dark, and the farther she went the more disheartened she became, the more she wished to end it all. But there wasn't even any traffic on this godforsaken road.

Then it seemed God heard her prayers. Helena heard a vehicle approaching and looked around. Behind her was a curve in the road; the driver wouldn't see her until the last moment. She clasped the fertility goddess she had hung around her neck that morning, when she still hoped that Hineahuone would bring her luck—perhaps even both of them, her and the baby. Her visit to the Neumanns could have changed everything.

But her last hopes were gone. The thin leather band tore as Helena pulled on it. She clenched her fist around the little *hei-tiki* as the sound of the car got louder. Then she let herself fall.

3

Miranda Biller drove similarly to how James flew: dangerously and at top speed. James, sitting next to her in her sleek Buick Roadmaster, clung to his seat.

When the ship had docked and he'd disembarked, the only man fit for duty among those wounded heroes, he'd been desperate. He would rather have been shot down over Germany than return to New Zealand like this. But he certainly didn't want to die in a ditch from his cousin's reckless driving on the outskirts of Lower Hutt.

Miranda seemed oblivious, noticing neither his desperation nor his fear. She'd greeted him joyously, with a boisterous hug. She'd shrugged off his anger at his father's manipulation. "You shot down some enemy planes, so you did your part. Didn't you get a medal too? And everyone's so happy to have you back!"

James wrinkled his nose in annoyance. His Distinguished Flying Cross for brave deeds in the face of the enemy seemed like a consolation prize. Wing Commander Beasley had organized the awarding of the medal quickly, just before the young pilot was sent home. James muttered that he could have done considerably more, to which Miranda replied that he could also have died.

She led him to her sharp car—the bright red sports car had been a present from her mother for her twentieth birthday—informing him that they would be going to her family home first. "There're no more ships to Christchurch this week. You could ask the air force to try to get a flight over, or you can just stay with us a few days and recover in Lower Hutt. You can go riding with my mom, or to the dig with my dad."

The Billers owned a weekend home in the mountains, and whenever a magazine did a story on Brenda Boleyn, Lilian Biller's nom de plume, they mused about how she drew inspiration for her new works from the spectacular landscape.

Miranda's mother always laughed about it: she really didn't need inspiration. Lilian could also have written her melodramatic novels in a train station—when she fell into her fictional world, she didn't notice anything else around her. She bought the house in Lower Hutt to keep her two horses and have a better place to ride than Wellington's city park. It was an archaeological find that settled the Billers on this specific cottage, though. Train workers had stumbled upon an old Maori *pa*—a village with defenses—in the area. It hadn't been destroyed, so the tribe must have abandoned it without a fight. Ben Biller had been obsessed with learning why it had been abandoned, and hoped to excavate spectacular artifacts from the early period of Aotearoa's settlement. During semester breaks, he had come to the site with a handful of students. Lilian hadn't relished the thought of her husband camping in the wilderness, and he was no great outdoorsman. Miranda's mother wasn't wrong to worry that he might start a wildfire with a camping stove, or cause a landslide setting up a tent in the mountains. The house, a mile or so from the dig site, was a safer alternative. Ben slept in a proper bed and set out to the *pa* every morning after a good breakfast. "Besides, this way my mom can check that Dad hasn't fallen into an old cooking pit and gotten braised," Miranda would joke.

So to Lower Hutt, then. On this gray, ignominious day of his return to New Zealand, James let Miranda lead without complaint. The last thing he wanted was to fly to the South Island with the air force. How could he explain his presence to his comrades in the squadron? Pilots were not usually given leave in this heated final phase of the war.

Miranda ignored her cousin's attitude. She chattered cheerfully about this and that, excitedly telling him about her work with the orphans in the Polish camp. Watching the road seemed to be of secondary importance, and James's stomach clenched as she took a sharp curve. Just then, someone appeared in front of them on the side of the road, and he tensed. Miranda didn't slow down, and suddenly the person fell into the middle of the road. Miranda responded immediately, turning the wheel sharply. As young as she sometimes appeared, she was an excellent driver. The car shot off of the paved road and lost contact with the ground. Improbably, it landed next to the road on all four tires, and continued speeding toward a group of trees. It no longer seemed to be under control, but Miranda stomped on the brakes and the car came to a stop in front of a rata bush.

"Well," Miranda said, relaxing. "What was that?"

"Everything all right?" James couldn't believe neither of them was hurt. They looked back at the person now sitting in the road.

"A young woman," Miranda said. "What's wrong with her? I didn't hit her, did I?"

"She's crying," said James. "I think she's crying."

Helena sobbed despairingly. She had prepared herself for the crash, longed for it—and then the little red car had missed her by a hair. Shaking with fear, she watched the driver and a woman come toward her. He would blame her. The car was probably broken, and it was her fault, and she'd be responsible for the repairs.

The young man reached her first, clasped her shoulder, and turned her toward him, more concerned than angry. Helena thought his slender face with freckles on the tip of the nose reminded her of someone. And then she thought she must be dreaming, because the woman who appeared at his side was none other than Miranda Biller.

"It's Luzyna!" she cried, amazed. "What're you doing here, Luzyna? Luzyna's one of the Polish orphans in Pahiatua." Miranda had turned to the young man when Helena didn't answer because she couldn't stop sobbing. "This is my cousin James," Miranda introduced him, taking Helena helplessly in her arms. "Say something, Luzyna. Are you hurt? How'd you get here? All alone and soaked to the bone! Where were you headed?"

"Back to Pahiatua, I bet," James speculated. "It's the right direction. Miss, were you, er, were you in Wellington, Luzyna?"

James didn't quite know how to address the girl. Miranda had called her an orphan, but she was clearly no child. When she finally looked up at him, James found himself looking into the tear-stained but beautiful face, framed with tangled brown hair, of a girl of about eighteen. Her formerly neat braids had loosened, and one was missing its band, letting wisps of hair free. Resigned, anxious, afraid, and hopeless—her big porcelain-blue eyes seemed to tell a whole story.

"Not Luzyna," the girl sobbed. James assumed she was correcting his pronunciation, but then she gave a completely different name. "I'm not Luzyna. I'm Helena. Luzyna is my sister. And I . . . I . . ."

James looked at Miranda, perplexed. "Do you know what she means?"

Miranda shook her head. "No. That's definitely Luzyna, or at least she's registered as Luzyna Grabowski in the camp. Though I don't think it matters right now. Whatever her name is, she needs to get out of the rain and off the street. She can tell us everything later." She asked seriously, "Luzyna, it looked like you threw yourself in front of my car on purpose. Did you?"

Helena sobbed again but couldn't answer.

"For now, we'll take you to my parents' house," Miranda decided. She tried to pull the still-shaking Helena to her feet, but then left that to her stronger cousin. "Help her up, James. I'll get the car. I think I can get it back on the road without any problems."

"Tell me your name again?" James asked, reaching for her hand to help her up. "Please don't worry. Whatever your name is, wherever you come from, wherever you're going—everything will be all right."

Helena looked into his soft brown eyes and could see that he really believed that. She didn't, though, and she didn't want to take his hand either. She never wanted to touch a man again.

"How could you know that?" she asked, suddenly angry, and pulled herself up. "You don't know me. You don't know what I've done or what I've been through."

Helena stumbled and James caught her. She flinched at his touch.

James wanted to brush the hair out of her face, to help her, to comfort her. She seemed so delicate, but strong. He felt that when he put his arm around her to support her. She didn't want him to, even though she needed help. He looked her directly in the eyes and tried to make his voice soothing.

"Helena," he began. He pronounced her name slowly and clearly, with a bit of a New Zealand accent. "I'm sure terrible things have happened to you, and maybe you've done something bad too, but it's war . . . It's impossible to judge. Some say dropping bombs on cities is justified because it'll end the war sooner. Others say it's a crime and has no effect on the length of the war. Who's right? You can tell me and Miranda, or me, or Miranda, or Miranda's parents, or whoever you want what you did and what happened. You can also forget it all and start over, Lu—Helena. I think 'Helena' is beautiful." James's heart fluttered as a shy smile stole over Helena's teary face. "And I promise you," he continued, "that you're safe now."

"When they find out, they'll throw me out of the camp," whispered Helena. "It would've been better if I had died."

James shook his head. "No!" he declared. "It won't be as bad as you think." He smiled. Miranda had gotten the car back onto the road and stopped next to them.

James reached for Helena's hand. "What do you have there?" he asked gently when he felt the figurine in her fingers. Instinctively, her fist tightened around it as though he would try to take it from her. He managed to catch a glimpse of it. "Oh, a *hei-tiki*." He recognized it. "I have one too," he revealed, pulling a necklace out from under his shirt. "A present from a friend."

Helena looked at the jade figurine. James's little god had wings like a bird. "A *manu*, a dragon, and this one is a 'birdman,' he explained. "Really, birdmen are much bigger, and made from bark or leaves. The Maori fly them at certain times to send messages to the gods. This one flew with me, keeping me safe." Helena wondered whether Miranda's cousin now expected her to tell him about her *hei-tiki*. She kept quiet. He seemed familiar with the Maori gods, so if she told him about Hineahuone, he would probably at once know her predicament.

"Well, let's get in the car," James suggested without pressing her further. "And Miranda, try and drive a little more carefully. Helena's been frightened enough, and I've had it with close calls today too."

Miranda wouldn't have let that stop her, had there been any more opportunities to race around curves, but the Billers' driveway wasn't far, and wasn't paved. Miranda had to be extremely careful with her low-set sports car. Half a mile later, they reached the house, which was painted blue and white with a veranda wrapping around the house, decorated with carvings. Beside the house were stables. In the last light of evening, they could make out two small, strong horses grazing in a nearby pasture, against the spectacular background of the mountains.

"You have horses," Helena said softly. Back in Lwów she had drawn horses in her schoolbooks and dreamed of someday learning to ride.

Miranda nodded. "Vince and Vallery," she introduced them. "Do you like horses? If you want, we can go riding tomorrow before we drive back to Pahiatua. They're very well behaved."

Helena felt something like yearning before the thought came to her that a fall from a horse could cause a miscarriage. Vince and Vallery, a sorrel and chestnut, didn't seem likely to throw a rider, though.

"Miranda, maybe Helena comes from the city and doesn't know how to ride," James said. He turned to face Helena, who sat in back, and smiled at her. "We don't really know anything about you."

Helena didn't return the smile. She had just moments ago wanted to finally say everything she'd been hiding, but now she only wanted to be quiet. She was completely exhausted.

"Well, come in, come in," Miranda said after parking the car in front of the stables. "My mother will be waiting. Though she probably only expected us."

James momentarily wondered how his aunt could relax, knowing how Miranda drove, but he forgot his thoughts right away when Lilian Biller threw open the door.

"Well, there you are! James, my boy, I didn't believe you were really back until now. And your mother's already called three times." Lilian Biller didn't let James get a word in. She danced down the steps of the veranda and hugged him. Helena was struck by how like her daughter Mrs. Biller was. Lilian seemed like an older version of her daughter. She was just as slender, red haired, and graceful—but shorter. James was a head taller than she was. "Did you have a good drive? I expected you would've gotten here sooner, but in this weather you can't really drive all out. I suppose it's good for you to drive carefully, Miranda."

James made a face.

Lilian spied Helena, smiled at her, and held out her hand in greeting. "And who is this here? You didn't find a girlfriend at the pier, did you, James? I know you air force boys are fast fliers, but Miranda was supposed to fetch you from the ship itself, so you wouldn't run away from us again." She threatened James jokingly with her finger.

Helena blushed.

Miranda started to introduce her, but James was faster. "Aunt Lily, this is Helena," he explained. "She's one of the Polish refugees Miranda works with. We picked her up on the way."

Lilian Biller furrowed her brow. She was as smart as she was joyful and spontaneous.

"Picked her up? This far from Pahiatua?" Lilian looked at Helena more closely. "You're wet as the cat that missed the fish, child," she said. "We'll get you warm and dry first, and then you can tell us what brings you this way."

"First of all we should call Pahiatua and say that Luzyna . . . that Helena is with us," Miranda said. "I don't know if you told the caretakers where you were, Lu—Helena, but you're supposed to be back at camp by seven, you know. If you're not, they'll miss you, and then there'll be trouble."

Helena shrugged. "There will be anyway," she murmured, but didn't object when Miranda went straight to the telephone.

Miranda informed the camp administration, without going into detail, that Luzyna Grabowski would be spending the night with her family. With a bit of luck, the secretary in Pahiatua wouldn't know where the Billers' summer home was, and as naturally as Miranda described an accidental encounter and an invitation from her parents, it could have happened in Palmerston.

Relieved, Helena followed Miranda's mother into the large living room, which along with the spacious kitchen occupied almost the whole ground floor. The room was made cozy by a large fireplace in which a fire hissed, although it was summer. The room was comfortably furnished with bulky wooden furniture and could have been in any farmhouse anywhere if it weren't for the Maori artifacts everywhere. Helena noticed statues of gods, instruments, and weapons. On the walls were weavings and one of the dragons on which James's *hei-tiki* was modeled.

"My father collects these things," Miranda explained.

Lilian laughed. "And I get to dust them," she declared dramatically. "Now sit by the fire, Helena, and I'll have a bath drawn for you. There's nothing like a hot bath on a day like this. And you, James, get on the phone and call your mother. Gloria and Jack are waiting on tenterhooks." James wanted to say something, but Lilian cut him off. "I know you're angry. You can curse at your father on the telephone for all I care—the main thing is you're safe."

4

Helena felt she was in a dream as she slipped into the softly scented mountain of foam in Lilian Biller's bathtub. The fact that Miranda's mother had a private bathroom seemed unbelievable to Helena. Lilian had expressly designated this luxurious bathroom as "mine," and it could only be reached through her bedroom. The bedroom was likewise impressive. Helena had read about canopy beds but had never seen one. But here one was, covered with a dark-blue comforter and many pillows and surrounded by a cloud of light-blue curtains.

Helena let herself relax in the warm water, enjoying the invigorating rose scent and letting her gaze wander over the rest of the room. Elegant standing lamps with Tiffany glass shades bathed everything in a soft, sleepy light. The bath mats were a cheerful, fluffy honey yellow, with matching towels. The sink looked to be made of marble, and on the washstand were seemingly expensive perfumes in colorful bottles. Miranda's family must be rich to have a house like this. Did professors in New Zealand make that much? Then Helena recalled that Miranda's mother was a successful novelist, so she was probably the one who made the money, and she clearly had no qualms about using her money for personal luxuries.

Helena thought Miranda's mother was nice, if a bit strange. Lilian Biller acted more like an older sister than an authority figure, and she seemed so much younger and more carefree than Helena remembered her own mother being. Even before their deportation, Maria Grabowski had been a serious person. She had joked with Luzyna only once or twice, and she never warmed up to anyone outside the family.

Lilian Biller, on the other hand, treated Helena like a member of the family already. Helena was a bit uncomfortable when she looked at the soft flannel pajamas and the fluffy bathrobe Miranda's mother hung on a hook for her. "Your dress is soaked through, and dirty. We'll have to wash it," she had said with an encouraging smile before she left Helena alone in the bathroom. "And my things—or Miranda's, for that matter—won't fit you. Just get yourself ready for bed. We're the only ones here, after all." Helena wondered if it was proper to be in nightclothes among complete strangers. On the other hand, this soft, luxurious bathrobe would cover more of her body than any dress did.

As Helena relaxed in the tub, washing her body with scented soap and her hair with rose water, her spirits were refreshed. She began to think clearly again—and her worries and guilt resurfaced. As welcome as she felt here, she had to decide how much of her story to tell the Billers. She would have to tell them the worst part, about the growing baby in her belly. And she had already told Miranda and her cousin her real name. She would have to tell them that she'd come instead of her sister, though she couldn't bring herself to confess her betrayal of Luzyna. Just the thought of how these kind people would look at her if she admitted to having abandoned her sister made her feel sick.

Helena reluctantly left the cooling water, wrapped the towel around herself, and brushed her hair in front of Lilian's mirror, which was framed with tendrils of stained-glass flowers. As she slipped into the pajamas and bathrobe, she went over what she would share and what she would keep to herself, though the thought of keeping secrets from this kind family was painful.

Helena padded downstairs in the somewhat-too-small slippers Lilian had put out for her. She stepped quietly down the winding blonde-wood staircase that led from the hall straight into the living room. More lamps had been lit, and Helena noticed a dining table as well as armchairs and sofas. James sat in front of the fireplace with an older man Helena guessed to be Miranda's father. They were drinking whiskey, while Miranda set the table. Through the open kitchen door, Helena saw Lilian pull a steaming casserole from the oven.

"I hope I didn't burn it," Lilian said lightly. "Mrs. Barker told me three times how long to bake it. She thinks I'm useless." Mrs. Barker was the Billers' housekeeper, Helena learned later. Mrs. Barker had prepared the casserole before taking the evening off with her husband and clearly didn't like leaving her employer alone in the kitchen. "But I can cook, you know," Lilian declared, placing the casserole on the dining room table. "When Ben and I lived in Auckland, I always cooked myself, didn't I, Ben? And it was good."

Ben Biller—a tall, thin man with blonde, wispy hair and a long, likeable face—gave her a warm look.

"We were head over heels back then," he said, not answering the question.

Miranda giggled.

Lilian looked from her daughter to her husband, feigning hurt feelings. "One more word from you, Ben, and I'll read everyone the poems you wrote for me back then."

James laughed too; Ben Biller's poems must have been infamous.

Just then, Lilian noticed Helena. "Helena, oh lovely, you've come down. And you look much better now. Ben, this is our young guest from Poland. A friend of Miranda's from the refugee camp. She ended up stranded here, somehow, but you can tell us the story later, Helena. Now, let's eat. Helena, you can sit across from James."

Helena moved to take her seat, self-conscious about her unusual dinner attire. Still, James pulled the chair out for her, as if she were a queen. He smiled at her again—this time with something like admiration in addition to the kindness in his eyes. Helena looked down, equal parts self-conscious, nervous, and flattered. Did he think her beautiful?

Anxiously, she tried to pull her hair back into an improvised braid. James winked, handing her a napkin with a mischievous grin.

"You can keep it down," he said, in his calm, warm voice. Helena, against her better judgment, felt suddenly that she couldn't lie to him. "It looks nice. You look like . . . like a girl in a painting."

Miranda glared at him, but Lilian agreed.

"He's right," she said. "Look, Miranda. Doesn't she look a bit like the Mona Lisa?"

Helena blushed.

"Or like a Madonna in a Catholic church," Ben Biller added after looking closely at Helena.

Helena didn't know where to look, so she turned her gaze to her plate. Professor Biller was assessing her with the same friendly interest Miranda had said he brought to everything; he clearly had no interest in anyone other than his Lilian.

James McKenzie's eyes would have betrayed his feelings, though, had Helena found the courage to look up.

"Oh, let her eat in peace." Miranda firmly ended the discussion "It's embarrassing to be compared to women in old paintings. She's a modern girl. And hungry too, I bet."

She winked at Helena and served her a large helping. Helena's mouth watered—she only now realized how hungry she was, and forced herself not to pounce greedily on the food.

The Billers didn't comment when she devoured a second, and then a third, helping. James ate with similar verve. He clearly hadn't liked the food on the ship.

By the time the table was cleared, Miranda could no longer contain her curiosity. The men had built the fire up again, and Helena had curled up in a corner of the sofa while Miranda and Lilian took their places in armchairs.

"Now, Helena, tell us," she said encouragingly, "how'd you end up on the road in Lower Hutt, and why're you Helena and not Luzyna, and what was so terrible that you"—Miranda stopped at the last moment before announcing Helena's suicide attempt to the whole family—"that you were crying so hard?"

Helena took a deep breath. "My name is really Helena," she finally said. "Luzyna's my younger sister." She told them about the opportunity to immigrate to New Zealand, and that she had been too old at eighteen. "I wanted a new life so much. But Luzyna didn't—"

"And so you switched passports," Miranda cheerfully interrupted. "Clever! As long as everyone who knew you kept quiet."

Helena nodded, relieved that Miranda had saved her from having to lie—or worse, tell the truth about leaving Luzyna. Then, her voice quiet and halting, she told them about Witold, burning with shame. She would never before have thought of talking about his assaults, let alone in the presence of men. She kept her eyes down, and blushed deeply as she fell quiet at the end of this part of the story. She was surprised that the Billers didn't seem shocked, or to think she was to blame. They were outraged by Witold's cruelty, but sympathetic toward Helena.

Miranda alone shook her head at Helena's naiveté. "Helena," she groaned. "You were already in Bombay. That fool could have said whatever he wanted; they wouldn't have sent you back or even investigated. I would've brushed him off as cold as you please. Or turned him in. He would've put his tail between his legs in an instant, count on it."

Tears filled Helena's eyes, and Lilian laid a comforting hand on her arm. "Helena was terrified, Miranda," she explained in a reproving tone. "None of us can imagine what she was going through. Just think what she had already survived. Deportation, Siberia, forced labor, the loss of her parents, being shipped to Iran, the camp." She turned to Helena. "Of course you were afraid, my dear. Don't let anyone make you feel guilty."

Tears streamed down Helena's cheeks anyway. "I won't." She swallowed. "I . . . I wanted to forget it. I would've forgotten it. He left me alone once we were in Little Poland. He's going to marry a New Zealander and naturalize here. Everything would've been fine . . ."

"Except?" asked James, as kind as he was oblivious.

Lilian looked knowingly at Helena's belly. "How long have you known?" she asked softly.

"Two weeks," Helena whispered. "I've known I'm expecting for two weeks."

Lilian, Bob, and James took this in with astounding composure, but Miranda's temper flared again.

"I'd report the bastard now," she said fiercely, after Helena had told them how Witold had reacted. "It's appalling for him to make you deal with this alone."

Lilian raised her eyebrows. "What, did you think he would suddenly develop paternal feelings? Or a sense of responsibility? It's a blessing for Helena that he didn't, really. You didn't want to marry him, did you? But you should report him, for justice's sake. I can't imagine anyone would blame you, Helena. You—"

"It would be complicated, though," Ben Biller objected. He'd filled a pipe and was puffing on it pensively. "You'd have to tell them what he'd used to control you. The false papers would come out."

"And?" Lilian spoke sternly. "Don't scare the girl. As if anyone would send her back."

"But she wouldn't be able to leave the camp," Ben continued, unbothered. "She would, of course, get new papers . . . Maybe she'd become a New Zealander straight away."

"Truly?" asked Helena, rubbing her eyes. "It seems too easy for a new passport. In Europe . . . in Europe people die because they have the wrong passport. Or none at all. They're constantly checked. And you need—"

"A birth certificate," Ben finished her sentence, unflappable. "Yes, I see the problem there. If Miss Grabowski is already eighteen years old . . ."

"Nineteen," murmured Helena. "I turned nineteen at the end of the year." Her birthday had passed uncelebrated.

"If Miss Grabowski brought a birth certificate along at all, it's her sister's. To get the right one, someone would have to write to Iran, contact Luzyna, and ask her to send it. That would take months."

And it would be impossible anyway. Helena again felt as though the ground was disappearing from underneath her. Luzyna and Kaspar weren't in Tehran anymore. It would be impossible to track them down.

"That's true," Miranda agreed with her father. "And Helena wouldn't be allowed to leave Little Poland. She'd have to give birth there."

"Everyone would know," whispered Helena. "About me and Witold. And . . . and what if they don't believe me then? Witold will deny everything."

"He could even claim Helena made it all up." Lilian the novelist had a mind for the dramatic. She didn't seem to notice how much she frightened Helena. "To explain her pregnancy and find someone to care for her baby. It would be he said, she said, and the passport picture would be evidence against you. I expect Luzyna doesn't look like you."

Helena saw Luzyna's face before her again, and began to sob.

"The simplest thing would be to leave everything as it is," Ben interjected with his usual calm. "Miss Grabowski could retain her sister's identity, stay quiet about Witold's crimes, and leave the camp before her pregnancy becomes obvious."

"But where will I go?" asked Helena quietly. "I . . . I would gladly take a job. In Wellington or anywhere. If . . . if I could get a work visa. Only when . . . what will I do when the baby comes?"

"Don't worry about work. Come with me to Kiward Station." James finally joined the discussion, astonishing everyone. "Kiward Station is my parents' farm," he explained to Helena. "On the South Island, far from here. No one will know you there. No one will care whether you call yourself Luzyna or Helena. As for the pregnancy . . ." He thought for a moment and then looked around at everyone. "She can say she was married, and her husband was killed in the war. My parents will have to know the truth, of course, but they're pretty understanding."

James looked around expecting approval, but his gaze settled on Helena, whose tears had abruptly stopped. Would she really be able to escape everything? Was there a way out? She was looking at him with wild hope.

"But how will I get out of Little Poland?" she asked. "If I . . . that is, if I do accept your offer." She rubbed her forehead.

"Oh, getting released from the camp is the easiest part," Lilian declared self-confidently. "I'll drive you there tomorrow and arrange everything. We'll tell them we're offering her a position. As a maid or something."

Helena and Miranda shook their heads at the same time.

"We're not supposed to work," Helena explained. "We're supposed to go to school as long as possible. I wanted to try to finish."

"And you will," James agreed. "I mean, I'm sure there are schools you could attend in Christchurch."

Miranda rolled her eyes. "James, it's not about finding her a school but getting her out of the camp." She laughed mischievously. "If you lose your head so much at the sight of her, why not just offer to marry her?"

Helena's breath caught.

"If there's no other way," James responded defiantly, turning red at once when he realized what he'd said.

Lilian laughed nervously; Ben furrowed his brow.

"He's in love, he's in love. I knew it. He's in love," Miranda sang, giggling giddily.

"Nonsense," James responded gruffly. "I just want to help. I'd like to do something, to really do something for the people in this war, not just goof around like you. Taking care of children in Little Poland, that's all very nice but not exactly decisive for the war."

"And marrying Helena would be decisive for the war?" Ben asked, confused.

Lilian rolled her eyes.

"Well . . . If I'm not going to be allowed to fight," James continued heatedly, "then I want to at least do what I can here. I—"

"You don't need to sacrifice yourself for me," said Helena quietly.

This evening had been a whirlwind of emotions, and she didn't know how to feel. James had been so kind to her, but now it seemed to be less about her and more about some lofty goals.

"I would gladly do it," James maintained, still looking at Miranda.

Helena's heart sank. This was nothing more than a quarrel between cousins—about her, of all things. She looked down again.

Lilian laid her hand comfortingly on Helena's arm and turned sternly to James and Miranda. "Both of you stop it right now. Helena's embarrassed enough already." She smiled encouragingly at Helena. "Don't take these two seriously. No one's a martyr here, and if someone's in love, that's no one's business but theirs. Don't worry, Helena. I'll take you to Pahiatua tomorrow and speak with the camp administration. Of course they'll let you go, even without a marriage."

Helena, however, remained despondent. Once again other people were taking control of her life. And James: she didn't know what to think of him. People in New Zealand were so different than those in Europe. More open, but at the same time less sincere? She wondered what would become of her on this farm on the South Island.

5

Of course, they didn't need to have a wedding to get Helena released from Pahiatua. Lilian Biller brought Helena and Miranda to Pahiatua the next morning and asked to speak with Major Foxley and Mr. Sledzinski. She told Helena to wait for her in the hall, and smiled encouragingly as she was called inside. Lilian looked exceptionally elegant that morning. She wore a black-and-white paisley pencil skirt and matching suit jacket that emphasized her slender build, with silk stockings and black pumps. Her red hair was pulled up neatly, and perched atop it she wore a stylish hat somewhere between a beret and a doctoral cap.

Mr. Sledzinski drank her in with his eyes as she walked in. Exactly what Lilian Biller and the administrators discussed, Helena would never know. She waited for a half hour on the edge of her seat—and then was stunned when Major Foxley and Mr. Sledzinski walked Lilian out, smiling, and held out their hands in parting to both Lilian and Helena. Both wished "Luzyna" luck going forward. Major Foxley sounded genuinely friendly, but the Polish administrator seemed restrained. Helena thought she also noticed a reproving look—perhaps Miranda's mother had mentioned the pregnancy after all. Lilian didn't seem inclined to tell Helena anything, though.

"Well, that's done." she said cheerfully. "Fetch your things, Helena, and say good-bye to your friends."

Helena left the administrative building in a trance and ran to her former residence. Her only friend was Natalia, who was bursting with curiosity when Helena told her she was leaving camp. Helena told her parts of the truth. She told her about the Neumanns and claimed to have met Miranda and James in Wellington Harbour. They had taken her to the Billers', and all had agreed that "Luzyna" would live with the McKenzies as a ward instead of in the camp. The story had some gaps, and Natalia filled them with wild speculation.

"James saw you and wanted to bring you home right away? Oh, Luzyna, that's wonderful. His parents must be rich? They have a farm? Oh, why can't something like that happen to me? Is he handsome? Are you in love with him too?"

Helena blushed. "It has nothing to do with love," she insisted. "It's just . . ."

Natalia frowned. "So you don't love him? Or he doesn't love you? Then don't go, Luzyna. Stay here."

"It's not what you think, Natalia," Helena murmured, packing her few possessions. "It's . . . oh, I can't explain it. But it's the right thing for me." With that, she hugged her friend for a long moment, and rushed out before Natalia could say anything else. "I'll write to you," Helena called over her shoulder.

Helena sighed, but Lilian was waiting for her in the car, and Helena was already thinking about her new life. Miranda would stay in the camp and do her job. Natalia was sure to bombard her with questions, but Helena didn't care. Once again, a new chapter of her life was beginning. Once again, she didn't know what the future would bring. But her heart carried a new quiet hope for happiness.

James McKenzie did everything possible over the next few days to relieve Helena of her fear and embarrassment. The ship to Lyttelton Harbour didn't leave until Friday, so the two of the them spent the week in Lower Hutt with the Billers family. Helena devoured Lilian's novels, which she found delightful if somewhat explicit. Soon enough, she let James convince her to explore the house's surroundings. Lower Hutt was named for the Hutt River and lay near its mouth on the Pacific. The Billers' house was located farther inland, near the Taita Gorge, where the river carved its way through towering hills. The area there was heavily forested, and the paths were narrow and too overgrown for easy walking. So James saddled Lilian's horses and took Helena out for a ride.

"It's not half as dangerous as driving with Miranda," he assured her when Helena expressed concern. "And other than flying, riding is the best way to get to see a place."

Vince, the gelding, did plod along calmly behind his stablemate, Vallery, and Helena was so entranced by the landscape that she never even thought about the possibility of a fall and a miscarriage. She did worry about being alone with James. He made her thoughts scatter with his unimposing friendliness. He treated her like a cousin, though, and never so much as gave her a look that would make her uncomfortable. So Helena found herself completely relaxed on the ride. James told her about the native New Zealand flora. The forest here was dramatically different from the fir, elm, and oak forests in Poland, and the conifers of the Siberian taiga. All around her were plants she'd never even imagined: giant ferns and red-blooming rata trees, palms and beeches, and so much lichen. There were trees trailing lengths of liana, and raupo growing by the river. The dried raupo leaves were used for Maori weaving— mats and *poi-poi* and the skirts of their dancing clothes, which rustled pleasantly when worn. There were also manuka trees, and Helena was proud when she recognized the plant. James confirmed that the tree's oil had medicinal properties.

"Every soldier in the Australian army has a little bottle of tea tree oil in his kit," he explained. "Or at least they did in the First World War, according to my father. It probably wasn't much use at Gallipoli, but it works wonders on blisters and other small annoyances."

Helena told him that her *hei-tiki* was carved from manuka wood, and James looked astonished.

"*Hei-tiki* are usually carved from *pounamu* jade like mine, or bone," he said. "I've never heard of a manuka wood one before. The *tohunga* made it especially for you?"

Helena nodded. "It was kind of her, wasn't it?"

James nodded. "It probably means something," he surmised. "People don't wear them just because they're beautiful. Traditionally, there's a ceremony when a *tohunga* makes one, singing *karakia* and calling upon the gods. The wearer is put under their protection."

"Like a cross blessed by a priest?" asked Helena. Her mother had worn a cross, but had traded it for bread in Siberia.

"Probably," replied James. "You must honor your little goddess. And ask Ben about the manuka wood." Helena nodded, clasping the figurine around her neck, and reached to touch a manuka tree as they rode past. Its raw bark seemed warm against her hand, as if the spirit she'd felt in the Ngati Rangitane's *marae* greeted her again. "Now I'll show you a kauri tree."

Kauri trees, James told her, were sacred to the Maori, and they didn't reveal the trees' locations to *pakeha*. Professor Biller, however, had found one near the old *pa*. James led Helena down densely overgrown paths of ferns and lichen, and the horses carefully made their way over fallen trees lying across the undisturbed forest floor. The ride took hours, and by the time they returned Helena would be aching and exhausted. The effort was worth it, though, as they came suddenly into a clearing and saw the kauri tree.

"It's . . . huge." Helena could hardly find words. The trunk must have been twenty-five feet around.

"Kauri trees can be more than a hundred and fifty feet tall," James explained. "The oldest are thought to be over two thousand years old."

Helena could hardly imagine such a lifespan. She felt small and insignificant in the presence of the tree.

"You feel small when you fly too," James confided as she tried to put her feeling into words. "You see how vast the land is. When you fly over it, you realize you could never have 'dominion' over it, like the Bible says. The Maori have the right attitude. They see nature with more awe than we do."

That evening, Helena listened with great interest as Ben Biller discussed Maori culture. He had two students visiting that week to help with the dig, and he gave talks in the evening. As James had predicted, he had an idea about Helena's *hei-tiki*.

"The *tohunga* must have sensed strength and generosity like the tree in you. Its spirits are guardians. They protect, watch over, and heal."

"Perhaps the tree is also supposed to protect the wearer of the *hei-tiki*," one of the students posited, and Ben nodded.

"There's always a give and take," he said. "The Maori see a constant exchange between man and nature, the corporeal and the spirit."

Lilian Biller thought more practically and invited Helena on a shopping trip to Lower Hutt. Though Helena didn't know what she could buy, she was pleased to be invited.

If one didn't arrive late on a rainy Sunday afternoon, Lower Hutt was a growing, bustling little town. Lilian took Helena and James, who had joined them, to eat in a restaurant with a view of the river's mouth. There she explained that she intended to buy Helena a few articles of clothing.

"Don't worry, nothing too expensive, nothing fancy," she assured Helena, when she timidly refused. "We'd need to drive to Wellington for that anyway. But I don't like sending you to Kiward Station like that. Gloria would think I'd grown stingy."

Lilian had told Jack and Gloria McKenzie, James's parents, that Helena was coming. She had assured Helena that they would be happy to have her, though Helena was nervous. She hoped the McKenzies wouldn't draw the same conclusions Natalia had. It would be terrible for them to think she'd gotten James to help her because of her feminine charms.

After lunch Lilian took Helena to a local department store, which sold ladies' fashion and accessories. They bought a simple dark-blue dress, two blouses, and a pert little hat. The hat also matched a high-waisted light-blue dress that Lilian picked out for her. The dress fell loosely, made her look very young, and would conceal her pregnancy for another few months. Lilian added a warm coat. Although it was summer now in New Zealand, winter could get quite cold on the South Island, according to Lilian.

"But not as cold as Siberia," Helena said quietly.

Lilian put her arm around her, smiling. "Thankfully not," she said. "But that's no reason not to dress warmly. Now, we still need a few sets of underwear and a suitcase, and then we'll find James. Do you have any idea where he could be hiding?"

When James had left the women on their own to go shopping, Helena had been relieved. The little compliments James occasionally offered, like when she put up her hair or wore Miranda's old riding dress, embarrassed her, and she didn't know what to make of them. But Helena hadn't yet been as embarrassed as she was that afternoon in the small ice cream parlor where they met James.

"Here," he said, shyly pushing a box across the table. "I thought maybe Aunt Lilian had forgotten, and I didn't want to ask my mother to do it. And from Kiward Station you have to go all the way to Haldon to shop. Compared to there, Lower Hutt is a metropolis. Better to take care of it here."

Helena thought James's clarifications strange. Curious, she opened the little box. When she saw the small gold ring inside, her face turned red.

"It's, it's a . . ."

"A wedding ring," James confirmed. "You did want to pretend you were married in Poland, right?"

"I was only fourteen when I left Poland," Helena whispered.

Lilian smiled. "Who cares?" she asked. "You don't have to give details. James is absolutely right. It'll make it much easier in Haldon if everyone believes you're carrying a war hero's child. A very good idea, James. What did that pretty ring cost? I'll give you the money for it."

James reddened at her offer. "You . . . you don't need to do that. I . . . well, I was happy to do it. It wasn't that expensive. Nor was it cheap—I mean, it is supposed to look nice, after all."

Lilian laughed. "So our Helena wasn't hitched to a cheapskate, or a poor wretch either. Seems like you've already thought up a suitable husband," she teased James. "You'll have to give us all the details about him."

Helena didn't know where to look. Just moments before, she'd been excited to show James her new dress. Lilian had insisted that she put it on immediately. "If it comes to it, it'll be good for work in the kitchen," she had mused, "or the stables. Though if Gloria takes you under her wing, you'll rarely see the kitchen. So I hope you like sheep more than for roasting."

Helena wasn't sure if she liked sheep, roasted or not. She'd never really had any experience with animals. She estimated that James's family owned a lot of them, as well as dogs, horses, and several hundred cattle. Helena was excited about the horses—she was already sorry to say good-bye to Vince and Vallery.

"You'll meet some of their family," Lilian said to comfort her, pleased that Helena liked horses. "Vallery's mother, Vicky, came from Kiward Station, and Vince is Vallery's foal. I could take another horse, James. Tell Gloria and Jack to pick out a handsome mare for me. From Princess's line if possible."

⁂

Miranda had asked for another day off from the camp to drive James and Helena to the port, and Helena had to agree with James: she would have much preferred to ride gentle Vince than trust Miranda's driving.

"Oh, just wait until you fly with James sometime," Miranda said, hurt, when Helena let out a fearful gasp at a curve she took particularly sharply. "Compared to how he zips through the mountains, I'm a snail."

Helena was confused until James explained that the McKenzies had a private plane on Kiward Station: a Piper J-3 Cub, which he fondly called Pippa.

"A plane of your own is nothing special on sheep farms," he insisted when he saw Helena's shock. She had gathered that the McKenzies weren't poor, but owning a private airplane seemed decadent.

"We have a lot of land for the sheep to graze," James said, justifying the purchase. "It's easier to keep an eye on them from the air and to herd them in for shearing and the winter. It used to be done on horseback—every time, it took days of hard work to herd the sheep into the highlands and then to find them in the mountains in the fall and bring them back. And it wasn't as safe. Winter can come suddenly in the mountains, along with unexpected storms and snow. With my Pippa, I can handle the herding practically alone, and far fewer sheep get away from me than from a whole gang of riders."

"So you learned to fly there?" Helena asked incredulously.

She still couldn't quite get used to the idea that the young man beside her climbed into his own airplane as naturally as others did a streetcar.

James nodded. "Of course. My dad also flies, but he can't really make it sing. Pippa drifts too easily when he flies, especially during landing. If you want, you can fly her sometime too. It's not hard."

Helena nodded halfheartedly. She was fighting nausea in the car and hoped it was Miranda's driving and not the pregnancy. Otherwise the ship was going to be very unpleasant.

The trip from the North Island to the South Island ended up being the most pleasant journey Helena had taken by ship. Cook Strait, between the islands, proved stormy, and Helena, like many other passengers, got sick. But after that they sailed along the South Island's coast, and the sea was calm. From the deck, passengers could see the island's green hills and dark beaches. Fascinated, Helena watched a dolphin pod circle the ship, and she clung, terrified, to the railing when, near Kaikoura, a sperm whale surfaced at the bow.

"They really are enormous," she murmured, after seeing humpbacks and other whales. "Are you sure they don't eat people?"

James laughed. "No, they're very gentle. Most whales don't even have teeth. They're just curious. Look how close they come."

Helena felt she was dreaming, the trip was so pleasant. Her happiness was only darkened by the thought that Luzyna should've been in her place. What unimaginable possibilities would her lovely sister have had in this wonderful country! She compared the friendly, worldly James with the crude, somewhat stupid Kaspar. Immediately a picture of a happy young couple materialized: a life in comfort, and a wife who was respected and loved. James surely would have fallen for Luzyna.

Helena wouldn't let herself hope that James found her beautiful, though he was extraordinarily nice to her. He spent the whole day talking with her on deck and even took her to dinner in the ship's restaurant. Helena enjoyed unusual fish dishes, and when the band started playing, she heard jazz for the first time. It was intoxicating and almost demanded that you dance. James immediately asked her to dance, but she declined. She still shrank from a man's touch, and besides, she'd never danced before. She would've made a fool of herself, and everyone would've stared and whispered. Luzyna, she thought with a smile, wouldn't be an embarrassment on the dance floor. She probably would have been the center of attention. Helena smiled until she reminded herself whose fault it was that Luzyna would never have this experience. She let her head sink down again, not noticing James's smile in return.

6

After two days the ship docked at Lyttelton. From the quay, one could see the entirety of the idyllic town stretched over a hill and along a bay. The natural harbor offered even large ships room to navigate and lay anchor.

"Christchurch is the bigger city," James explained as Helena marveled at how small the town was compared to the large harbor. "It's about seven miles north of here, but Christchurch doesn't have a harbor. Ships with passengers and cargo bound for Christchurch anchor in Lyttelton. Eventually Christchurch and Lyttelton will probably grow together; more and more land between them is being settled. It used to be that all that connected the two cities was a hard mountain road. It was called the Bridle Path because guides led all the horses by their bridles since it was too hard to ride. Our family's matriarch, Gwyneira, rode it, though, over a hundred years ago. She had just settled her horse after the three-month sea voyage, trusted her, and rode over the pass. And her dog, Cleo, herded the twenty or forty sheep that made up Gwyneira's dowry, by herself. She came to New Zealand to marry Lucas Warden, heir of Kiward Station. She'd never even seen him before, and they were, unfortunately, unhappy. The story of her ride over the Bridle Path is one of our oldest family tales. Gwyn's a legend anyway. I don't remember her, though; she died when I was three. She was well over ninety." James looked over the harbor as the ship docked, and pointed at a woman waiting beside a pickup parked on the quay.

"There, look, that's my mother."

Helena had expected to recognize something of Lilian and Miranda in James's mother, but there was no trace of that red hair, slender waist, or sharp nose in Gloria McKenzie. Helena would never have guessed Gloria and Lilian were related; Gloria must have taken after a completely different branch of the family. She was sturdier compared to Lilian's fairy-like delicacy, and although her whole face lit up when she saw her son, her features looked stern. She didn't seem as open and outgoing as Miranda or Lilian either. Gloria's blue eyes stood a bit too close together, and her lips were thin and sharply defined. Her thick, light-brown hair was cut short, a style that suited her well. Gloria wore jeans and a plaid shirt under a leather jacket, and from a distance she could've passed for a man. But James's mother wasn't unattractive; she possessed an austere beauty that was revealed only on second glance.

Looking closely, Helena realized Gloria wasn't alone. Next to her was a long-haired black-and-white dog looking adoringly up at her, until it heard James's voice.

"Ainne!"

The dog's bark sounded like a cheer. James seemed considerably less excited to see his mother than he was his dog. Ainne, too, immediately lost all interest in Gloria McKenzie. She practically flew to James, who rushed down the just-lowered gangway. When they reached each other, Ainne sprang into his arms, howling, while he called her name over and over and rubbed her fur. He couldn't have looked happier; not just he but the dog, too, drew back lips and smiled.

Helena took her suitcase and threw James's bag over her shoulder; he'd dropped it when he saw Ainne. She followed him slowly, anxious about meeting his mother. Gloria McKenzie sauntered toward them, happy but at ease—clearly the impulsivity of someone like Lilian or Miranda lay far from her—and she made no attempt to interfere in the joyous reunion when she reached James and his dog. Instead, she smiled at Helena and offered her hand. She must have seen her with James at the railing.

"It seems we're not needed here," she remarked wryly, looking at James and his dog. She introduced the latter. "That's Ainne, James's sheepdog. He trained her himself. Before he ran off to fight other people's wars, they were inseparable. I'm Gloria McKenzie. And you are Miss . . . Graybauski?" She pronounced the Polish name as incorrectly as imaginable.

Helena returned her handshake self-consciously. "Grabowski," she corrected her. "But please, call me Helena."

James's mother smiled and took the duffel bag from her. "Lovely. And how nice that you speak English. I was afraid I'd have to dust off my French. Someone told me that was the language they spoke more of in Poland."

Helena nodded and explained that her mother had taught English. James finally hugged his mother, his happiness falling stiffly away.

"This is Helena," he said. "She's one of the people who, unfortunately, can't fight her own war." James was apparently ready to start the family argument right away.

Gloria sighed. "Fight with your father," she said with restraint. "I can't judge these things. I'm just happy to have you here again. And you're welcome too, Helena. We're happy to take you in and excited for the baby. Maybe we can help make the world a better place without having to let our son get shot at."

"Helena didn't have that choice," James said fiercely, ready to fight. "Her parents are dead."

Helena, uncomfortable about being an excuse for a family fight, stroked Ainne. "Does she fly your plane too?" she teased, seeking a distraction and pointing at the dog. "I mean, you did say you herd the sheep together, and she is a sheepdog, after all."

Gloria McKenzie smiled, visibly grateful for the change of subject.

"She helps sort them afterward," James explained, unable to suppress a smile himself. "But she's not afraid of the plane, so I take her with me when I fly."

"Which is fine by me," Gloria added with a crooked grin. "He flies more carefully with Ainne in the cockpit. After all, he doesn't want anything to happen to her. Oh, James, I know you're angry, but it's so good to have you back. Are you two hungry? Should we get something to eat here, or in Christchurch? Or do you still have some shopping to do, Helena?"

Helena shook her head. "We ate breakfast on the ship," she said. "And I . . . I have everything I need." She pointed to her new suitcase.

"Good." Gloria sounded relieved—shopping didn't seem to be one of her preferred activities. "Let's drive straight to Kiward Station, then. It'll take a few hours, Helena. Of course, it used to take days to get from Haldon to Christchurch, let alone Lyttelton. With cars, though, the distances have diminished."

James's mother looked just as natural in her pickup as Lilian and Miranda had at the wheels of their sleek sports cars. She also drove fast, but carefully, and Helena felt considerably safer. She still struggled with nausea, aggravated by the fact that Gloria's truck smelled strongly of dog and perhaps also a little of sheep.

The road led straight through the mountains, and Helena was glad when James suggested they stop at a lookout point on the way.

"From here, immigrants first looked out at Christchurch and the Canterbury Plains," he explained. "The city was much smaller a hundred years ago, of course." Christchurch, large by New Zealand standards, lay on the banks of a river. Helena could see a number of stone buildings, and assumed a few of them were churches. Why else would they call the city Christchurch?

James confirmed her guess, partially. "The first settlers were religious, and they built churches right away, an Anglican as well as a

Catholic one. You can go to mass at the cathedral, if you're religious. You are Catholic, right?"

"Yes." Helena nodded without elaborating.

"The city isn't named after Christ himself, though, but after Christ Church college at Oxford. Don't know who picked it, but he must have been really proud of his college." James smiled. "They also founded a university right away, and the campus looks just like Oxford. I'll have to take you sometime; they say a stroll through Christchurch can save you a trip to England. Another thing worth seeing is the streetcar. It's quite a novelty here, though of course there are undergrounds in Europe already."

While he talked, he moved to lead Helena back to the truck, but she wanted a bit more time to take in the landscape stretching away behind the city. There was so much green grass and, farther out, snow-capped mountains. They were partly hidden by clouds, and James seemed disappointed in the view. "When it's sunny, it's spectacular."

"Your farm is over there somewhere?" Helena asked, pointing to the plains beyond the city.

Gloria, who had seemed a bit bored by James's discussion of Christchurch, eagerly chimed in. "For over a hundred years," she declared proudly. "And always in the family's possession, although with a very dramatic history. We primarily breed sheep—the land's perfect for grazing. It doesn't rain enough for crops, and the soil's not good for growing. Tussock grass grows well here, but once the sod is destroyed, it's hard to grow anything else. So we let sheep graze on it—primarily for wool, but we raise some for slaughter. The last few decades we've raised cattle too. It's good business, especially now in wartime when the meat's being exported. And Kiward Station is known far and wide for it collies." She pointed to Ainne. "The most prized sheepdogs in the country. Their ancestors came from Wales with Grandma Gwyn. People still talk about Cleo and Friday. Shall we get going? We still have a long road ahead." Gloria didn't seem to care much for the outlook.

For the rest of the long trip she and James told stories about the legendary Gwyneira McKenzie, whose first husband, Lucas, became posthumously famous as a painter.

"He passed that on to his great-granddaughter," James added, pointing to Gloria. "My mother is quite talented. I can't draw at all, though."

"If he really was my great-grandfather," Gloria qualified. "Grandma Gwyn once hinted that Paul Warden was actually Lucas's half brother— that they had the same father. Lucas's father may have been so disappointed with his son that he took the production of an heir into his own hands."

"You mean, he and Grandma Gwyn . . . ?" asked James, dumbfounded. This was apparently news to him.

"I don't think it was her choice," Gloria replied. Helena felt a pang of empathy, but also some relief. Maybe she wasn't the only who had to live with such a scandal. "Lucas disappeared sometime after that," Gloria continued. "He died somewhere on the West Coast."

"And Gwyneira married her true love," James said, revealing the happy ending. "James McKenzie, known as the Robin Hood of New Zealand. He was a livestock rustler. He's my grandfather on my father's side; I was named for him. So it shouldn't be such a surprise that I'm no dove like Dad."

James seemed to want to bring the family quarrel back up, but Gloria McKenzie wouldn't take the bait.

"Tell us about your family, Helena," she encouraged.

Helena told them about Lwów, about her parents, and a little about Luzyna. Gloria didn't seem to wonder, any more than her cousin had, whether a sixteen-year-old should be left to herself. They simply accepted that Luzyna had wanted to stay in Iran. Of course, they couldn't really have understood what that meant for a young woman. Gloria, Lilian, and Miranda took New Zealand's opportunities for women for granted.

While Helena talked, Gloria navigated through seemingly endless grassland. From the Bridle Path, it hadn't looked far, but the Canterbury Plains stretched on for miles—a sea of grass dancing in the wind, only occasionally interrupted by a copse of trees, a stream overgrown with reeds, or rocks that seemed to have been placed randomly about. They saw very few farms, though they did pass some signs. James explained that there were hardly any small farms here, mostly large, wealthy farms off the highways, with paved private drives.

They reached Kiward Station around noon. Gloria turned onto a private road that first led alongside a small lake and then around a hill. Helena's breath caught when she saw the main house for the first time. Kiward Station looked nothing at all like a farmhouse. It seemed more like an English manor house—the seat of a lord or baron as described in novels, Manderley from *Rebecca*, or Thornfield Hall from *Jane Eyre*. The building was built from gray sandstone and full of large bay windows, some with small balconies. The driveway was wide, doubtlessly planned for coaches and horse teams. It wound around a circle one could easily imagine planted formally with roses. The McKenzies didn't seem to pay it any attention, though, and left it to the rata bushes.

"Well, what do you think?" James smiled.

"It's beautiful," Helena murmured.

"It's showy," Gloria judged. "The man who built it, Gerald Warden, wanted his wealth on display, to rival the British nobility. That's the context for his marrying his son to Gwyneira too. She was a Silkham, from an old Welsh noble family. Her father wanted to marry her to an actual lord and not some New Zealand sheep baron. She was promised to Lucas Warden in a blackjack game during Gerald's sheep-buying sojourn in Wales: Warden and Silkham played for Gwyneira's hand. Her father didn't take it seriously; Grandma Gwyn could have said no. But leaving for New Zealand would be the adventure of a lifetime, and she loved adventure."

With a little shove, Gloria opened the door of her pickup, which seemed to stick a bit. James let Ainne leap down before he climbed out himself and then held the door open for Helena.

"Don't look too impressed. We don't have a butler or anything," he teased. "But I'll gladly carry your suitcase up."

Helena followed him nervously up a few steps and through the entryway, which led into a grand foyer. It was certainly intended to be more impressive than its current disorderly state allowed it to be. The McKenzies seemed to put everything here and then forget about anything they didn't need immediately.

"We mostly use the entrance as a closet," Gloria McKenzie said apologetically, hanging her leather jacket on a coatrack already nearly buried beneath a pile of coats. From the foyer, they passed into what seemed to be an office: the walls were lined with file cabinets, and the desk was somewhere beneath a pile of receipts, notepaper, and pencils, along with a typewriter and a cookie tin. "This was the formal parlor," Gloria explained. "Grandma Gwyn turned it into an office. Who on a farm needs a whole room for calling cards? Being close to the entrance, it's more useful for receiving deliveries and paying wages. The formal atmosphere helps if you need to fire someone too."

Gloria McKenzie smiled sadly. She didn't seem to relish the thought of having to fire anyone.

From the office, they passed into a long salon full of heavy old English furniture. They were certainly exquisite antiques, but heavily worn from regular use. From there a wide staircase led to the second floor. Doors led off the salon into various side rooms, one of which passed through to the kitchen and so served as a dining room.

"This used to be the study," said James, showing Helena a living room while Gloria popped into the kitchen to exchange a few words with an employee puttering around there. "We use it as a living room now, especially in winter. The salon is hard to heat." A large angled sofa and bulky armchairs dominated the room, and a rocking chair was positioned in front of the fireplace, with dog blankets nearby. A dog was lounging on the sofa and leaped down with a guilty expression when James and Helena came in. "Wednesday! Shame on you," James admonished, rather halfheartedly. It seemed hard to be angry with the little tricolor collie, who greeted him almost as excitedly as Ainne had before. "She's pregnant," he explained to Helena, "so she thinks she can get away with anything." Helena turned red at once, and James was embarrassed. "And she . . . uh . . . of course she can. I mean, one ought to indulge expectant mothers a bit." Embarrassed, Helena played with the golden wedding ring she had dutifully worn since leaving Wellington. "I'll just show you your room, then," said James quickly, leading Helena up the stairs.

As James opened the door to her room from the wide hallway, Helena gasped.

"That's . . . that's . . ." She tried to smile. "That's what I call indulging."

The large, light-flooded room was furnished with delicate blonde-wood furniture. The walls were covered in bright yellow wallpaper, and the windows were draped with antique rose-colored silk curtains in remarkable condition. Yellow pillows and a matching comforter covered the bed. Someone had put a few books—novels by Brenda Boleyn—and a picture book of Maori art on the night table. A door led into a separate dressing room with mirrors and built-in drawers, through which lay a small, elegant bathroom. On the other side was a small sitting room with inviting bay windows. From the armchairs placed around a tea table in front of them, she would have an extensive view of the garden, which was thoroughly overgrown. The McKenzies had let the native plans run wild, and only maintained paths through the garden to the stables and other farm buildings.

"Do you like it?"

"It's incredible," Helena whispered, overwhelmed. "But I really don't need such big rooms."

James shrugged. "These rooms were Grandma Gwyn's. That's her." He pointed to the painting dominating one wall of the sitting room. It was a portrait of a beautiful woman with red hair and indigo-blue eyes. Miranda and Lilian were the spitting image of her, the only differences in the shades of their blue eyes and red hair. Miranda looked almost exactly like her; Gwyneira must have been about her age when it was painted. In the picture, she perched impatiently in an armchair that Helena had seen in the living room downstairs. "The only picture of her painted by Lucas Warden. She preferred to be photographed, because she didn't need to sit still as long. Since she passed we've saved these rooms for guests, and I guess . . . everyone thinks she should watch over people." He smiled apologetically at Helena.

"What a lovely thought," Helena said quickly.

"My parents have a suite on the other side of the house," James continued, pointing. "They have a view of the drive. Those were Gerald Warden's apartments when he was master of the house. I live in what were Lucas's rooms, and otherwise the house is empty. The house is immense; old Gerald Warden probably planned it for a ten-person family, so don't worry about the rooms. Just make yourself at home. Dinner's at seven, and I can come get you, if you want, so you don't get lost."

Helena wasn't worried; she had a clear sense of direction. But she was nervous.

"Should I dress for dinner?" she asked, concerned. "I mean, you have a cook."

The house seemed so much like a noble manor that she wouldn't have been surprised if everyone came to dinner in evening gowns and tuxedos.

James laughed. "The cook doesn't care what you wear," he said. "And neither do my parents. I'm sorry the house is so intimidating. Other than this place, we're completely normal people. I mean, we do have help—a cook and two maids, all of them Maori. My mother couldn't handle this giant house alone, and she doesn't want to. She and my father run the farm together, but Kiward Station is hers legally. Her mother was the heiress but didn't really want it. She was a world-famous singer; I think she still performs. Kura-maro-tini Martyn. Maybe you've heard of her?" Helena shook her head no.

"Well, she was before your time. Anyway, she lives in the United States. She was successful too; otherwise she would've sold Kiward Station. For years, that was Grandma Gwyn's biggest fear. But when my parents married, she signed the estate over to Gloria. We haven't heard much from her since, except things in the papers about her performances. I don't think she even said anything about my birth. She didn't like the thought of being a grandmother, I guess. She was extraordinarily beautiful, and I'm sure growing older didn't suit her." Helena could imagine Gloria McKenzie suffering under such a mother. It wasn't easy to hold one's own in the shadow of a beautiful, talented family member. Again she thought of Luzyna. "As I said, make yourself at home," James called to her once more before he finally left Helena alone.

Helena put her few possessions in the drawers and sat at the bay window. But instead of looking at the garden, she stared at the portrait of the young woman on the wall.

Gwyneira Warden had also become pregnant by rape. Had she felt as dirty as Helena did? Had she felt burdened by her own complicity? And was it possible that her second husband had truly loved her anyway?

7

James knocked on Helena's door exactly at seven, rather agitated. Apparently, he had quarreled with his father immediately after leaving Helena.

"I shouldn't have come home," he growled as he escorted her downstairs. "I should've actually gone to Greymouth and taken a job in the mines. Then we'd see how much they wanted me back."

Helena didn't say anything. It seemed to her that James's parents wouldn't have cared whether James spent the rest of the war on the West Coast, on the North Island, or even in Australia, so long as no one shot at him.

"But this young lady would've been sad," she finally said, pointing to Ainne, who followed James adoringly.

James's angry expression gave way to a smile. "You're right," he said, and Helena felt better at once.

James's outburst had unsettled her, but the ease with which he regained his composure confirmed her sense of the young man: James McKenzie could be quick to anger, but it didn't last long. His parents had hurt him, but they would surely make up soon.

Jack and Gloria McKenzie had already taken their places at the table when Helena and James came down, and Jack stood politely to greet his guest. He was a tall, slender man with curly red-brown hair, calm green eyes, and skin considerably darker than his son's. His face was square and lined with wrinkles—many were clearly laugh lines, but this man had also, Helena knew, lived through difficult times. Jack McKenzie seemed good-natured and reserved, and Helena found him quite likeable. He guided Helena to a place next to James and made friendly conversation while the food was being served. A young girl in a dark dress and apron but without a cap on her long black hair brought the meal out. She clearly had Maori ancestry, but Helena wondered if she might have white ancestry too.

"Thank you, Anna," Gloria said as the girl served the soup.

That's not a Maori name, in any case, Helena thought.

"So, you come from Poland, Helena?" Jack McKenzie asked, interested. "Where from, exactly?"

Helena lowered her spoon. Clearly her hosts only wanted to be nice, but it was still hard for her to speak of her lost home in Lwów.

"From Lwów," she finally said. "The name is a bit hard to say in English, but it's also called Lemberg. The city has many names, you see, because so many different peoples lived together there. Mostly in peace." Helena forced herself to take a spoonful of soup and swallow it. It was good and tasted of sweet potatoes, but her memories left a bitter aftertaste. "Lwów is in eastern Poland," she continued. "There were always lots of different people: Belarusians, Ukrainians, Jews, Poles. Now there are probably just Russians there, since . . . after the deportations." She rubbed her forehead. She felt ill just discussing it, but the McKenzies didn't mean to distress her. She saved herself by discussing the city's culture and architecture instead of the horrors of the war. "Lwów is an old city. There were many different churches, museums, and theaters. The opera is famous. My . . . my parents took us there— when we were old enough to sit still, that is." She smiled nervously.

"Did you have a big family?" Gloria asked.

Helena nodded. "Aunts and uncles," she said quietly, "and cousins, and there were four of us: my father, my mother, my sister, and me. We . . . we had a lovely house in the middle of the city. My father's practice was next door; my mother's students came to our house. Luzyna and I were never alone."

Helena couldn't keep her voice from breaking, and Gloria realized that her interest in Helena's hometown was causing her more distress than happiness.

"You don't have to talk about if you don't want to," she said understandingly, and called Anna to clear the soup bowls. "Memories can cause pain, even when they're happy. How are things with the Billers, James? Does Miranda know what she wants to study? And is Gal still excited about mining?"

James had been quiet, but he answered patiently—if also monosyllabically—Gloria's strained questions about their relatives on the North Island. He knew, of course, that these questions were just an attempt to break the silence. Lilian had telephoned several times in the last few days, so Gloria was already caught up on how the Billers on the North Island and Galahad in Greymouth were doing.

Jack finally ventured a harmless subject. "It's been unusually cold the last few days," he commented.

This tactic proved fruitless—James was taking every opportunity to bring the conversation back to the war.

"If you think it's cold here," he said sarcastically, "ask Helena about Siberia."

Helena lowered her head, embarrassed. She didn't find it cold on the Canterbury Plains at all.

"You were interned there, right?" Jack did ask, with friendly concern. "In a work camp?"

Helena nodded. "At a mine," she said, stiffly. She didn't like to talk about life in Lwów, much less their years in Vorkuta. "They usually sent us girls into the forest to break branches off trees. It wasn't such difficult work."

"That sounds difficult enough for young girls," said Jack, touched, "especially in the ice and snow. Your parents didn't make it?"

Helena nodded again. She absolutely didn't want to talk about that. But James had his father where he wanted him. "You see what happens when people don't stand up to Hitler?" he crowed. "Men like that have to be stopped. It's up to everyone. Every man who can carry a weapon."

That sounded lofty, but an expression of amusement promptly lit Jack McKenzie's square face. "But it was Stalin who deported you, wasn't it, Miss Grabowski?" he asked with emphatic friendliness. "Hitler only entered Poland after breaking the nonaggression pact with Russia. And then Stalin joined the Allies, and now fights on the same side as your Royal Air Force."

James reddened.

"Of course, that could quickly change," Jack spoke on, at ease. "The Germans will soon be defeated, after all, so we can just continue right along eradicating evil from the world, by bombing Moscow next, for example. Brand new flight plans, James. I'm sure it'll be fun flying."

Heated, James started to respond, but Gloria intervened, firmly changing the subject.

"Well, I'm glad James will be flying his Pippa again to help herd the sheep in. I've decided to bring them back from the highlands early, Jack. All the forecasts are calling for an early and hard winter. I think we'll bring them back in four or five weeks at the outside. If we wait too long, it'll be risky. Tomorrow, you could show Helena the farm, James. Lilian says you enjoyed riding, Helena? I'm glad. We'll pick a nice horse out for you."

Helena bit her lip. She couldn't possibly accept all this.

"I . . . I'd like to do more than ride and . . . and read and relax," she said quietly. "The rooms are so beautiful, Mrs. McKenzie, but I would like to make myself useful. If you have some kind of work I could do."

Gloria smiled. "Oh, we'll find something. First, get to know the place. You've never been to a farm before, have you? No one stays idle here for long. There's just too much to do for that."

And it was true. Helena had slept fitfully, despite her exhaustion. She hadn't had a room to herself since leaving Lwów all those years ago, and now found she missed the sounds of others. When she did get up the next morning and leave the house, she realized immediately that the management of the farm left Gloria no time to even think about the household. Even though most of the sheep were in the highlands, leaving only a few in the yard and the surrounding pastures, there was plenty to do. The cattle had to be fed and watered, and mucking the stables took a long time. Jack was already on a tractor when James and Helena began their tour of the farm, and Gloria was busy moving sheep around. The large stables that housed the fatlings during summer were being cleared for the ewes coming in from the mountains. Helena watched, fascinated, the way the dogs worked with Gloria. She directed her three collies with curt commands, and at a whistle from her, James's Ainne joined them and nipped at the heels of a ram who had run off.

"You two can bring the horses into the house pasture," Gloria called to James and Helena. "Peter and Arama have to muck the stables. Why don't you go for a ride and take these sheep to the Ring of Stone Warriors?"

Helena was glad Gloria had included her in the instructions, though she didn't think she'd be much help herding sheep. As it turned out, she didn't have to do anything. James and Ainne, joined by Wednesday, performed the task on their own, and Helena rode a well-behaved old horse that trotted after James's powerful gelding without needing direction on her part. She could simply relax and enjoy the ride. James, on the other hand, followed the sheep as they were driven by the dogs. Helena wondered how they knew the way. There were no narrow, winding paths here, as there had been in Lower Hutt, just endless pasture. Did James orient himself by the sun?

"Oh, nonsense, I use the landmarks," he laughed, when she finally asked. "The little grove there, for example—those are southern beech trees, which are everywhere here. And there are rocks here and there. Those over there we call the Ring of Stone Warriors."

He pointed at a strange rock formation that lay in front of them and right away whistled the dogs back. The sheep were to graze freely in this area.

"Did someone place them there?" asked Helena.

The massive boulders formed a circle, as if gnomes had gathered to dance and then turned to stone.

James shook his head. "No, they've been there for thousands of years." He dismounted and held Helena's horse so she could follow suit. She swung herself awkwardly out of the saddle. She was sure it was easier in trousers like Gloria wore, but Helena had never seen women in pants before the war, and certainly not in Iran or India, nor in the small town of Pahiatua. Only in Wellington had she first noticed a few sophisticated-looking women wearing wide, elegant pants.

"They got their name from Grandma Gwyn. The Maori have a different name for the formation. For them, this is sacred ground. They pray to the gods and spirits in rocks and rivers."

"So this is a Maori graveyard?" Helena inquired. She recognized gravestones in the clearing in the center of the rocks.

"No." James led his horse between the boulders to the gravestones. "Actually, it's ours. James and Gwyneira McKenzie are buried here. The Maori gave Grandma Gwyn permission to bury James here. He'd always been an ally to them, and even spoke their language, which was rare back then. Burying him here was a delicate matter, though. There's a family cemetery on Kiward Station, but Grandma Gwyn didn't want to be buried next to Gerald Warden, and she wanted to be buried beside James. My parents have already asked for permission for when they die. It was easier to get, too. Grandma Gwyn outlived Tonga, and Koua only wanted money."

Helena wondered who Tonga and Koua were, but as she approached the graves she grew quiet. She felt close to the woman who lay buried here, and even to the man at her side. The Maori were right: this was a magical place. Helena had never felt so moved at a grave before. Even when her parents were buried, she had only felt sadness and emptiness, while she now thought she felt the presence of a higher power.

"Don't the sheep mess things up?" Helena asked, glancing at the animals that had strewn themselves around the stone circle and were now grazing peacefully. "I mean, they could knock over the gravestones."

"That's the strange thing about the sheep," James mused, sitting down in the grass. "Grandma Gwyn wouldn't pasture them here for years because the local Maori chieftain opposed it. Tonga believed in the traditions, and the Ring of Stone Warriors was *tapu*. It was really just a power game. Grandma Gwyn and Tonga fought their whole lives over who had say over this land. My parents were able to put that behind them, though. My mother has Maori ancestry, and she lived with the Ngai Tahu for a long time and knows their traditions. She proved to Tonga that half of his sacred land on Kiward Station was in fact not *tapu*. Since then, this area has been used for grazing. But the sheep won't touch the grass inside the stone circle. No idea why—Moana thinks they sense something spiritual, but I don't buy it. It's probably just bad to them. In every pasture there are parts that just don't taste good."

"Who is Moana?" Helena inquired.

"A friend," James answered evasively. "Koua's daughter."

"And who's Koua?"

"The current chieftain," James said. "The *ariki* of our local Maori tribe. A *hapu* of the Ngai Tahu."

Helena nodded. She had listened to Ben Biller's talks closely for days. The Ngai Tahu were the tribe to which almost all Maori on the South Island belonged. On the North Island, on the other hand, there were many different tribes. Members mostly lived together in one place, but very large tribes divided into several *hapu*. Originally, every *hapu* had a *marae*, but now many tribal members lived outside the ancestral villages.

"So there's a *marae* near here?" Helena asked, testing her knowledge. James nodded and whistled for the dogs. It was time to head home.

"Right next door," he answered. "The Ngai Tahu used to live on the grounds of Kiward Station, beside the little lake along the driveway. Later they moved to their own land. They're on the old O'Keefe farm that borders on Kiward Station, and no one can drive them from there, no matter what they're always calling for in Haldon."

"Why would anyone want to force them to leave?" Helena asked, shocked. She thought of the Maori at Palmerston. "I mean, they're not bothering anyone."

James shrugged. "From what I hear, a lot of people in the village think they're trouble. We've always gotten along well, though, despite any differences with Tonga. But we have family ties—my great-grandmother on my mother's side belonged to the tribe. She had children after Kura-maro-tini, so my mother has aunts and uncles in the *marae*, and I have more cousins than I can count. My father has friends in the tribe, too, and my mother—they say she almost married Koua's older brother, Wiremu. I could tell you so many stories, but let's go to the hangar and I'll show you Pippa."

⚘

Helena found the McKenzies' family stories much more interesting than the bright yellow single-motor prop plane, which sat in a port of corrugated metal. But James was excited to explain all the workings of the plane and would've liked nothing more than to take her up. It was getting late, though, and Jack and Gloria were expecting James to help feed and care for the animals.

Though Helena was sore after the long ride, she tried to help. She was delighted to bring hay to the horses' stables, and she was happy when they whinnied and snorted expectantly when they saw her approach with the bucket of oats.

"They really communicate their feelings," she said enthusiastically at dinner.

The dinner talk was significantly less forced than the previous evening's. Even James lost his reticence and answered questions about the sheep and farm. Ultimately, conversation came back around to the Maori.

"Where is Moana, anyway?" he asked his mother, serving himself some sweet potatoes. "She used to be here almost every afternoon."

"In Dunedin," Gloria told him. "Studying to become a teacher. Remember, she applied to the university? And not long after you left, she was accepted. I don't know if she came back for break. Perhaps she stayed with Wiremu's family."

"But"—Helena recalled that one of Ben's lectures and one of Lilian's novels focused on a chieftain's daughter—"didn't you say Moana's the *ariki*'s daughter?" She turned to James. "How can she leave? I thought— that is, Professor Biller said chieftains' daughters are like priestesses for the tribes. That they have great, um, spiritual significance." Helena stumbled a bit on the word, which was new for her.

The others laughed.

"Ben lives in another world," Jack said. "A hundred years ago, the chieftain's families were subject to strong *tapu*. There was a lot they weren't allowed to do, and things they were required to do. Ben can talk about that for hours, and it's really interesting. But the Ngai Tahu had relaxed these traditions even before Kiward Station was founded. They assimilated with the colonizers more thoroughly than the tribes on the North Island—because they were so outnumbered, for one, and it was simply more practical. The culture they brought from Polynesia wasn't really suited for New Zealand's climate, especially on the South Island. People froze in traditional clothing, they had no domesticated animals and lived entirely by hunting, and they couldn't do much farming, since other than *kumara* their crops didn't really take. And then the colonizers arrived with sheep and cattle, warm clothing, blankets, household goods, and seeds. The Ngai Tahu began to trade with them right away. They were often taken advantage of, though, and more than a few crooks tricked them into exchanging thousands of acres of land for a few blankets and household items."

"Don't speak ill of our forefathers," Gloria teased her husband. "Gerald Warden was one of those crooks, you see," she explained to Helena.

Jack grinned. "Not one of my forefathers," he said. "Just yours, my love."

Gloria smiled. "Grandma Gwyn compensated them later. Jack's right, though: virginal chieftains' daughters sending their tribe's men to battle in elaborate rituals haven't existed here for at least a century. Assuming the Ngai Tahu even had time for that nonsense, I think they had enough to do just finding food. Moana is trying to reawaken her people's spirituality, though. She sees herself in the tradition of the *ariki tapairu*, and teaching is among the duties of a *tohunga*."

"If European princesses are repairing cars now," Jack added, referring to the wartime activities of the British heir apparent, Elizabeth, "why shouldn't our chieftains' daughters study?"

Both Helena and Gloria noticed that James let the mention of the war go without using it to start an argument. James's mother winked at Helena when they finally said goodnight.

"Sleep well, Helena. It's nice to have you here."

Illusions

CANTERBURY PLAINS, NEW ZEALAND (SOUTH ISLAND);
PAHIATUA, NEW ZEALAND (NORTH ISLAND)

JANUARY–JUNE 1945

1

Helena wouldn't admit how afraid she really was when James insisted on taking her for a ride in Pippa a few days later. Gloria, however, could see it on her face.

"Stick to a reconnaissance flight," she warned her son. "No herding sheep, even if you're itching to. Otherwise that girl will never fly with you again."

Helena took it that herding the sheep required some daring maneuvers, and thought she would have died of fright. Though Gloria might have just been thinking about her stomach. Helena did feel sick right after takeoff, when James took the first hard turn. The little airplane banked sharply, and Helena was pressed hard against her seat behind James and had to keep herself from screaming. After that, she focused with determination on the view instead of thinking about the potential dangers of flying. She took in the expanse of the Canterbury Plains, which made even Kiward Station look like a dollhouse. James showed her the courses of the Waimakariri, Rakaia, and Selwyn Rivers, and she noticed tiny sheep and cattle grazing on their banks. They saw a few sheep farms—recognizable from the air by the hall-like shearing sheds—and one or two groupings of run-down-looking huts and houses.

"Those were once *marae*," James commented. "Hardly anyone lives there now. They just sit there rotting."

Helena had a lot of questions about that, but with the propeller's noise, conversation was impossible. He flew them over the small town of Haldon, saying something about the mines there, which she didn't quite catch. Then he steered toward the mountains. Helena's breath caught when they reached the southern foothills and the snow-decked peaks lay directly ahead. From their height she could see down into ravines and over high ridges. Of course James couldn't help himself when they spotted the first sheep in foothills. Excited, he immediately dove to drive the sheep from the slopes into the basin. It was only when Helena screamed in fear that he remembered his mother's warning.

"It's not dangerous," he insisted, righting the plane.

She forgot her fear quickly at the sight of a mountain lake and spectacular rock formations.

"Well, wasn't it beautiful?" asked James triumphantly when they had finally landed.

Helena nodded cautiously. The mountains' beauty had impressed her, but she was relieved to be on solid ground again. Ainne, who'd been waiting in the hangar, was happy to see them. She greeted Helena like a member of the family, and Helena's heart swelled. In the short time Helena had been on the farm, the dogs, cats, and horses had already found a place in her heart. Her family never had pets, and with the war she was grateful for that—they would've starved in the empty house in Lwów. But Helena loved spending time with the animals, and every day she managed to become a little more useful in the stables.

Dinner with the McKenzies was a pleasant affair. That evening James told them about the flight and how brave Helena had been. She blushed.

"What did you say about Haldon?" she asked, to divert attention from herself. "I couldn't quite hear you. Are there really mines there?"

"There were," Jack answered. "A long time ago, though. In the 1850s a few mines were opened around Mounts Hutt and Somers. Mostly coal, but a handful looked for gold too. Miners poured in, hoping for deposits like on the West Coast. Even sleepy little Haldon had a few mines, and for a while, the town seemed to be growing. There was work to be had, and stores opened. But the coal dried up, and one after another the mines were shut down. There're only two or three left in the area, and they'll shut down soon. It's not worth it; they get triple the returns on the West Coast."

"There was never much gold here," Gloria added.

"And that little boom didn't do the towns any favors," Jack continued. "Some of the miners moved on, but a lot had started families, put down roots, and stayed. The population of Haldon is much higher than before the mines. And now there's a lot of unemployment."

"But there doesn't have to be," objected James. "There's a war, and if the men were to volunteer . . ."

Jack McKenzie rolled his eyes. "Then the city would have war orphans and widows to take care of too."

"But James is right," Gloria interjected before the quarrel could flare up again. "There doesn't need to be any unemployment in New Zealand. The men could move to the cities and find work. There's all kinds of factory work, especially with the war, processing meat and vegetables to send to Europe. I only have so much sympathy for those boys who hang around Haldon doing nothing. There's always some idleness behind people's complaining. On both sides."

Helena wondered what Gloria meant, but changed the subject again. James and his father got along much better when the topic was dogs or horses.

A week later, Helena joined James on a shopping trip to Haldon to pick up supplies for repairs, among other things.

"Wouldn't you rather go yourself?" Helena asked Gloria shyly when she saw that the long list included toiletries and clothing. Of course, the selection of wool sweaters in a small-town general store wouldn't be overwhelming, and Helena didn't imagine she could go too far astray when it came to fashion and taste. But most of the women she knew preferred picking out their things themselves. And getting away from the remote farm as rarely as Gloria McKenzie did, every excursion could really be an event.

Gloria shook her head, claimed she had too much work, and called for the dogs. Ainne, however, jumped into the pickup next to James.

"My mother doesn't like to shop," he explained as they drove off. "She doesn't really like to go anywhere at all. It was a feat that she picked us up from Lyttelton. Usually Dad would've gotten us, but she was probably worried we'd tear each other to pieces on the ride home. You can believe it when she says she'd rather stay on Kiward Station. She's probably thanking heaven you're here; otherwise, she'd have to venture into the lion's den herself."

Helena furrowed her brow. "What's so dangerous about a store in Haldon?"

James shrugged. "Nothing, if you ask me. The owner is a gossip, and she always peppers Mom with questions. She'd probably gawk a bit too, since Mom doesn't bother to put on a dress to come to town. It's all torture for her. She just isn't a people person. Must have something to do with her childhood. She went to an English boarding school with Aunt Lilian, and Lilian had a wonderful time, but it was awful for Mom. She only came back to Kiward Station when the First World War was almost over. Her parents had taken her to America, where they were living. I don't know what happened after that. She doesn't talk about it, but she must have moved heaven and earth to make it home, by way of Australia. And now she never wants to leave again."

Helena wondered at the strange story, but didn't say anything. Though the streets were only partially paved, they were almost to Haldon.

The town really was a backwater. There was a lumber and hardware store, a general store, and a post office, as well as carpentry and smithy shops. But only the liquor trade seemed to really flourish. Helena noticed three pubs already open, though it was still morning.

"Like Mom said, the men don't have anything to do," James explained disapprovingly, noticing Helena's surprised face. Clearly he shared his mother's opinion about unemployment in Haldon, which was visible not just in the pubs. A few young men were hanging out in front of the hardware store as James parked the pickup.

"Back already, McKenzie?" one of them asked. "Shot down all the Nazis?"

The other men laughed.

"Or were you called back?" asked another. "I heard your daddy had you fetched. Vital to the war effort, your Kiward Station is."

There was further laughter.

"Don't suppose you'd need a few hands, seeing as things are going so well?" the first man added.

James shook his head, visibly relieved to have a practical question. "Sorry, Jeb. We've got men enough. Might be my mother will hire a few men to help herd the sheep next month, but she always wants experienced people. You could ask her."

"She only ever hires Maori," objected the man who mocked Kiward Station's importance to the war. "She likes those savages. They're cheaper, I bet."

James seemed to want to say something, but held his tongue. Helena realized she'd only gotten to know one of the workers on Kiward Station so far: Maaka, the foreman. He was Maori and good friends with Jack McKenzie. The other shepherds she only knew by name. She remembered Peter—unquestionably an English name—and Arama.

As they went in, James greeted an employee of the hardware store, a Maori, with a friendly *kia ora*. The two of them spoke a bit in Maori; Helena had learned that James spoke it fluently.

"This is Helena Grabowski," he said, switching to English, probably for the benefit of the other customers too. Helena blushed and looked nervously at the wedding ring she was wearing. James had reminded her to wear it. "Mrs. Grabowski is a refugee, from Poland," James continued. "Her husband was killed in the war."

Helena bit her lip, hoping no one would ask questions.

The young Maori nodded. "*Haere mai*, madam. I'm Kori. I'm sorry to hear about your husband. I hope you like it here in our country."

He and James began discussing nails and screws. Once they settled on a price, Helena helped James carry everything to the truck. Neither Kori nor the men outside offered to help.

"Can the Maori join the army too?" Helena asked James as they crossed the street toward the general store.

James nodded. "Of course. They're citizens, at least in theory, though our two cultures have had a lot of tension in the past few years. There'd be trouble if there were *pakeha* and Maori soldiers the same unit. But the British made special Maori battalions, and they have a reputation for excellence. The Maori are born warriors. They fight like the devil when they want to. Not many volunteer though; understandable given the way whites treat them."

He looked meaningfully at a pub where two Maori had just stepped out. She couldn't see the bartender, but heard customers jeer until the men were out of sight. All this while another Maori was unloading boxes of liquor and carrying them through the pub's back door.

As they entered the general store, a Maori girl was stocking the shelves.

"Reka, can't you work any faster? You look like you're about to fall asleep," came the sharp voice of the store's proprietress, as the girl exchanged a friendly *kia ora* with James. "If I watch her closely, I can see her start dreaming with her eyes open," the woman remarked, in an apologetic tone, to James and Helena. "She's just as dumb and lazy as the one I had before her."

She spoke loudly enough for Reka to hear her, and Helena hoped James would defend the young woman. He ignored it, though, turning all business.

"Mrs. Boysen, allow me to introduce Helena Grabowski." Helena tried not to blush as James told her about Helena's war-hero husband. "Mrs. Grabowski will be with us for a few months, working for my mother," James continued. "Please help her find everything on this list my mother gave her." He smiled at Helena as well as Mrs. Boysen. "Just put everything on our tab."

Mrs. Boysen's haggard, thin-lipped scowl transformed into the picture of friendliness as she eagerly showed Helena textiles while rudely ordering Reka to gather the other items on the list. Reka took the paper without comment; she could read, so she couldn't have been all that stupid.

"I'm headed to the smithy." James took his leave. "I'll pick you up here when I'm done."

As soon as they were alone, Mrs. Boysen began to sound out the "McKenzies' Polish boarder," as she called her. Helena soon understood Gloria's dislike for visiting Haldon. This was more an interrogation than a conversation. She fought back by pretending not to understand the questions when they were too intimate. She replied monosyllabically to questions about her family's deportation to Siberia, and claimed to have met her husband there. She said he joined the newly formed Polish army immediately after they were released.

"He died soon after," she finished, touching her ring and looking down, in the hopes of seeming believable.

"So, you're not with James McKenzie?" Mrs. Boysen asked brazenly, letting her gaze pass over Helena's stomach.

Helena felt embarrassed again. Her pregnancy wasn't really visible, but Mrs. Boysen seemed to have a magic gaze.

She shook her head. "No, of course not. James was in England. I was in Iran, and then in Pahiatua. I know James through his cousin Miranda Biller."

That appeared to satisfy Mrs. Boysen, and she left Helena in peace long enough to choose a blue sweater and two checkered work shirts that would suit Gloria. Helena chose a shirt in her own size and, making a quick decision, asked bravely about trousers.

Mrs. Boysen pursed her lips disapprovingly. "That's not an attractive look, child," she admonished, before showing Helena a few articles of clothing that were meant for young boys and loosely cut.

Helena tried on the work pants with a blue-and-yellow-plaid shirt. Standing in front of the mirror, she almost didn't recognize the woman looking back at her. Her slender figure had filled out, making her look more feminine, surely because of the pregnancy. Helena couldn't pass for a boy as she might have a month ago. Fascinated, she let her gaze wander over her round cheeks and her gleaming hair, tied into a ponytail; then her full breasts; then her still-slender waist and still-flat stomach. It was amazing that Mrs. Boysen had already noticed her pregnancy. Helena's long legs looked shapely in the trousers. She smiled and at that moment noticed that James had come back to the store.

She saw a spark in his eyes. Could it be that he admired her? She was almost expecting a compliment, but James held back.

"Taking cues from my mother?" he asked nonchalantly. "Certainly more practical for riding."

"And, and working in the stables. Maybe I can . . ."

Helena suddenly became self-consciously aware that she had been about to put these clothes on the McKenzies' bill without asking. She was about to suggest to James that she could work them off, but he interrupted her with a smile.

"You should definitely get them. Mrs. Boysen, please put every-thing on our account. My father will settle it at the end of the month as always. Are you done, Helena?"

Helena blushed when he talked about the bill. "I . . . I should change."

James shrugged. "Why not keep them on? Reka, would you pack up her dress for her? Thank you."

He gave Reka a smile and then signed Mrs. Boysen's receipt. Helena followed him self-consciously onto the street. James greeted by name two matrons coming toward them, and they gave Helena a look of mixed disapproval and curiosity before disappearing into the store.

"They'll be gossiping about you for sure." James grinned, holding the passenger-side door open for her. As he helped her in, the indifferent expression gave way to something else. "You look . . . well, I hope I'm not overstepping my bounds, but you look stunning."

2

"Where are we going now?" asked Helena when James turned off the road before Kiward Station. The truck rumbled over a dirt access road pitted with potholes.

"To the Maori village," James told her, stopping before a stream that trickled across the road. He drove the vehicle through it carefully.

"Looking for help for the herding?" Helena asked.

James smiled. "Good guess," he said. "We really do prefer the Maori to loafers like Jeb Gardener."

"Everyone does, right?" she said. "The hardware store, Mrs. Boysen . . ."

James looked surprised. "You don't think we're anything like that old dragon Mrs. Boysen?"

Helena bit her lip. "No, of course not," she stammered. "I . . . I only meant, well . . . Mrs. Boysen didn't seem to like her employee much. Why doesn't she hire someone white if she doesn't like the Maori?"

"Because whites ask for more money, don't work any harder, and wouldn't let her kick them around," James replied. "She treats poor Reka horribly. Reka's a smart girl who did well in school. Moana tried to convince her to go to high school and then on to the university. But she got pregnant. Her husband drinks, and Reka has to support them all. So she lets Mrs. Boysen treat her terribly."

"She has a baby," Helena marveled. "She looks so young. I wouldn't have thought she was more than sixteen."

"I think you're right," James said. "But that's not unusual. Maori girls often get pregnant early. And over and over. They have too many children, too little money, and only a few ever learn a real profession. The men don't either. So all that's left is poorly paid jobs among the whites who treat them terribly, and they work just hard enough to not get fired. Reka's an exception. She works really hard, but Kori at the hardware store, he never does more than necessary."

"That's so sad." Helena thought of the colorfully painted meeting-houses and the mysterious stories of the Ngati Rangitane. Even Ben Biller's stories were about proud warriors, strong chieftains' wives, and clever gods; about carving, kite making, fishing, and hunting. Why were the Maori here so different? "Why are they so . . . so apathetic?"

"The Maori or the whites?" James teased her, but turned serious quickly. "The old ways of life are falling apart," he said. "At least that's how Uncle Ben sees it. The Maori live like the *pakeha* but only because they have to. The colonizers destroyed their tribal structures, so now they have to make money but don't have the same opportunities to go to school and get a good job. Most Maori don't finish school and then have to leave their tribes to find work at factories in the cities. It makes them miserable, and then they drink too much. It's a vicious cycle."

With a dark expression, James steered the pickup carefully through the arched entrance to the *marae*. Once, statues of gods must have stood there, like at the village near Palmerston.

"They don't have *tiki*?" Helena asked, playing with her little amulet.

James smiled. "You sound like one of Uncle Ben's Maori Mythology 101 students," he teased her anew. "But that's just history. Most Maori have long since converted to Christianity. There's only a little superstition left—a few elders who cling to their gods and cast a spell now and then on request. But the majority go to *pakeha* churches or don't believe in anything anymore."

As the pickup passed the first few houses, Helena saw how much despair there was in the village. The Ngati Rangitane's *marae* had looked run down, but the community buildings had still been functional. This village was completely dilapidated. James had to dodge free-roaming chickens and pigs. Barefooted, half-naked children stared at the new arrivals despondently, as did the elders sitting outside their houses, many with a whiskey bottle beside them. The occasional lean horse was tied up between the huts, but mostly they had cars, looking fitter for the scrap heap than the road. Only the few mutts that chased the truck, barking, showed any signs of life.

James brought them to center of the village, which looked like an old farmhouse.

"O'Keefe Station," he said. "It belonged to Howard O'Keefe, founded around the same time as Kiward Station. Warden and O'Keefe were rivals, although O'Keefe didn't do all that well. Kiward Station flourished, but O'Keefe made bad investments and had huge setbacks—he didn't really know anything about money or sheep. But the Maori still talk about his wife, Helen. She founded a school and worked for the natives here. When Howard died, she sold the land to Grandma Gwyn, who then gave it to the Maori. Tonga never used the house, so it fell apart. He rejected all *pakeha* culture, but apparently Koua sees things differently."

James pointed to the entrance of the house, which had hadn't been painted in decades but looked sturdy, where a man sprawled in a rocking chair. He was younger than Jack McKenzie, but it was hard to estimate his age exactly. Unlike all the other Maori Helena had met so far, his face was tattooed. Under his cautious watch, James parked the truck, and they climbed out.

"*Kia ora, ariki,*" James greeted him.

He grinned. "*Kia ora*, Jimmy Boy. Back from war, eh? Did you cut off a few enemies' heads and smoke them properly?"

Helena bit her lip. Ben Biller had mentioned these tribal traditions too, but Lilian had prevented him from going into detail during dinner.

"No one does that anymore," James answered curtly. "My mother sent me, Koua. We want to bring the sheep in soon. The weather in the highlands is supposed to shift for the worse before autumn comes. You probably know."

The chieftain nodded and pointed to a radio next to him playing tinny swing music.

"The gods revealed it to us," he quipped.

Helena saw James roll his eyes and wondered if the chieftain might be drunk.

"We'd be obliged if you could send a few people," James continued matter-of-factly. "Hare and Eti, if they can stay sober a few days. And Koraka and Rewi."

Koua shrugged. "I'll ask them, if I don't forget." He let his gaze wander over to Helena. "What do we have here?"

Helena was embarrassed standing there in her pants and flannel shirt, but realized Koua wasn't looking at her lustfully. If anything, his gaze seemed mocking. The chieftain of this strange tribe wore jeans and a plaid shirt. His hair fell in long, greasy strands, black with some gray mixed in, down to his shoulders.

"Your *wahine*?" Koua grinned. "War spoils?"

Helena didn't understand, but James became visibly angry.

"A guest, Koua, a guest. Who men should treat politely," he said stiffly. "Gloria will come by herself to see about the workers and say when we'll need them."

Koua yawned. "Oh, look at the time. *I nga wa o mua*." He waved at them dismissively and reached for the bottle beneath his chair. "D'you want a belt, Jimmy Boy? How about the *wahine*?"

James shook his head. "Thanks," he said coldly. "None for us. It's early in the day, and we have a future we don't want to drink away."

He took his leave with a wave of his hand, just friendly enough not to seem rude.

"That was the chieftain?" she asked in disbelief as they drove away. "Was he . . . I think he was drunk."

James nodded, sighing. "Yep. That's why my mom will have to come, and my father will probably have to stop by too. Koua is unreliable, but he's the only one who can get the men to work. When we talk to them ourselves, they say 'sure, sure' and only come if they happen to remember. Still, they do good work. We don't hire them because we can pay them less, but because they handle the sheep with skill. The dogs and horses too."

The vehicle thundered through a pothole.

"What did the *ariki* say about me?" Helena turned the conversation back to Koua. "What does *wahine* mean? And *I ga* . . . ?"

"*I nga wa o mua*," James supplied. "*Wahine* means woman, also wife or sweetheart. Koua used it in a disrespectful way, though. That's why I got angry. And *I nga wa o mua* has to do with the Maori understanding of the past. Translated literally it means: 'from the times that lie before us.' I don't really understand it, but my mother learned a lot about the Maori worldview as a young woman. You could ask her, or Uncle Ben, if you want a linguistic analysis and comparisons with related Polynesian cultural concepts."

He smiled. Clearly his mood was improving.

Helena found the Maori philosophy less interesting than the thought that James had defended her, demanding Koua show her respect. But she'd read enough English novels to know that it was probably just part of being raised as a gentleman, and James would treat any woman with courtesy. He was such a gentleman he even flattered a stranger pregnant with another man's child. Helena felt strangely disappointed—and suddenly angry that the unwanted baby had robbed her of any chance for James to think of her romantically. She quickly reproached herself. She couldn't let herself fall in love with James; feelings for him would only complicate things even more.

When James and Helena arrived at Kiward Station a few minutes later—the Maori village was very close—they didn't find Gloria McKenzie in the stables as expected.

"Gloria's inside," said the worker listlessly filling the troughs with oats in her place.

Helena was immediately concerned. Was James's mother sick? She always oversaw the feeding, and would be sure to on a day when James wasn't there. James seemed unconcerned, though. Instead of going to see her, he took Helena and Ainne to bring in the horses.

"What would be wrong with her?" he asked when Helena expressed concern. "Someone's probably visiting. Some farmer or someone going out with my father to see the sheep, so Mom has to entertain his wife. She'll be in a delightful mood later." He winked at Helena, who smiled in return, relieved. If Jack was off with the visitor, that would explain why there wasn't another car in the yard. With the help of the shepherds, they took care of the horses quickly, and went into the house. "And to completely ruin Mom's day, we'll go tell her about Koua," James quipped. "She'll be thrilled to have to go there herself."

As they came in, they heard voices in the old study, and Helena turned to go upstairs to change. She would've liked to show Gloria McKenzie her new attire, but she'd be embarrassed in front of another woman. And the voice was unmistakably a woman's. James, however, recognized the voice immediately, and Ainne ran happily to greet the visitor.

"It's Moana," James declared, obviously happily surprised. "Come on, Helena, you don't need to change for Moana."

Helena followed him a bit reluctantly and stopped awkwardly when she saw Gloria and Moana. She wanted nothing more than to just turn around and go. Never before had she so regretted meeting someone without at least straightening herself up a bit. But even with her hair done and in her finest dress, she would have looked mousy next to Moana. Even the beautiful Luzyna would pale compared to this young woman. Moana sat with Gloria in front of the fireplace, under siege from Ainne's happy licks. She was the most beautiful woman Helena had ever seen. She had brown skin, an oval face, blackberry lips, and a straight nose. Her eyes were very big and very dark, and behind them a soft, friendly fire seemed to burn. It flared perceptibly when Moana saw James, and flickered strangely when she saw Helena. Moana wore her thick black hair loose and parted in the middle, and it brushed the tops of her hips. *Black as ebony.* Helena couldn't help thinking about Snow White. Her mother had read her the fairytale as a child, and Helena had always pictured the princess just so.

"Moana, how long's it been?" James beamed at the young woman. "I thought of you every day I flew, you and your kites." Moana stood up rushed over to him. "To what do we owe the honor of this visit?" James asked. "Isn't summer break over already? Did you hear that I was back?"

James put his arm around her, and Moana offered him her face for *hongi.* Helena sensed they didn't want to part again.

"*Kia ora*, James," Moana said in her soft, velvety voice, a voice like honey, more singing than speaking. "I'm happy you're back."

James's face clouded. "I shouldn't be here," he said. "The war isn't over."

A gentle smile settled on Moana's lips. "I've never seen you as a warrior," she said. "You want to fly, not to kill. The *manu* are our messengers to the gods."

Moana played with a *hei-tiki* she was wearing around her neck. Helena noticed it matched James's amulet, and realized Moana must be the "friend" who'd made it for him.

James laughed bitterly. "Well, I'm not about to become a priest," he countered. This comment struck Helena too. Of course he didn't want to become a priest; he belonged to this gorgeous girl. "But forget about the war for now." James changed the subject. "What're you doing here, Moana? I mean, of course I'm happy to see you."

"She's visiting me, not you," Gloria interjected. "Moana, you're going to have to rip yourself away from James if you want to continue our talk. I want to go check on the horses soon."

Moana blushed while James assured his mother that the animals were fine.

"I'm just here for the weekend," Moana explained. "I'm supposed to give a presentation on the Maori relationship to time. We discussed it in class to help prospective teachers understand their Maori students better. We talked about *I nga wa o mua*, the *pepeha*, and about the meaning of *maunga* and *whakapapa*—all the stories of our ancestors coming to Aotearoa. Suddenly everyone was looking at me, and I couldn't explain it either. So I came home."

"Because there's not a single *marae* left around Dunedin where a *tohunga* lives who could explain it to you?" James asked incredulously.

Helena thought he meant to tease Moana. He probably knew her reasons for coming to Kiward Station were only pretenses, and she was there to see him.

Moana, however, wasn't amused. "It's true," she said soberly. "At least, I don't know of any. The Otago Maori don't live in their own villages anymore, they're all in cities and suburbs, and trying to find a *tohunga* there would have taken longer than the train to Christchurch. So I'm imposing upon your mother. I'm coming, Gloria. Let's go on." She moved to sit down again.

James seemed to remember Helena only then. She still stood shyly to the side. He smiled at her and made an inviting gesture.

"Weren't you interested in this too, Helena?" he asked. "We just heard '*I nga wa o mua*' from Koua." Helena flinched when James softly put his hand on her back and gently pushed her toward the fireplace. He seemed to have forgotten that she shrank from being touched. Moana looked her over carefully. "Has Mom already told you about

Helena, Moana?" James asked. "Our guest from Poland? Helena's very interested in Maori culture. She caught the bug from Uncle Ben, I guess. Helena, this is Moana."

"The *tohunga* in a *marae* of the Ngati Rangitane gave me the bug," Helena corrected him with a smile. "She gave me this too."

She showed them her own *hei-tiki*, and Moana's gaze grew interested.

"Hineahuone?" she asked. "The fertility goddess? Carved from manuka wood? How unusual."

Helena smiled shyly. "It's supposed to protect me," she murmured, and let the amulet disappear back beneath her shirt.

Gloria noticed her outfit and smiled approvingly. "You look good, Helena. Riding clothes suit you. Sit down and join us. And do tell how our esteemed *ariki* came to say '*I nga wa o mua.*' Let me guess. He used it in the sense of 'if you don't come today, then you'll come tomorrow.'"

James laughed and bowed jokingly. "The gods reveal the truth to you, *tohunga*," he teased her. "I'll leave the three of you to it and go check on Pippa. I want to make sure she looks good before the flight into the highlands tomorrow."

"But you'll come to dinner?" asked Moana. "I . . . Your mother invited me."

James nodded and smiled at her. "I wouldn't miss the chance to dine with a chieftain's daughter for anything in the world." He was maintaining his jocular tone.

Helena kept her gaze lowered. She wondered if Moana would spend the whole weekend at Kiward Station.

"*Whakapapa,*" Gloria McKenzie began to explain, "to simplify, means ancestry." She spoke carefully and in a quiet voice. Clearly she lacked Ben Biller's enthusiasm for lecturing. She seemed to find it difficult to share her knowledge with others. "In that respect the canoe your ancestors used to come from Hawaiki to Aotearoa is more important than anything, because it's where it all began. It's also the first thing told when someone tells their personal story, their *pepeha*. More important than the ancestors themselves are the paths they took and the places they lived. So, less the existence and more the experience. In the same way you could say that the tribes' past and future flow together. The past determines the future. It's not finished; it doesn't let go of us."

Helena rubbed her forehead. She thought about Siberia, and she thought about Luzyna.

"Then we are never free?" she blurted out. "One can never move on from something? Never put something behind you?"

"Forgetting is never easy," said Gloria, and her face took on a far-away look.

Up until then, Helena had seen James's mother as completely self-possessed. Now she sensed that Gloria, too, struggled with demons from her past.

"But isn't it also an opportunity?" Moana asked in her gentle voice, which was like a caress. Despite her twinge of jealousy, Helena felt drawn to the young woman. "If the past isn't finished, there's always the possibility of changing it."

Helena became suddenly enraged. "What if someone's dead?" she asked bitterly. "They stay dead."

"Their death can take on a new meaning, though," Gloria explained. "That's *toku*: 'how important is what I'm describing for me?'"

"Or *taku*," Moana added. "'How important am I for what I'm describing?'"

Helena lost the thread of conversation when the two of them began discussing *maunga*, a place between the past and future. For Moana and Gloria, the Maori philosophy seemed to be comforting. For Helena it caused anxiety. Her past irrevocably determined her future. Because of Witold she was bound to a baby she didn't want. And as if that weren't enough, what she'd done to Luzyna would follow her forever. Her future was bleak, while Moana surely had a happy life with James on Kiward Station ahead of her.

Helena had fallen hopelessly into these thoughts when Gloria and Moana finally ended their conversation as James and Jack came in for dinner. James seemed to be happy, with the wind still in his tousled auburn hair. Of course he hadn't just checked on his plane, he'd taken a short flight around the farm. He was about to tell them all about it until he noticed Helena's despondent look. "Helena, what's wrong?" he asked with genuine concern. "Was it too much past for you?"

The question cut Helena to the core, and her face fell—that was exactly how she felt. She didn't know what to say, or what to make of Moana's gaze. The young Maori watched every interaction between her and James closely. Helena thought she saw alertness in her eyes, sympathy, pain, and also sadness. It was as if Moana's mood changed every time she blinked.

⚜

"Well, forget all that nonsense." James attempted to cheer Helena up, pulling her chair out for her at the table. "Whatever the Maori say, what happened yesterday is over and done with. The future's what matters. The war will be over soon, Helena. Churchill, Roosevelt, and Stalin are meeting in Yalta over the next few days. They're going to set guidelines for order in Europe after the war, whatever that means. In any case, there'll be peace when your baby is born." Helena was grateful for his concern for her—and his paying her any attention while Moana was there.

The young Maori woman looked surprised but said nothing about Helena's pregnancy, and she watched James's behavior toward Helena without jealousy. Not that there would have been cause; Helena was no competition for Moana.

"As soon as the Germans surrender," James continued moodily, "everything will take a turn for the good."

Helena weakly nodded when he looked at her for approval. She didn't really care whether her child was born during war or peace. She still couldn't imagine being a mother, and she tried not to think about it.

War and peace in Europe didn't seem to hold much interest for Moana. Instead, she asked about James's flight, and he described it enthusiastically.

Jack McKenzie's mood wasn't as good as his son's. There had been work to do near the old O'Keefe Station that afternoon, and he'd used the opportunity to stop by the Maori village on the same errand as James.

"I spoke with Hare and Rewi," he said. "They want to come herd— let's just hope those aren't empty promises. Their wives were there, and they'll certainly remember and try to keep them halfway sober. I wouldn't hold out hope for Koua, though, Gloria. Even if you catch him sober, he just doesn't care about anything. Tonga would roll in his grave." It seemed only then to occur to Jack that he was sharing a table with Koua's daughter. "I'm sorry, Moana."

Moana shrugged. "He drinks too much," she agreed. "The tribe should recall him. Only there's no one better. Besides Uncle Wiremu. And he'd rather be drawn and quartered than come back here."

"Is he well?" Gloria asked, her voice a bit forced.

Helena recalled that James had once spoken of Wiremu, saying that his mother had almost married the chieftain's son.

"Very well, thanks," Moana replied. "He's going to be chief doctor soon. Dr. Pinter is retiring, and Wiremu will lead the clinic. My uncle works in a children's clinic near Dunedin." She had turned to Helena to explain politely. "He likes it there, and his family is there. He would never come back to lead a run-down Maori tribe in the plains. However sad it may be."

Moana folded her napkin. Helena had already noticed that afternoon that Moana had impeccable manners.

Gloria smiled at the young Maori. "Then it'll be up to you, Moana. You could be the *ariki*."

Moana arched her brows. "On paper," she scoffed. "But in reality? Do you really think these drunken louts with nothing on their minds but whiskey, fishing rods, and hunting rifles would ever elect a woman chief? Let alone one that would whip the village into shape? No. They'll choose one of their own, so that everything in the *marae* stays as it is." Moana pushed her plate aside. "James, will you drive me home? I don't want to get home too late. Who knows what state my room's in. I haven't been there in ages, and my father's probably been letting his drinking buddies pass out there."

Moana had seemed reluctant and hopeless, but now she was beaming again, clearly looking forward to a ride with James.

James stood up and looked indecisively at Helena. "Would you like to come, Helena?" he asked.

Helena shook her head. She definitely didn't want to be a third wheel. "I'm too tired," she demurred, without managing to look up. And so she didn't see the light in Moana's eyes go out.

3

The next six weeks flew by. Everyone was busy morning til night preparing for the herd's arrival at the farm, cleaning stables and ramps and checking fences. Helena made herself useful in the house as well as the stables, and on the day before the herding, she asked shyly if she could somehow help with that too. Gloria said yes immediately.

"We need all the help we can get. You can ride with the food wagon and help feed the two-legged beasts. The men are starving when they come in from herding, and I'm no good at cooking, so I enlist our maids every year. But they don't have much initiative; they have to constantly be told what to do."

Anna and Kyra, who had both Maori and *pakeha* ancestry, were sweet but not very bright. Helena had noticed that the meals at Kiward Station lacked variety; it seemed the cook only knew a few dishes. The housekeeper Helena's family had employed in Lwów had been much better. Helena, who had liked to help with the cooking when she was a child, had already been thinking about offering to make dinner one night. She was delighted to help with the catering, and went with Anna and Kyra to stock the wagon. To her surprise, they used a tureen very similar to the one she remembered from Iran.

The next morning, everyone gathered at sunrise in the yard near the shearing sheds. Soon it was crawling with men, horses, and excited dogs, and Helena's hands were full giving out coffee and sandwiches.

Most of the men came in large, rusty pickups, with their horses tied down in the beds. Two were already nipping on a whiskey bottle, and Jack took it from them without any fuss.

"You'll get it back tonight," he said firmly. "I need you sober during the day."

Gloria led two horses, one for her and one for Jack, into a trailer hitched to the family pickup. Jack hitched the soup dispenser to the truck that carried hay for the horses and also could be used to transport sheep.

"The sheep come back on their own four legs," he explained to Helena, still moody about the workers' whiskey, accepting a second cup of coffee. "But if one's injured or weak, we can load it into this. We used to slaughter sick animals right away. Before we had trucks, the herding was much harder. You'd ride two days before you even caught sight of the first sheep. Now everything is easier. We drive the horses up, then gather the sheep James herds out of the mountains with Pippa. It still requires skill, but there's no more riding for days in bad weather to find the stragglers."

James was still filling the vehicles with fodder, tents, and fencing to build provisional pastures; herding still took a few days. Finally, he came to get some coffee.

"Are you sure you don't want to fly with me?" he teased, taking a grilled cheese sandwich.

Helena filled his mug. "Has Moana flown with you before?" she asked, feeling brave. She'd already heard much appreciation for her help; apparently last year they'd had problems in the morning before the herding.

James furrowed his brow. "Moana?" he asked. "Herding sheep? No. Why?" He took a second sandwich.

Helena blushed. "Because she . . . because she has the same *hei-tiki* as you."

166

James smiled. "Yes, but she's afraid of flying. She only flies kites. We used to build *manu* every year before Matariki, the Maori New Year's festival, to fly with requests from the gods. Moana's really good at it. That's why I whittled her the *hei-tiki* one day. It represents Nuku-pewapewa, a chieftain who's supposed to have escaped his enemies by climbing into a *manu*. Then, before I went to war, she gave me this one." He fished out his little patron spirit.

Helena nodded and bit her lip. So. They had exchanged *hei-tiki*, surely as tokens of their love. She was relieved when Jack called for everyone to set out.

"When will I see you?" James asked while Helena packed everything up.

She shrugged. "I think we're camping somewhere," she said, and gestured in the direction of the highlands.

James smiled. "I'll find you," he said, waving good-bye casually with one hand on his pilot's cap. All the men were wearing hats against the sharp cold of that fall morning. But it was clear, so at least the shepherds wouldn't have to contend with rain or snow.

Helena watched James go. She didn't understand what he'd meant; he didn't need to spend the night camping. It would be much safer for him to fly home and land the plane on the paved runway instead of a field. And then he could sleep in his own bed.

Helena talked with Jack McKenzie as the pickups and trucks rolled leisurely westward. The peaks of the southern mountains that had seemed so close to Helena on Kiward Station grew only slowly closer.

Jack laughed when she marveled at their distance. "It seems that way to everyone. Gwyn liked to tell the story of her first ride at Kiward Station. She thought she could ride to the mountains quickly, but she rode for hours and hours without reaching them. We've got a few dozen miles to go before we see the first sheep. And even then we won't really be in the mountains, just the foothills. The sheep don't wander deep into the mountains. There's hardly any grass there, just moss and lichen—and snow." He smiled at Helena. "Look, it's James."

Jack pointed as James performed a daring aerial maneuver, then shot away toward the mountains where he would get straight to work.

When the workers from Kiward Station reached the plains, the first ewes were already grazing there with their lambs, while others came over the hills, bleating angrily.

"They already know where to go," Jack noted. "James doesn't need to do much. When they hear the airplane, they get going."

"They come willingly back to the farm?" Helena marveled. "They're so ready to give up their freedom?"

"They trade their freedom for a safe stall and plenty of hay." Jack laughed. "It's a good deal, don't you think? Seriously, it'll get nasty out here soon. It's no fun for the sheep; not all of them would survive a winter in the mountains."

Slowly so as not to scare the sheep, the shepherds parked on the edge of the plain, and started unloading and saddling the horses straight away. The sheepdogs leaped out, eager to get to work. Helena watched, fascinated, as they drove groups into a herd with lightning speed and then separated the Kiward Station sheep from the others. Helena wondered how Gloria, Jack, and the Maori shepherds knew which of the animals were theirs.

"They have earmarks," Gloria explained when she came to get her first coffee. Helena and Kyra had gotten sandwiches ready for a second breakfast, and Anna had begun cutting meat and vegetables in the improvised field kitchen. "We do it when they're lambs. It's the best way to keep them separated as adults, at least for people who know their stuff—to a beginner, they all look the same." Gloria bit into her sandwich and looked over the catering station, pleased. "You've got a good grip on this, Helena. Well done. This is the first time I haven't worried about the food."

Helena beamed and turned to preparing a stew for lunch with gusto. To her surprise, she found that she liked working outside with the shepherds. She'd always thought of herself as a city person, and never would have guessed she'd enjoy cooking outside and eating at a campfire.

"We used to cook on the campfire," Gloria recalled. "That was a pain." Now, it was just for warming up, much needed as it got colder by the hour.

The change in the weather seemed to encourage the sheep, which came out of the mountains faster and in ever greater numbers. Soon, the whole plain was filled with bleating creatures large and small. By late afternoon James came over the ridges in Pippa and crossed briefly over the field kitchen.

"That's the signal that he's got them all together," Gloria said, pleased. "There'll still be some stragglers in the hills, though. Someone will have to gather them together tomorrow before we ride out." She smiled at her husband. "Shall we do it, Jack?"

Touched, Helena watched as Jack McKenzie returned the smile. "Always happy to when it's with you," he said.

⚜

The riders and dogs drove the sheep to Kiward Station over the next few days. The food wagon would go ahead and wait for the herds at preselected resting places, so Helena and all the other hands were spending the nights in the wilderness. Jack sent shepherds to help the girls set up their tent, and by dark everyone was sitting around roaring campfires. The men passed whiskey bottles around, and soon people started singing, and then telling stories. Helena let herself be swept up by the atmosphere. A few *pakeha* shepherds had brought along harmonicas and guitars, and the Maori played along on the flute. The music mixed with the bleating of sheep and the snorting of horses trotting back and forth in the makeshift paddocks. The cold, clear air, the dark silhouettes of the mountains, and the star-filled sky overhead—Helena almost felt something resembling happiness. But whenever she began to feel comfortable, Luzyna sprang into her thoughts, and she felt pangs of conscience anew. This was stolen happiness; it wasn't meant for her.

"Looking at the stars?" Gloria had turned to her. She hadn't joined in the singing and stories with the men either, contentedly lost in thought instead. "They must look strange to you. I was always disappointed by the stars in Europe."

Helena hadn't had a chance to notice a difference between the European and New Zealand skies yet. In Lwów there was too much light, and during the ice-cold nights in Siberia she didn't venture outside unless she had to. She had looked at the stars—particularly in Siberia, where they'd hung above the camp with a monstrous brightness—but she didn't know their names.

"I don't know them well," she admitted.

"I do," Gloria said dreamily. "My teacher, Miss Bleachum, would take me out at night and point out the stars. We even had a telescope. And Marama, my grandmother, was Maori. She explained to me what the stars meant to her people."

"They're inspiring," murmured Helena. "And comforting. They don't ever change. No matter what we've done or will do, the stars stay just as they are. They were there before we were born, and they'll be there after we die."

Gloria shook her head. "That's just how they appear to us," she said. "Miss Bleachum taught me that we don't see them as they are. Their light takes hundreds of thousands of years to reach us. So we only see them as they were all that time ago, not as they are now. Some of the ones we see today have long since gone out."

Helena sighed. "Does that have anything to do with *I nga wa o mua*?" she asked.

Gloria laughed. "In a way, maybe, even though the Maori wouldn't have known about the vast distances between stars. For them, stars were gods who guided them along their way. They would navigate in their canoes by the stars, so the light from thousands of years ago directed their futures, if you think about it that way. Maybe it's more to do with our interpretation of the past . . . but I'm no philosopher, my dear, and the night's too beautiful for brooding. Let's just enjoy the present, even if it does make us fall for a false image."

Gloria leaned back and told Helena about the stars, but Helena only half listened to her stories of gods and seafaring. She wasn't going to romanticize the past, and no present, however lovely, would eclipse what she had done.

The shepherds set out early the next day, and Helena didn't struggle to do the same. The night had grown sharply cold, even in the tent she shared with Anna and Kyra. Despite thinking she'd never freeze again after surviving Siberia, Helena had woken up several times shivering, even in a flannel shirt, breeches, and a thick sweater James had lent her. She looked forward to hot coffee, even if she had to prepare it herself.

It wasn't much different for the men. Shivering and rubbing their hands together, but still in good spirits, they gathered around the food wagon. As they warmed up, they got to laughing, jokes flying back and forth. Helena and the maids received heaps of compliments, which Anna and Kyra enjoyed. As usual, Helena was embarrassed when men said how pretty she was. Though she could still hide her pregnancy, she was already plumper than the maids. And her skin, which had always been smooth and rosy, now had blemishes. After her night in the tent, her hair was stringy, and her quickly braided pigtails did nothing to improve her looks. Helena knew she was anything but pretty, and she didn't trust men who paid false compliments.

After breakfast Gloria and Jack rode out with their dogs to gather the last stragglers from the foothills, while the rest of the shepherds started the herds back toward Kiward Station. The others drove ahead in the trucks. A young Maori, who like Anna and Kyra seemed to also have *pakeha* ancestry, drove the catering wagon and flirted shamelessly with the maids. That he didn't try it with Helena only confirmed her sense that she was becoming dowdier every day. She tried to ignore the banter, as it slipped from Maori to English and back again, by staring out the window. The weather that day suited her mood; the sky had become cloudy and gray.

"There's snow coming," Jack had said that morning, and the men had nodded knowingly. The shepherds worked to leave the foothills behind as quickly as possible. Once they reached the Canterbury Plains, they would be free from winter. It rarely snowed on the plains, mostly raining instead.

Jack and Gloria didn't extend their ride as they had planned, instead rejoining the group before lunch. They led fifty sheep, herded by four dogs. Ainne leaped excitedly on Helena, looking for praise for her day's work, while Gloria and Jack were served stew. For the first time Helena thought how nice it would be to have a dog like Ainne of her own. An animal who would love her no matter what. That must be a nice feeling.

"You're proud you helped bring the sheep in, aren't you, girl?" Helena patted her and gave her a piece of sausage.

Gloria nodded and laughed. "She's bragging. It wasn't all that hard. The sheep came running to us on their own. They couldn't wait to be herded. They sense when the weather shifts and know it's safest to seek protection with the whole herd. So don't act like you did anything so brilliant, Ainne."

She scratched the dog, who answered the scolding with unconcerned tail wagging. Gloria accepted a bowl of stew, praised the food, and gulped it down quickly, staring at the sky with furrowed brow.

Everyone saw the dark clouds, but it seemed likely they could escape the weather.

Jack ordered the men to herd the sheep downhill quickly after lunch. They were, nonetheless, caught in a heavy downpour that afternoon, and everyone was soaked and sour when they finally reached the campsite. At least they were spared the full force of winter in the mountains. An old but intact cabin offered some protection from the weather. There wasn't room for everyone to sleep there, but at least everyone could warm up inside before the men retired to their waiting tents. Gloria decided that only the women and a few older farmhands who felt the cold deep in their bones would sleep inside. That was how they did it every year.

Helena unrolled her sleeping mat and blankets between Anna and Kyra and as far from the men as possible. She knew she wasn't in any danger, and that Gloria and Jack would surely keep an eye on their workers. Still, Helena couldn't relax in the overcrowded room, which smelled of wet clothing and sweat. Maybe the close quarters and the sounds of the other sleepers reminded her of the barracks in Siberia, where she and dozens of other women and girls were crammed into a drafty room. She could hardly sleep. When she did nod off briefly, memories of her dying mother, her promises, and Luzyna's reproachful face woke her with a start.

Eventually Helena couldn't stand it. She peeled the blankets back, wrapped one around her shoulders, slipped into her shoes, and quietly left the cabin. Feeling the grass beneath her feet and breathing the fresh air, with the scent of horses and sheep nearby, she felt immediately better.

The clouds had parted; the sky was clear, and the stars shone like new. Helena looked up at them and searched for the differences between the northern and southern skies Gloria had described.

She suddenly heard a man's voice behind her. "That's the Southern Cross."

Helena spun around, terrified, though she had recognized the voice right away. James wore a long rain jacket, and his auburn hair was tousled. He grinned at Helena as if he had prepared a surprise just for her.

"Where . . . where did you come from?" she asked.

"From Kiward Station, of course." James smiled. "I rode out this morning before dawn. Wanted to catch a bit of the real herding. From the plane it's pretty boring."

Helena frowned. Recently she had heard quite the opposite from him.

"Hey, you're not pleased to see me?" James sounded disappointed. "I told you I'd find you."

"It couldn't have been too hard," Helena replied, immediately annoyed with herself. Why did she have to be so difficult? But the situation felt strange, almost as if James was flirting with her. "Don't your workers always rest here for the night?"

James made a face. "True. You caught me," he admitted good-naturedly. "How do you like the herding? When it's not raining, I mean?" Helena saw in the moonlight that his waxed jacket gleamed wetly. Why had he come despite the weather? Did he come back every year? "Are you enjoying the cold, clammy tents, and smoky cabins that get colder all night so you wake up as a block of ice, assuming you can even get a second of sleep with everyone else snoring?" He winked at her. Helena realized he was teasing her. "Those glorious nights, in the bosom of nature, that my parents couldn't stop raving about?"

Helena didn't quite know how to answer. "I like the stars," she said evasively.

James nodded and stood next to her. "Then let's see what we've got up there." With seemingly strict scientific intent, he looked up into the sky. Helena's heart began to beat more quickly. She felt a mixture of joy and fear. "The Southern Cross, like I said," he began to explain. "Do you see it? Five bright stars that form a cross. That's how the Christian seafarers saw it, anyway. The Maori saw it as a canoe. It's on the flag of New Zealand. Did you know that?"

Gently, James put his hand on Helena's shoulder. She shivered at his touch. A short time before, she would've pulled away at once, but now she surprised herself with the desire to lean against him. She did neither, instead standing perfectly still and trying to concentrate on James's words, until one dog barked and then all the others joined in. Ainne, who had been watching the sheep with the other dogs, must have heard her master's voice. She came running to James and leaped on him, whimpering. James knelt and greeted her—though Helena thought he seemed less happy than usual to see her.

Barking came from the cabin, where some men had their dogs sleeping beside them, and more came from the paddocks by the horses.

Gloria McKenzie appeared at the cabin entrance, and the beam of her flashlight lit on Helena's face. "Helena?" Gloria asked, alarmed. "Did something happen? The dogs . . ."

Helena started, feeling like she'd been caught out, although she hadn't done anything wrong. She didn't even need to be embarrassed about her outfit; like everyone else, she had slept in her clothes. On the other hand, it was night, and she was standing there in the dark next to James. Gloria must have thought she had slipped out to see him.

"James!" Gloria had recognized her son. "What are you doing here?"

She was surprised—so James had clearly not caught up with them here in previous years.

"I, uh, thought I'd make myself useful." James's confidence had vanished before his mother. Apparently, he hadn't thought about how to explain his presence.

"With a tired horse, galloping through the night?" The beam of Gloria's flashlight fell on James's brown gelding, tied to a tree, damp with sweat and still breathing quickly. "Who you completely forgot at first sight of a young woman?" Gloria's voice was stern; the horses were dear to her. "Take Kenan to the paddock, brush him, feed him properly, and then look for somewhere to sleep." She watched as James went to his horse, took off the saddlebags, and threw them over his shoulder to take them into the cabin. "In a tent, son," Gloria added.

"I . . . we didn't do anything," Helena defended herself. "Just . . . just looked at the stars."

"That shine falsely, as we know," remarked Gloria. "Now, come inside. We need to get up early tomorrow."

4

After the encounter with James, Helena was worried. She hardly dared look Gloria in the eye, although she had nothing to be ashamed of. She cared deeply about the McKenzies' opinion of her, and didn't want them to believe she was after their son. As an unmarried pregnant woman in Poland, she would already have fallen into disrepute. In her very Catholic homeland, no one would've believed her about the rape unless she had proof. She still couldn't believe that the Billers and McKenzies had never doubted her. But now that she had been discovered in the company of a young man at night . . .

Helena kept her distance from James the next day, and for the following weeks as well. She grew fatigued more quickly, and used that as an excuse to help less in the stables and more in the kitchen. That way she was almost never alone with James.

At Easter Moana returned from Dunedin to her *marae*, and the next day she visited Gloria and her family to tell them about a special project. Helena listened as she enthusiastically explained that she had been excused from the teaching seminar to spend the rest of the semester turning a former meetinghouse, one of the central buildings of the *marae*, into a school. It had been empty since the tribe had begun living in family groups in individual houses. Moana's eyes flared, and she punctuated her speech with graceful gestures as she described her plans.

"I thought you might help renovate it, James. It's been a bit neglected, but the structure is solid. Really only needs cosmetic work: a few nails, some paint. I'm not sure how we'll pay for it yet, but I'll think of something. Maybe the parish will donate, or Koua will be generous."

Gloria and James exchanged a doubting look, apparently thinking that neither was particularly likely.

"Are there enough children for a school?" Helena asked, trying to show interest.

She had seen children playing during her visit to the *marae*, but surely a school needed more than just a partially renovated house. Books and teachers, at the very least. It would only make sense, Helena thought, if there were a lot of students.

Moana swung her hip-length hair over her shoulder, and Helena felt a twinge of envy. Even this simple gesture seemed so graceful.

"I think so," Moana answered enthusiastically. "We have a lot more children than the *pakeha*—the school in Haldon would burst if they all went every day. I'm not thinking of it as a regular school, though, more like a . . . a camp, or after-school studies. Or maybe also regular schooling, or something in place of it when the kids don't go to Haldon. I just want to start, and see what happens. I can always teach during the semester break, and a few of my classmates are coming from Dunedin to help. Maori education is a major topic; the government supports these kinds of projects."

"I wonder whether the children will share your excitement," Gloria mused. She didn't seem to have liked school herself. "After all, classes would be voluntary."

Moana nodded but smiled. "The children will come. It'll be very different from the school in Haldon. We won't just teach the usual subjects, but we'll have Maori art, kite making, weaving, braiding, and gardening. We'll play music, dance, do fun things. And when we tell stories, they'll be our stories, not the *pakeha* literature that's so distant from the children's reality. We have to try to engage them somehow.

Things can't go on like they are. Half the children in the *marae* can barely read or write."

Helena recalled that James had mentioned something similar. The Maori children didn't feel comfortable in the Haldon school and skipped whenever they could. There were plenty of reasons. It was a long way from O'Keefe Station to Haldon; the subjects were often irrelevant to their lives; and the *pakeha* children excluded them. There was tension between the *pakeha* and Maori children to start with, but the worse the Maori children did, the more the whites bullied them. Even teachers occasionally were cruel, perhaps hoping to make the Maori children more ambitious. Of course it had the opposite effect: the Maori children just stopped going.

Teachers sometimes tried to intervene with the parents. Even though school was mandatory in New Zealand, the Maori traditionally never forced their children to do anything, and only a few parents understood how important it was to learn to read and write. Now and then the Ministry of Education would send inspectors and threaten to take the children from their homes if they weren't forced to go to school. In the past the whites had often forced Maori children into boarding schools to alienate them from the tribal culture the whites found threatening. But that had worked well, and now no one feared the downtrodden Maori living in small run-down tribes. So it wasn't worth the trouble or cost of tearing children away from their tribes, placing them somewhere else, and forcing them to go to school. The parents understood that and calmly listened to the threats, said good-bye to the officials politely, and continued letting the children do as they pleased. Moana wanted to provide another option.

"You'll help, won't you, James, if I can raise the money?" she asked. "And you too, Helena?" She turned amicably to Helena. "I know, I know, you shouldn't climb ladders anymore." Moana smiled at Helena's now-unmissable pregnant belly, and Helena blushed. "But a little painting, maybe the tables and benches that James will hopefully make for us? I hope some people from the village will help too."

Helena chewed her lip. The thought of being among a group of young people the way she now looked was terrifying. She felt sure they would all whisper about her and the baby's absent father. The McKenzies had told her again and again that everything was different among the Maori, but she couldn't believe it. Helena hardly even showed her face in Haldon, although she always wore her wedding band and everyone knew the story of her "husband." Still, she found it unpleasant.

"I'm not much for carpentry," James claimed, halfheartedly. In truth, Helena thought he'd long since been won over—Moana's charm would compel any man to pick up a hammer and nails.

⚜

Drumming up the money for the project proved more difficult. The collection in the church parish was a failure. Gloria asked the pastor of the Anglican church take up a collection, and the priest gave a lovely sermon about neighborly love and helping people help themselves. Afterward, though, they only found a few shillings in the collection box. The attitude of the parishioners was so hostile that Moana immediately decided against her ideas for a charity picnic, a bake sale, or a flea market. The local school, the parishioners thought, offered a proper education, and Sunday school was likewise open to all. If the Maori didn't appreciate these opportunities, that was their fault. As Bernard Tasier, owner of the hardware store, put it, no citizen of Haldon had a spare penny for anyone.

"And they'd teach them that pagan nonsense," Mrs. Boysen said, giving the pastor a reproachful look. "Maori culture and traditional skills. What exactly are those?"

"Well, what do you think?" Tasier interjected. "Carving weapons and smoking the heads of enemies. 'The tribes must find a way to new self-awareness.' What utter nonsense. I can't believe I heard it at church. Do we want them to start bashing in their neighbors' heads or suing them for land again?"

The crowd of parishioners nodded excitedly—they seemed to think one just as bad as the other, although the Maori wars hadn't reached the South Island. There had only been peaceful protests by tribes against wrongful displacement, which eventually the courts had decided. Gwyneira McKenzie wasn't the only one compelled to pay reparations to the tribes.

In the end, Helena figured that the donations to fund Moana's project came primarily from the McKenzie and Biller families. Gloria mentioned Moana's plans to her cousin Lilian on the phone, and shortly afterward a generous anonymous check arrived. Once they had the funds to buy materials, Moana just needed to find volunteers to do the work. She met almost as much resistance in the Maori village as in Haldon. Other than James and Helena, who'd agreed as soon as Gloria suggested she help, she found no reliable volunteers. Every so often an old man would come by to lend a hand, or an old woman would offer to teach the children weaving or braiding, but the children's parents remained, for the most part, disinterested. Even Koua didn't support the project, mocking it instead. As a last resort, Moana sweet-talked two young Maori into building a few school benches. She couldn't completely conceal her disinterest in Hare's and Koraka's advances, though, and soon enough they realized what Helena had already seen: Moana only had eyes for James.

The situation improved a bit when two more education students from Dunedin arrived, both just as energetic and excited as Moana and also of Maori ancestry. They started right away on the repair work, and even began teaching after just a few days. Laura drew children in by making simple musical instruments and singing fun songs. Janet told stories of Maori gods and heroes and had the children act out scenes from them. Moana taught the children to build kites, *manu*.

They would fly them at the end of May, when the Pleiades appeared in the night sky and the Maori celebrated Matariki.

"The *manu* serve as messengers between heaven and earth," she explained.

Janet suggested the children write wishes for the gods on bits of paper. "Then you can send them into the sky with your *manu*," she told them.

The Maori children undertook the writing of their wishes with delight, and those who couldn't write well didn't protest when Janet corrected their spelling. After all, the gods had to be able to read the messages.

Moana laughed. "The reverend wouldn't be thrilled, but in this case the ends justify the means."

The energy of the budding teachers and students was so infectious that even Helena put a kite together in the end. She couldn't bring herself to write a wish list, though. She no longer believed in the Christian god, but her whole life she'd been taught that she could have no other gods. Writing wishes for the Maori gods felt like blasphemy. Besides, she didn't know what to wish for. Every attempt to find Luzyna had failed. Helena written repeatedly to Iran, as well as to Poland once the country had been liberated. The Red Army had marched into Warsaw on January 17, and organizations were working to reunite families. But no trace of Luzyna and Kaspar could be found. Asking some foreign god to protect her sister couldn't possibly help.

She told James this after he seemed confused and a little disappointed when she flew her kite a week before Matariki without a message.

"You don't have any other wishes?" he asked. "Something not to do with your sister? Something for yourself or for your baby?"

Helena stopped herself from saying that she would like to wish the baby away and shook her head silently. She had just started feeling it move, and knew that she should feel some kind of love for this little human growing within her. But she couldn't. She tried to think about the baby as little as possible—about neither its birth nor what might follow.

She concentrated on planning the Maori New Year's festival, which would be celebrated the night of the first new moon after the Pleiades appeared. The Maori saw the constellation as a mother and her children. Many traditions surrounded their reappearance, including the making and flying of kites and communal reflection on the highs and lows of the previous year. The tribe was supposed to celebrate the festival together, but there hadn't been any plans made in many years. Koua didn't care about traditions—he greeted the Pleiades more often with a whiskey bottle than with *karakia*. Moana and her friends were determined this year to hold a proper Matariki festival and make the tribal traditions come alive for the children.

"Are you really going to prepare a *hangi*?" Helena asked Laura.

They were planning the feast, and Laura had explained that a communal meal cooked in the earth was part of the Matariki tradition. The food should be finished as close as possible to the exact moment the stars appeared in the sky, so that it could be offered to the mother and her children after their long journey. There wasn't any volcanic activity around Haldon, so they would have to dig a cooking pit and fill it with red-hot stones. It was a lot of work, and Helena, who would be preparing the food, didn't really see the sense in it any more than James had.

"We must have one," Laura declared, eyes dancing. "The children need to experience it once. It all depends on James helping. Will you talk to him, Helena? He'll listen to you."

Helena frowned. She didn't know what Laura meant by that. If it was about who was closest to James, Laura should have asked Moana.

Laura laughed when Helena suggested this. "I think he sees things differently," she noted with a mischievous expression. "But it doesn't matter. Moana has already found herself a digger. Her cousin Ropata is coming from Dunedin to celebrate with us. He's never had a proper Matariki festival either. And Janet convinced Rewi to dig. I'm hoping to persuade Koraka, myself. You see: you need to ask James. And he's the most important; he's guaranteed not to be drunk before noon."

Helena didn't need to do much to convince James to help. Though he grumbled a bit that North Island traditions were being transplanted and he would be left carrying the water for them, Helena found support from Gloria.

"You won't be carrying the water; you'll be holding a shovel," she chided James, laughing. "And I've never been to a *hangi*. We'll all come to the *marae*, I'm sure Jack will help too. Don't be lazy, James. Maybe we'll find some gold."

"You can't eat gold, as everybody knows," James muttered. "Who said that, again? Some Native American, right? There's a reason gold lies *in* the earth and food grows *out* of it."

⚜

"I hope it at least tastes good if we're going to work so hard," James grumbled anew as he drove Helena into the *marae* with the truck full of spades and shovels. "You should handle the cooking. Your stew for the herding was exceptional, and what you make is much better than the cook's. The Maori always skimp on the spices." Helena blushed at the praise. She hadn't spoken with James much lately—once the repair work was finished, he hadn't come to the meetinghouse every day. That was fine with her; the worse she thought she looked in the mirror, the more she avoided him. "And you still don't want to fly your kite?" James asked. "I can do it for you if you're too tired."

Helena blushed anew, this time from shame. He might as well have said "too fat." It was now the end of May, only six or seven weeks until the birth.

"Or I can take a message up to the gods for you in Pippa and let it float on a cloud," James suggested, smiling.

Helena bit her lip. During the last few days, absolutely everyone had been encouraging her to ask the gods to bless her baby at Matariki—sometimes jokingly, like Gloria, but also seriously, like Janet, who was taking on the role of priestess for the rituals. Her grandmother had been a *tohunga* of the Ngati Kahungunu, and Janet felt called to it. Helena refused unwaveringly, giving her Christian upbringing as an excuse. She felt like a hypocrite, though, because it wasn't Jesus but James that made her unwilling. She'd given it a lot of thought and ultimately had to admit, at least to herself, that her only real wish was that James might feel toward her the way she felt toward him. No matter how Helena fought against it, she could still feel his hand on her shoulder the night of the sheep herding. Day after day she relived the magic of that moment, only to tell herself that it was all in her head. After all, James hadn't made any further attempts to get close to her.

Instead, he had spent lots of time with Moana during their work on the meetinghouse. Helena didn't want to, but she noticed every laugh they shared, every conversation, and every offer of help. They worked side by side, and each seemed to sense instinctively what the other meant to say or do next.

On the morning of the Matariki festival, James left Helena right away to join the group around Moana. He greeted Ropata, a tall Maori in *pakeha* clothing, and they began to discuss how they would first heat the stones and then transport them to the cooking pit. Helena turned away and joined the women preparing the food. Reka, the young mother who worked in awful Mrs. Boysen's store, handed her a peeling knife right away and pointed to a mountain of sweet potatoes. She was busy weaving the cooking baskets out of reeds. She didn't seem to have confidence in her craftsmanship, though.

"I hope everything doesn't get full of sand." She sighed. "Sure, Ahurewa says the baskets will keep everything out, but I don't know how. I would just hang a kettle over the fire. That's also traditional."

"I thought before the *pakeha* came there weren't any kettles," Helena offered for consideration.

Reka took a sip of beer and returned to the braiding. "When you're right, you're right," she said, grinning. "Well, many thanks, *pakeha*. Glad you're around."

Like Reka, most of the Maori men and women sipped beer or whiskey all day, and so by sundown, the mood in the *marae* was already quite festive. Moana and the other teachers were delighted that it looked to be a clear night, and gathered their students with their kites around the fires.

A few elders had already taken seats around the fire and were keeping a lookout for the stars. Moana noted with joy that they weren't too drunk to tell the children stories. Ahurewa, the village midwife, told the story of the stars at Matariki: The mother star is Whanui, and every year the sun asks her for help. The sun is exhausted; will Whanui and her daughters come to her aid, so that the winter won't be too hard? Whanui gathers her children. If they joyfully lend a hand and shine brightly, the winter will be short and seeds can be planted early. If they are pale and reluctant, however, then it will be a longer winter.

Helena listened to the legends of the stars' journey as spellbound as the children, and held her breath alongside them as the Pleiades finally shone clearly in the night sky above the plains.

"A short, mild winter," Ahurewa interpreted, and took a drink of her beer. "We'll be able to plant early and have a good harvest."

Helena wondered how much the Ngai Tahu still sowed and reaped. Other than a few shabby vegetable gardens next to the houses, the Maori on O'Keefe Station seemed to have hardly planted anything.

Nevertheless, she nodded and joined in the song that the teachers struck up with the children.

Ka puta Matariki ke rere Whanui.
Ko te tohu tene o te tau e!

Matariki is back! Whanui continues her flight.
The new year begins!

The old people began to cry, though whether from sorrow or joy it was hard to say. As was traditional, Moana had asked them, when the stars first appeared, to speak the names of the previous year's dead and mourn them one last time before the tribe turned toward new life. The children were to learn this ritual. The women complied but kept the ritual short.

"No one died last year," one of the old women confided in Helena. "Not counting Peta, who finally drank himself to death. But he wasn't from here. He came from Kaikoura."

When the sky was painted thick with stars, holding its full beauty, Moana, Laura, and Janet had their students fly their kites. The children unfurled them proudly into the wind. Helena hoped their parents and the others from the tribe weren't too drunk or uninterested to praise their work, as James and Moana had instructed them to do.

James—where was he, anyway? Helena hadn't seen him in quite a while. And then she knew why. She heard the sound of a faint motor growing louder and louder, then recognized the position lights that moved like the glowing eyes of a dragon across the sky. James was seeking his own connection to the stars. Pippa flew over the festival grounds at a low altitude, though far above the children's kites. To their astonishment, the airplane towed a kite behind it. Helena recognized the *manu* kite in the shape of a wing, painted in her favorite colors.

"It's yours!" shouted a girl. "Look, Helena, yours is flying higher than the others."

Now Helena recognized it: James was flying her kite. She waved at him together with the children.

"Let's sing the kite song, really loud, so James and Pippa and Helena's kite can hear it all the way up there," Moana encouraged her charges.

Helena marveled again at how incredibly certain of James's love she must be that she didn't mind her boyfriend flying another woman's kite.

James landed Pippa on the access road to the Maori village and came over to the celebrants, laughing. He had brought Helena's kite back in good shape and gave it to her.

"Here, it just had to get up in the air today and have a chat with the gods."

"And what did they say?" Ropata inquired before Helena could answer. He handed James a cup of beer. For both men, it was the first of the evening. Neither James nor Moana's cousin had drunk any alcohol before the celebration began. Koua, on the other hand, was already rather drunk.

James happily clinked glassed with both of them. "Basically what the radio says too," he replied and winked at Koua. "It's going to be a good year. There's finally peace on earth." Germany had surrendered; the war was over. "Maybe people driven from their homes can go back." Helena bit her lip. Was that directed at her? Did he want her to go back to Poland? "Many families that have been separated will reunite." Now he did turn to face Helena. "And children will be born into a better world. Here, the gods gave this to me for you." He held out a *hei-tiki* of jade.

Helena took it with gratitude. "I . . . I do already have one," she murmured awkwardly.

James grinned. "But your baby doesn't," he explained. "And who could protect it better than Mother Earth and Father Sky?"

When Helena looked closely, she recognized the two gods in their intimate embrace. Papatuanuku and Ranginui, the first parents of the world.

5

Moana's Matariki was a complete success. Koua and most of the other Maori got drunk, but they played music, laughed, and danced as perhaps they had before. Moana and her teachers made sure that their students made it to the meetinghouse to sleep—the communal night inside the school was another high point of the festival—before the drinking got out of hand. They hadn't even eaten much. The rocks in the cooking pit hadn't been enough to cook the meat, and it was still half raw when the men dug it out. Thinking quickly, Reka had put everything into a kettle and made a stew of it, though another hour passed before it was done. And the reeds had warped in the heat, so sand did end up between the celebrants' teeth. Still, the children were delighted, and the drunk revelers probably didn't even notice. Helena and the McKenzies left before the stew was done. Though dinner hadn't been prepared at Kiward Station, there were cheese and cold cuts in the refrigerator and bread was baked fresh every day. James grinned when Helena bit hungrily into a sandwich.

"Now, admit it. You shouldn't let the earth prepare your food unless you live next to a volcano." He smirked.

Gloria arched her brows. "It was worth a try."

Jack laughed. "Besides, you can't say that across the board," he said, leaping to his wife's assistance. "In Europe, the best cheeses ripen in holes in the ground."

James rolled his eyes. Helena tried not to look at him. She thought about her kite and his present for her baby. Could it be that he did feel something for her? Or were his attentions meant to make Moana jealous? That made more sense to her. Probably James hadn't liked that Moana had spent the whole day with her cousin from Dunedin. She had danced gaily with Ropata, and he was undoubtedly in love with his cousin; that was unmistakable. James had certainly noticed it as the day went on, and was reacting to it. In any case, Helena needed to keep aloof. It would hurt too much to get her hopes up and then be disappointed.

❦

Helena kept her promise to engage with the school. She supervised the children, spoke English with them, and learned some Maori herself. This way she rarely crossed paths with James, even less than when she helped out in the kitchen or stables on Kiward Station. Moana and the other teachers were more than pleased to have Helena's assistance. The project was proving a total success. Every morning Janet gathered those who skipped school and tried to make up the material they'd missed, and in the afternoon the meetinghouse was always lively. The teachers helped with homework for the regular school and offered arts, music, and reading classes.

And then, shortly after Matariki, something completely unexpected happened: suddenly, along with Maori children, there were white girls and boys on the benches in the meetinghouse.

"I want to make a kite too," said one of the boys. Helena recognized him as Marty Tasier, the son of the hardware store owner.

"And I'd like to dance," added a girl. A young Maori showed her a few simple steps right away, swinging *poi-poi*. She was clearly proud of finally being able to do something better than the *pakeha*.

Moana greeted the newcomers. "Of course, you're all welcome here. Finally there's a chance for friendship between us and the *pakeha*."

"This is more than I expected," Moana said to Helena. She was happy about the growth. "Never in my wildest dreams did I think *pakeha* children would come."

Soon enough the young *pakeha* learned their first words of Maori. They sang *haka* and danced and played out the stories depicted in the songs. James donated his old rugby ball and Moana explained to the children that, though this was a *pakeha* game, it had many elements in common with the Maori game *ki-o-rahi*. An old man remembered how to make the ball for that game and taught the children. His wife had others busy with weaving and explained the tribe's traditional patterns.

Everything was going wonderfully until the parents of the *pakeha* children found out where their Martins and Davids, Janes and Elizabeths had been spending their afternoons. The citizens of Haldon proved less than enthusiastic about their children's forays into the world of the Maori. A few of them complained to the pastor and the teacher in Haldon, and then came to the village to retrieve their children. Many became insulting—they acted as if Moana, Janet, Laura, and Helena had kidnapped their children or enticed them to act against their parents' wishes.

The teachers calmly faced their anger; they were confident enough in their work that harsh words didn't sway them. Helena, on the other hand, was afraid of men like Bernard Tasier. His screaming reminded her of the overseers in the Russian camps, and Jack and Gloria reinforced this by calling Tasier a Nazi. Throughout the war, the man had been loudly in favor of the ideology of the Third Reich. Helena grew angry, though, when he described the Maori as dirty savages who shouldn't be allowed near his son, and this almost gave her the strength to talk back to him. Still, fear outweighed her anger. She knew she wouldn't be able to continue the school when Moana, Janet, and Laura returned to Dunedin, and that was coming up.

Their teachers had supported their project, but now the three of them had to return to report on their experience before the semester ended. There were also exams before winter break, and the young women had to catch up on the material they'd missed. They knew they had to return but were sad to leave the children behind. On the day before their departure, they pleaded with Helena to at least help with homework in the afternoons. Though Helena would have liked to, she did not feel strong enough to face the enmity of Haldon's citizenry. She couldn't count on Koua's help either. The chieftain, like most of the *marae*'s residents, tolerated the school but wouldn't defend it.

"I don't know. My baby is due soon now," Helena said to excuse herself. "It's too much of a strain."

Helena knew this wasn't a good excuse, since otherwise she almost never mentioned the baby and its impending birth. Although there were only a few weeks left, she seemed determined to continue her life as before. She still rode, although she had to climb on a chair to get into the saddle and her breeches hadn't closed over her belly in a long time. She borrowed a sweater of Gloria's, which frequent washing had stretched, and it hid the loose cord wrapped around Helena's no-longer-existent waist.

"Isn't riding more of a strain?" Laura teased her immediately. "You don't seem to worry about that. If you were to fall . . ."

"I'm not going to fall," Helena replied calmly. She had learned to ride quite well over the past few months, and she only ever rode on a calm horse. "And Gloria says it's fine."

Helena was extremely proud of this fact. She'd gone out alone that morning for the first time, after Gloria expressly encouraged her to do so. For Helena this was high praise: she admired James's mother and rejoiced at any approval. Also, Gloria was the only one who didn't want to talk about the baby. They spoke about dogs, horses, and running the farm. Gloria was body and soul an animal breeder and could talk for hours about whelps and foals, so surely she was interested in each new life. But if Helena didn't want to talk about her pregnancy, Gloria accepted that, and left it to Helena to decide what she did and didn't want to do.

"Gloria probably rode until the day she gave birth herself," said Janet, who had never quite warmed to James's mother. She was open and talkative but also very feminine. Gloria's gruff, reticent manner and men's clothing grated on her.

"And put James in the kennel with the puppies when there wasn't anyone else to watch him," Moana said, revealing one of the McKenzie family legends, unsmiling. Gloria's easygoing approach to pregnancy and child-rearing seemed to make her uncomfortable too. "You mustn't imitate her, Helena," she added sternly. "I know you think everything Gloria does is perfect, but you mustn't take it as far as riding horses until the day you give birth. It'd be better to keep the school going. Helping with homework is much less difficult than riding."

Helena held her tongue. Personally, she thought an angry Bernard Tasier considerably more dangerous than the gentle mare Megan. She was long past wanting to induce a miscarriage, but still: this baby wasn't welcome. When it was born, she would care for it; she would do her duty as she always had. She would sacrifice herself for this baby, if she had to. But so long as it was possible, she ignored it.

One day, after Moana and her friends had said their good-byes with heavy hearts, Gloria finally broached the subject of birth. "We'll need to find you a midwife, Helena," she said as the family sat around the fireplace one evening. Winter had the plains fully in its grip: it was rainy and bitterly cold. Helena blushed. She found it embarrassing to discuss the birth in front of the men, but James kept thumbing through his pilot magazine, and Jack puffed placidly on his pipe. "I would suggest Ahurewa," Gloria continued. "The *marae* is much closer than Haldon, and Ahurewa has a lot of experience. She's helped many more children into the world than Mrs. Friedman." Mrs. Friedman was the nurse and midwife in Haldon.

"If she's not drunk," Jack objected. Helena, too, had noticed that Ahurewa usually had a whiskey bottle by her side.

Gloria shook her head. "Even drunk she's a better midwife than Mrs. Friedman is," she said. "You can trust her, Helena."

"And if there are complications, we'll take you to the hospital," James joined in. He also seemed to have thought this through already. "I'll keep Pippa ready to go. In a worst-case scenario, you'll be at Christchurch in fifteen minutes."

"Will you be landing on Manchester Street?" Gloria teased him. "Or should she parachute down? Don't worry, Helena. You're young and healthy. Everything will be fine."

Helena nodded indifferently. Throughout the conversation, she felt as though they were talking about a completely different person. It still seemed impossible that she, Helena Grabowski, the well-behaved daughter of Polish Catholic parents, could get pregnant without wanting to or without a husband. She occasionally thought she would suddenly wake from this nightmare and be slim and flexible again, not flopping about like a beached whale.

"Oh, and could one of you fetch the cradle from the attic?" Gloria seemed ready to plan every detail related to the baby's arrival.

Helena was grateful that she remained so matter-of-fact. Laura and Janet had tended to coo with delight as soon as babies were mentioned, but Helena knew no such enthusiasm. She knew things had to be ready for the baby, but there was no joy for her at the thought of picking out baby clothes or a cradle. And she didn't have to worry about that either. Everything needed for a baby was already there at Kiward Station. The bassinet James brought to Helena's room the next day had been made for Gloria—a beautiful carved little bed of inlaid wood, upholstered with fine linen and a lace canopy. Helena said she thought it was worthy of a princess and Jack agreed, laughing.

"Kura-maro-tini and William certainly thought so. Gloria's father saw her as a princess who would one day rule the world. That's why they chose such a lofty name for her. She was always a bit ashamed of it as a kid. Her parents, on the other hand, were too proud to feed or change the baby themselves. Caring for her fell to my mother—and to me. I've always loved Gloria. First as a little sister, and then, after being apart for many, many years, as a woman."

Later, Gloria gathered her own baby clothes, along with those of Jack, James, and Jack's older sister, Fleurette. Gwyn had never bothered to throw anything away, and Gloria had never had time to go through everything.

"It's probably not the current fashion," she said, holding up a baby's dress, "but it's still fine if you don't want to sew anything yourself, Helena."

Helena shook her head. She would dress the baby in what was already there.

6

"What do you think you'll to name him or her, anyway?" Jack McKenzie asked casually, taking a sip of whiskey.

The family was again sitting around the fireplace, and as happened more and more lately, James's father was trying to talk to Helena about her baby. He seemed to see how uninterested she was in planning for the child, and was clearly worried about this. Perhaps Helena's lack of interest reminded him of his experiences with Gloria's parents, Kura-maro-tini and William; he had more than once mentioned their shortcomings. Then he'd ask, as if by chance, about Helena's plans for her baby, and she would have to come up with some excuse about why she didn't have an answer. That became harder and harder the closer they got. It was the last week of June, and Helena felt that she couldn't get any bigger. Her stomach was already grotesquely curved and her legs swollen. She sometimes lost her balance just walking, and struggled with back pain almost every day. She couldn't continue to ignore the baby, but neither could she admit that she felt more anger than anticipation, and certainly not love. If Kura-maro-tini had felt the same way, she had Helena's complete sympathy. Although Helena would never neglect the baby; she was far too responsible for that.

She was about to mutter something about how one can always name the baby after a relative, but the telephone rang. Gloria took the call in the office, but she reappeared at once.

"It's for you, Helena. It's Miranda. She sounds very anxious."

Helena wanted to leap up, but her state prevented her. Miranda was upset? Had she heard from Luzyna? As quickly as she could, Helena hoisted herself up and followed Gloria into the office, taking the receiver awkwardly. She still wasn't used to telephones.

"Hello, this is Luzyna Grabowski."

Helena had considered answering with her real name, or just saying hello. She worried she might have to speak to an operator first, or that someone might be listening. Miranda seemed to entertain no such thoughts.

"Hi, it's Miranda." Her clear voice did indeed sound alarmed. "How are you and the baby?" she politely asked, but hardly gave Helena the chance to answer before she blurted out her news. "Helena, Witold Oblonski is dead."

Helena reached for the small table on which the telephone stood to steady herself. Just hearing her rapist's name nauseated her. Only then did she realize what Miranda had said. Witold was dead? How? He was only a few years older than she was.

"Did you hear me, Helena?" Miranda asked. "I said, that shithead Witold is dead."

Helena nodded wearily. Then she realized that Miranda couldn't see through the telephone. "Yes," she confirmed flatly. "But, but how . . . how can that be? He . . ."

"He was beaten to death," Miranda informed her, "with a Maori war club."

The world began to spin around Helena. All of a sudden, she saw the excursion to the *marae* near Palmerston; the girl, Karolina, who wanted to be a warrior; the weapon that Akona had given to the child; and her triumphant words: *You can kill someone with this.*

"Karolina?" she asked.

"How did you know?" Miranda was dumbfounded. "Did you hear already? I didn't think it was in the papers, but it's certainly newsworthy.

A thirteen-year-old girl who beat her teacher to death. And not in the heat of the moment, either; she planned it. She hit him in the back of the head with the club, and then, as he fell, she kept hitting him. With excessive brutality, the police report says."

"I'm sure she had good reason," said Helen, thinking of her own fantasies. How often had she killed Witold in her thoughts? Karolina had actually done it.

"She says he touched her. Twice. And a third time he'd wanted more than just to feel her up. So she planned to kill him. That's just how she said it. Which was stupid. If only she'd claimed to have panicked . . . but it was premeditated, and she admits it. Helena, they're going to lock her up."

Helena leaned against the table, overwhelmed. It was too much. A vast nothingness spread through her mind, but she fought against it. She needed to think; she needed to help Karolina.

"Don't they believe her?" she asked quietly. "The police, the school administration, they have to see she was defending herself."

"It's difficult," Miranda explained. "On the one hand, they can see that she wouldn't beat a man to death for no reason. On the other, Witold's wife is hysterical. She's presenting him as a saint, as a defender of the children. He'd never touch one of his charges, she swears. And Karolina, it's on record that Karolina was abused during the deportation. She was seriously injured when she got to Iran. She was treated in a hospital, but she was already traumatized. Now Miss Sherman, I mean Mrs. Oblonski, is claiming she's crazy. They say something Witold did must have reminded her of those scumbags in Russia, and she lost her mind, so to speak. If that's what the officials believe, Karolina will be sent to the madhouse."

"Nonsense," Helena burst out. "Of course that pervert touched her. It wouldn't be the first time."

"Exactly," Miranda said, and sounded as pleased as if Helena had solved that day's crossword. "And you need to tell them that, Helena.

You need to bear witness for Karolina, and to tell them what he did to you. And your sister. You said something happened to her too, didn't you?"

"But I . . ." Everything in Helena shirked from publicly discussing what Witold had done.

"I know. I know we wanted to forget the whole thing," Miranda acknowledged impatiently. "But there's no reason anymore. He can't hurt you anymore, Helena. Your secret is safe. Nobody is going to question your papers. You can testify as Luzyna Grabowski about the rape, just leave out the extortion. The main thing is, Karolina isn't the only one making these accusations. You have to come here, Helena. As soon as possible. You just have to."

"The journey is too difficult for you right now," Gloria decided. Helena had returned to the McKenzies' living room pale as a ghost and told them what happened. "Of course you should testify; that poor girl needs all the support she can get. But you're in your ninth month. You can't travel to the North Island now." Gloria's tone was clearly regretful; she obviously felt for Karolina.

"Maybe she can testify here," Jack suggested. "To the police, or a notary. Then a notarized testimony could be presented in Pahiatua."

"It's not as good as testifying in person," Gloria said. "Particularly if his wife makes a scene. They need to see Helena's face to believe her—and not just her face." She let her gaze fall on Helena's pregnant belly.

"I could fly you there," James offered, completely at ease. "If that doesn't sound too terrifying."

He knew that after her first flight she'd been happy to have her feet on solid ground.

"Absolutely not," declared Gloria. "With all that shaking, she'd go into labor immediately."

"I'm not afraid," Helena clarified. "I actually liked it. I just felt sick. But I always felt sick then. On the train, and in the truck, and on the boat too."

"If the wind's halfway decent, Pippa flies practically without a tremor," James said. "Flying is much more comfortable than the ferry. And I don't even have to make any turns. It's a straight shot. We could leave tomorrow morning, and we'd be there in two hours or so."

Helena bit her lip. The thought of testifying horrified her, and her pregnancy would be a good excuse to avoid it. But she couldn't leave Karolina to her fate. That brave girl had taken revenge for Helena—and for who knew how many other girls before them. Helena couldn't give in to fear now.

James interpreted her hesitation differently. "If you don't trust me . . ." Disappointment showed in his eyes.

Helena shook her head. "We leave tomorrow," she decided.

Helena wasn't surprised when Gloria was waiting for her in front of her rooms later.

"I wanted to ask you, my dear," she said, almost embarrassed. "I mean, it's brave of you to go, but are you sure that's what you want to do?"

Helena rubbed her forehead. "I'm really not afraid," she said. "James is a good pilot."

Gloria made a dismissive hand gesture. "That's not what I mean. Of course James can fly. And if you go into labor while he's flying, he'll get you to a hospital sooner than we could have the midwife here. I've seen the boy land on a postage stamp. It's a question of your testimony. The airplane only has two seats. I can't go with you. Lilian can't either; she and Ben are on the Cook Islands. You'll be all alone." She looked Helena in the eye, and her gaze could mean only one thing. Gloria

McKenzie knew of what she spoke. "You'll have to talk about things you wanted to forget."

Helena chewed on her lower lip. "*I nga wa o mua*," she said quietly. "You never really forget."

Gloria smiled. "You're right. Maybe it's better to say it out loud. There are doctors, psychologists, who say it helps to talk about it. I . . . I never could." She lowered her gaze.

"Something like this happened to you too?" Helena asked. She had long since sensed it, even if Gloria had never said anything directly.

Gloria pressed her lips together. "I was in America and wanted to get back to New Zealand," she said. "I didn't have any money, and I was only nineteen. Getting home was more important to me than anything else. You can imagine the rest. I'd rather die than say it out loud."

"I'm, I . . ." Helena wanted to say that she was sorry, that she understood. She knew exactly how Gloria felt. But it wasn't Witold she was thinking of in that moment. Helena hated him, and it was his child that would destroy her future. But what stopped her from saying more was the thought of Luzyna. The betrayal of her sister she thought she would never be able to confess. "I'll manage," she finally said.

Awkwardly, Gloria stepped closer. Was she going to hug her? It only then occurred to Helena how rarely Gloria touched other people. Even now she shied away from an embrace and at the last moment only laid her hand lightly on Helena's arm.

"Good luck," she said.

⋆⊱✦⊰⋆

Helena was understandably nervous the next day, sitting behind James in his plane as Jack saw them off. She'd been embarrassed at how hard it was to get into her seat with her huge belly, and felt keenly her lack of grace. She was also aware of her unshapely appearance in her gray maternity dress, which looked like a sack. Haldon didn't exactly stock the latest fashions in maternity wear. To top it all off, she'd washed her hair the day before, but it already hung in lifeless stringy strands.

James didn't even seem to notice; he grinned at her just as he had on the day she bought the breeches and shirt in Haldon.

"Let's go. If anything's wrong, holler," he instructed. "It'll be a bit loud in the cockpit today." It had rained all night and didn't seem to want to stop. The weather worried Gloria, but James assured her the rain wasn't a concern. It was wind that would make the flight rough. The rain fell steadily as though the clouds would never leave the plains. It was deafeningly loud, and it still hadn't gotten light out yet. "And don't worry," James continued. "It's only about two hundred and fifty miles to Wellington. We'll make that in three hours or so, and land at the military airfield. We can fuel up there and fly on."

"Or take the train to Pahiatua," Jack said sternly. "Don't take any risks, James. It's an orphanage in Pahiatua, not an airport. Who knows if you'll be able to land."

James grinned, touched his pilot's cap in farewell, and sprang into the cockpit. "We'll be seeing you," he told his father insolently. "Keep an eye on Ainne for me."

Then he switched on the motor, the little plane rolled down the runway, and Helena closed her eyes. When she opened them again, they were airborne.

James had not been wrong. The flight was smooth and steady, and Helena didn't feel sick at all. They didn't fly very high, and followed the coastline, so Helena could look down and see the beaches and cliffs. At first everything was hidden under a veil of rain, but it cleared after a bit, and when they reached the Cook Strait, the sea sparkled in the sunshine. Here it became a bit rougher; it was almost always windy between the islands. Helena kept her courage up as promised.

"Your baby will be a pilot," prophesized James when they landed in Wellington and he saw that she hadn't been nearly as frightened as during her first flight on Kiward Station. "I'll teach it as soon as it can see over the steering wheel."

"Maybe it'll be a girl," Helena said, surprising herself. It was the first time she'd spoken of the baby without difficulty, and she'd even pictured a little girl who looked like her.

"And?" asked James. "Amelia Earhart was a girl. And Elly Beinhorn flew around the world in the thirties. Your daughter could do that. Or she'll fly to the moon. That'll be possible soon, mark my words. We'll be up there in twenty years."

Helena tried to smile, and tried not to think about where she and the baby might be in twenty years. Would it have an opportunity to make a life, or would it fail like its mother?

"Do you want to take the train from here?" James asked.

He'd taken Helena to the officers' mess to get her a coffee and something to eat. To her surprise, the flight had made her hungry.

Helena shook her head. "I don't mind if we keep flying," she said, although she would've been happy to put off reaching Pahiatua. The winding stretch over the Rimutaka Incline would be much bumpier than their flight had been so far.

But as James and Helena left the mess hall, a young sergeant informed them that someone had asked for them. "A young woman, sir, with a nice car. She says she's here to pick you up. Her name was . . . one moment . . . Miss . . . Miss Biller."

James and Helena looked at each other.

"Miranda," James said. "Now it's really getting risky."

7

Miranda was devilishly pleased with her successful surprise. She was waiting by the runway and pounced on James and Helena, hugging them both warmly.

"God, you've gotten huge," she said bluntly when she let go of Helena. "Now I understand why Aunt Gloria didn't want to let you come. The baby could be here any minute. Well, maybe it's the dress. Who knows what people in Haldon take to be the fashion for pregnant women? It's a miracle women there still have children at all."

Miranda looked ravishing that morning. She wore a turquoise suit with a barely knee-length skirt and a jacket with padded shoulders. A simple round little hat sat on her head. This seemed like Miranda's idea of being dressed for a serious occasion.

James rolled his eyes when he saw Helena blush. "Some women want to be able to move in their clothes." Was he defending Haldon, or Helena? "The dress might not be fashionable, but at least Helena could board a plane in it, which would've been impossible in the skirt you're wearing, Miranda."

Miranda made a face when Helena smiled at him shyly. "It's a good sign," she noted meaningfully, "when a man likes a woman in any dress. Now, get in the car; I said we'd be there this afternoon. Major Foxley and Mr. Sledzinski scheduled us at three. Mrs. Oblonski demanded to be present too when you testify, Helena. I don't know if they'll let her, but you should be prepared for anything. She can get pretty nasty." Since Helena was too big to squeeze into the backseat, James folded his long legs as best he could and Helena lowered herself into the front. Miranda slid gracefully behind the wheel and hit the gas at once. "It's so brave of you to fly in your condition," she declared, taking the next turn sharply. "I don't know if I could've done it."

"How's Karolina?" Helena asked apprehensively.

She hoped conversation might distract Miranda, and maybe then she'd drive a bit slower.

"The poor thing." Miranda did let up on the gas. "At least she's still in Little Poland and not in prison. No one quite knows who's responsible for her. The camp is under army management, and the police in Palmerston aren't exactly chomping at the bit to lock up a little girl. But they do think Karolina might be dangerous."

"Why?" asked Helena.

"They had two doctors examine her," Miranda said. "Psychologists or psychiatrists or something. And one of them says she killed him to defend herself and isn't a danger so long as no one attacks her. The other thinks there was some sort of displacement or a flashback or something, and that it could happen again without warning. It's not exactly helping that Karolina herself won't say much. She just sits there and looks at the wall, and the only thing she said was: 'I told him I'm never doing that again.' It seems clear enough to me, but the doctors chew it over for hours." Miranda was again driving breakneck over the winding mountain road. Helena felt sick.

"The other children's testimony hasn't helped," Miranda continued. "Major Foxley started looking into how Karolina even got the club. He probably wanted to blame the Maori somehow, which is nonsense, of course. Karolina could've just taken a knife from the kitchen or something. But this brought up the trip to the Ngati Rangitane, and that Karolina acted strangely there."

"Because she'd rather throw spears and row canoes than weave?" Helena asked sarcastically, thinking about James's claim that women could fly just as well. "She probably even threw the spears farther than the boys. I suppose that makes her a murderer?"

"They told him she called herself a warrior and insisted they paint her face like the men," Miranda said. "And that the man who trained the warriors in the *marae* gave her the club as a present. I'm sure the boys were envious and took their revenge with the testimony. So Foxley sent people to the *marae* to ask questions, but the *tohunga* sent them packing. She said the club was made for women's hands, and her grandson Hoani gave it to Karolina because it spoke to the girl. The weapon wanted to protect the girl. I think if Foxley had his say, Akona would be first to the madhouse." Miranda stepped on the gas as they started climbing uphill.

"Where's Karolina now?" James wanted to know. He sounded as concerned as Helena felt, though Miranda seemed to attribute that to Karolina's story rather than her driving.

"She's still in her room," Miranda said. "The other girls were moved. Some of them are afraid of her too. Mrs. Oblonski has been vilifying her, and the gossip from the boys from the trip to the *marae* has only made it worse. We're trying to be with her as much as possible—the caretakers, that is. We're all on her side. Someone has to keep an eye on her, anyway. One of the psychologists thinks she's at risk for suicide. It's an ugly situation. I hope they see reason after you testify, Helena."

Helena and James thanked all the gods and spirits when they reached Pahiatua in one piece. Helena was still dizzy, but labor hadn't started.

"Good baby," she murmured, addressing her child for the first time. "You have to hold on a little longer. We have a wrong to set right."

The baby kicked as if in response; it was apparently healthy and in good spirits. Helena sighed with relief, forgetting how she'd hated these little kicks until now.

Not much had changed since Helena's departure. The houses and playgrounds didn't look quite as new, but the children seemed happier and better fed. A few of them were going to move in with host families in Wellington that summer, mostly older children who wanted to study in the city or start an apprenticeship. For the younger ones, adoptions were being considered. The original plan for sending the children back to their homeland after the war wasn't an option anymore. Though Poland had been freed from German occupation, the Soviet army was in control there; Stalin's henchmen might just deport the children again if they returned.

Natalia was going to move out in the summer. A farming couple from Greytown was going to take her and her siblings in, and she was ecstatic. Helena was more than happy for her. She'd feared her friend would make a fuss about the pregnancy, but Miranda had apparently already told her about it, and Natalia's interest was minimal. Helena sensed Natalia was hurt that she hadn't been let in on what had happened with Witold. None of the other Polish refugees sought Helena out when she and Miranda had lunch in the dining hall. It was almost as though they were afraid of her. She understood. In Siberia, anyone could be next, and the children hadn't forgotten that lesson. If someone was in trouble, it was better to look the other way. Miranda and the other New Zealand caretakers confirmed this thought.

"We tried to find out if Mr. Oblonski molested other girls," one of the young women said. "We suspected at once that Karolina wasn't the only one, and you've confirmed it, Luzyna. But the children are quiet as the grave. No one will open her mouth."

Helena nodded, comforted that the New Zealanders were certain of Karolina's innocence. Though Witold had never approached any of them, something about him had still given many of the young women the creeps.

Finally it was time for Helena's hearing. Helena followed Miranda, with a pounding heart, to the office, and was happy when James joined them there.

"You won't be able to go in," Miranda told him. "I'm not even sure they'll let me in."

As she suspected, they both had to wait in the hall when Mr. Sledzinski politely asked Helena in. The major also greeted her amiably; only Witold's wife eyed her with hostility. She was allowed to attend the hearing, but not to speak or ask any questions. Helena quickly forgot she was there when Mr. Sledzinski asked for her personal information and the major attempted to break the ice by asking after the Billers. Helena answered quietly at first, but once she started talking about what Witold had done, the words came pouring out. She made sure to mention what he'd done to her sister on the ship between Russia and Iran.

"Why didn't you come to us, Miss Grabowski?" the major asked when she explained her pregnancy. "You could've trusted us with this."

Helena blushed and looked down. "He didn't do anything to me once we got here," she murmured, "and I couldn't prove it." Her voice became fainter when she described her conversation with Witold. "He said he was going to marry Miss Sherman to get a New Zealand passport. And if I reported him, he'd deny everything. And he . . ."

She bit her lip and was suddenly seized by an icy fear. What if Witold had told his wife about her? Nevertheless, she went on. "He said that if I reported him, he'd fight back. 'I'll claim you faked your papers,' he said. 'You have no right to be here.' He was going to say I was already pregnant when we got on the ship to New Zealand, and that I was a stowaway. He threatened to tell people that he knew me from before. And that part is true; we were in the same camp in Siberia. He said he would say I had been easy, even then. I was afraid."

The major nodded and turned to his secretary, who had acted as stenographer. "Please type that up, Miss Nola, and please stay here a moment, Miss Grabowski, to sign the statement. Thank you. You've been a great help."

⚜

Helena stood to leave while Mrs. Oblonski cornered the major and Mr. Sledzinski to refute Helena's testimony. Helena tried not to listen; she was just happy it was over. With a sigh of relief, she opened the door. And then something completely unexpected happened. Miranda was waiting, agitated, with a blonde girl about twelve years old, who immediately reminded Helena of Luzyna. She clung to Miranda's hand, hiding her tear-soaked face in Miranda's jacket.

"This is Barbara," Miranda said loudly to Helena, clearly hoping that the major and Mr. Sledzinski would hear her. "She would like to testify as well. Come on, Barbara, you need to look at Major Foxley. Pan Sledzinski and Pani Oblonski won't hurt you."

She used the Polish words; the children were used to addressing their teachers as Pan and Pani instead of Mr. and Mrs. She stroked the girl's hair soothingly.

Barbara looked up at her. "You has to with me come," she demanded in broken English.

Miranda gave the men a piteous look. She hoped they understood Barbara's fear, and the girl pulled her along into the room. Helena stood quietly by the door so that only James remained waiting in the hall.

"Well, come in, Barbara." The major addressed the girl kindly. Mrs. Oblonski began to speak, and he looked at her sternly. "Please, be quiet. It seems as though this is a third victim. You won't be able to wash your husband's name clean after this. Go ahead in Polish, Barbara. Pan Sledzinski can translate for me. Or Miss Grabowski."

"If that isn't the most outrageous—" Witold's widow began, but Barbara had already started to speak. Mr. Sledzinski interpreted simultaneously.

"The other girls told me not to tell since Karolina is crazy anyway," she whispered, "and Pani Oblonski says I only imagined it because lots of girls imagine things when they hear things like what happened to Karolina. But I didn't imagine anything, and my mama . . . my mama said I should always tell the truth." Tears were again running down Barbara's tender face.

"Go on, now," the major encouraged her. "Don't be afraid."

"I'm not good at math," Barbara responded, seeming to change the subject. "I almost failed the last test. But Pan Oblonski said I . . . that there were other things that I could do well. If I showed him, then he would change my grade." She sobbed. "I kissed him. And, and touched him, down there. I didn't look. He used my hand."

"That's enough." Major Foxley stood up. "Barbara, thank you. We've heard enough. You've helped immensely, and it was very brave of you to come. Being brave is far more important than being good at math. We're all proud of you. You can go back to your room now. I'm sure Miss Biller will accompany you. And you, Mrs. Oblonski, are suspended from duty, effective immediately. Although it does you honor to respect your husband's memory, it is unconscionable to manipulate children and damage their faculties for truth. The Ministry of Education will find some other use for you. You won't be teaching children here anymore."

Witold's widow seemed to want to say something, but thought better of it. Major Foxley waited until she'd left the office. Miranda and Barbara waited too; they didn't want to run into her again. James stood outside the now-open door.

"What to do now about Karolina?" Major Foxley directed the question to no one in particular. "After everything we've heard, I think it's safe to say she acted in self-defense. Do you agree, Mr. Sledzinski, that the camp should forgo any further legal action?"

Mr. Sledzinski nodded. "Still, we can't keep her here," he said in his flinty English. "After everything that happened. I suppose we could send her back to Poland." He sighed.

Miranda interrupted him, self-confident as ever. "If I might make a suggestion. Rather, it's a suggestion my aunt Gloria McKenzie made on the telephone this morning. She said she'd be willing to take the girl in, maybe even adopt her if that was a possibility. She told me that if you allowed it, I should take her to Kiward Station on the South Island. I could leave with her tomorrow."

Helena felt as though she'd been dealt a blow. Gloria wanted to adopt Karolina? A girl she'd never even seen? Meanwhile, Helena must have just been a temporary visitor to Gloria. It seemed that she had more in common with Karolina than with most anyone else. Helena's heart raced, but she tried to breathe steadily. Of course, there would be an extra room at Kiward Station soon. Helena was expected leave the farm after the birth of her baby. There had been some vague talk of high school or studying, but now it was time to face reality. Helena would have to find a job to support the baby, and Karolina would take her place on Kiward Station—in Grandma Gwyn's bright friendly rooms, protected by her portrait and beloved by Gloria. *I nga wa o mua*— Gloria's past determined Karolina's future. Though of course Helena didn't begrudge Karolina this. She had been brave; she had defended herself. She had not betrayed her sister. Helena stumbled.

"Hel—uh, Luzyna, are you all right?"

James's voice sounded concerned. He wrapped his arm around Helena's waist to support her. Helena was tempted to lean on him—to give in, however fleetingly, to the illusion of safety.

"But we have certain responsibilities for the girl," Mr. Sledzinski said. He likely hadn't approved of Helena's residence on Kiward Station without reservations either. "These psychologists think she'll need supervision. Special treatment. She's disturbed."

The major waved dismissively. "Oh, Mr. Sledzinski, everyone here's disturbed. These children have lived through countless horrors. The war in Europe didn't leave anyone unscathed. Psychological observation is likely to make the girl worse, anyway. And back to Poland? How would that work? Who would take her in? And why go to all that trouble when she could go to a good family now, people who mean well by her?"

"Moana can help look after her," said Miranda, who was never without an idea. "Moana is going to be a teacher. So if Karolina needs educational assistance . . ."

"This Moana is a member of the family?" Mr. Sledzinski asked sternly.

"Not exactly," Miranda answered, but then she put on her mischievous smile. "But we all assume that James will marry her."

"Miranda!" James roared.

Helena flinched, shaking his arm off.

"It sounds ideal," Major Foxley said, trying to smooth everything over. "The change of scenery will do Karolina good. On the South Island no one will know her, and she's guaranteed educational supervision. We won't find anything better, Mr. Sledzinski. The only alternative would be the asylum in Wellington."

"No." Helena raised her voice, working hard to speak firmly and surely. "You can't do that to her. I was with Karolina in the Maori village. She isn't crazy. She is a wonderful girl, and she will have a wonderful life. Gloria and Jack McKenzie will care for her, as will James and . . . his wife."

⚬⚬⚬

Helena struggled to keep herself upright and not to let any pain or disappointment show as they left the room.

She was so intent on acting normally that she never quite noticed James's outrage. He pounced on his cousin as soon as the door had closed behind them.

"Miranda, how could you! What you said about Moana and me?"

Miranda grinned from ear to ear. "Oh, come on, James. I had to say something. And it wasn't even a lie, really. I still remember how you used to play house when we were little."

"Miranda." James balled his fists.

"I have to take Barbara home now," Miranda said, talking herself out of the argument. "And then I'll check on Karolina. Could you two take the train to Wellington? Because, uh, I'll be leaving with Karolina tomorrow morning." She waved at James and Helena, smiling. "I'll see you at Kiward Station." With that, she fled.

"Helena." James sounded distraught, almost helpless. "Helena, I . . ."

Helena forced a smile. "It's . . . it's all right, James. I don't mind. I don't mind taking the train."

8

James and Helena didn't end up having to take the train after all. They caught a ride in an army transport, and James talked with the driver the whole way about the consequences of the German surrender. Helena lost herself deep in thought. The truck's suspension wasn't nearly as good as Miranda's car, and despite the young soldier's careful driving, she felt she'd been through the wringer by the time they arrived.

"We'll get a room in a hotel," James suggested, noticing her pallor. "You can rest a bit, and then we'll go for dinner. I know a few good restaurants in Wellington. We'll . . . we'll just have a nice evening."

Earlier that morning Helena might've said yes and even thought the offer promising. Now she heard hesitation in James's voice, even anxiety. He was worried that she'd accept, and then he'd have to take this fat, poorly dressed girl out in public, where people might recognize him.

Helena shook her head. "If we can, even though it's dark, I'd rather fly back," she murmured.

James laughed. "Of course we can fly. Remember Matariki? And of course all the bombing runs in Europe . . . those weren't flown midday when anyone could've seen the planes miles away. We can be home in three hours or so."

Everything went smoothly, but Helena still sighed with relief when Pippa came to a stop on Kiward Station's runway. Her back hurt, and she needed to put her feet up. She had a piercing headache, but at least she hadn't gone into labor. Despite how weak she felt, she wouldn't let James help her.

"I'm pregnant, not ill," she said, more sharply than she intended, and was immediately ashamed at his wounded expression.

"Helena, about what Miranda said—" James began, but at that moment, they saw headlights coming toward them. Gloria's pickup. Helena sighed with relief; she wouldn't have to talk or walk to the main house.

Gloria stopped and leaped from the vehicle. "My lands, it's true." She was beginning to work herself up. "Jack thought he heard the plane during the final stables check, so I came to see just in case. James, have you completely lost your mind, flying in the middle of the night? Making the trip twice in one day? And with someone about to have a baby? Not to mention driving with Miranda through the mountains. Helena, you must be completely exhausted." She helped Helena into the vehicle. James looked despondent. "At least everything went well," Gloria continued, pulling out a blanket for Helena. "Here, wrap up, dear. It's cold."

"You know how it went?" James asked.

Gloria rolled her eyes. "Of course. Miranda called right away. As soon as she gave Karolina the good news, she drove to the nearest pay phone. You know the Billers. If there's a telephone, Lilian and Miranda are the first ones there."

James laughed. "Is she really setting out with Karolina tomorrow?" he asked.

Gloria nodded. "Someone from child welfare is coming to look around, but yes, she'll be allowed to live with us. Not that there was ever much doubt. They're glad to be rid of her."

"I hope Karolina can speak a little English," James said doubtfully. "The other girl, Barbara, had a lot of trouble."

Gloria looked at him thoughtfully. "I don't think she'll talk all that much," she said.

❧⚜❧

Gloria's prediction proved true. When Miranda arrived a few days later with Karolina, she told them the girl hadn't said a single word the whole trip. Nor did she say anything at the sight of the house; it seemed to neither intimidate nor impress her. Helena joined the new arrivals as Miranda led Karolina into the house.

"Maybe you could try Polish," suggested Miranda. "Maybe she just doesn't understand."

Helena didn't believe that. In the Maori village near Palmerston, Karolina was able to communicate easily in English, better than most of the other children. Nonetheless, Helena smiled and greeted her in their mother tongue. Karolina didn't respond. Helena remembered that among the Ngati Rangitane she had seemed delicate—undernourished and short—but full of vitality. Now Karolina seemed downright fragile. Her pretty, heart-shaped face was clouded with sadness, and her long, curly black hair hung down limply rather than framing her face as it had when she'd discovered her inner warrior.

"Where's Aunt Gloria?" Miranda inquired.

"Here." Gloria hurried down the stairs. She was wearing her stable clothes: breeches, riding boots, and a checkered shirt. "I had to take care of something in Karolina's room." She winked as if it was a secret she'd shared. Then she became serious as she caught sight of Karolina, and her face reflected sympathy and pain. "Come here, my little one," she said quietly to the girl after exchanging greetings with Miranda. She laid her hand lightly on Karolina's bony shoulder. "I'm Gloria. I'll show you where you'll be living. I'm sure you want to rest."

Helena translated, though it was unnecessary—she could see that Karolina understood. The girl looked at Gloria anxiously but gratefully. After a two-day journey with Miranda talking at her ceaselessly, she must have been longing for some quiet. At least, so Helena supposed.

Gloria had prepared one of the former nurseries for Karolina. Helena thought it must have been Gloria's—the furnishings were simple and suited Gloria, who didn't tend to surround herself with unnecessary things. There were a few children's books on the shelves, and a sketchbook and paints lay at the ready on the desk, alongside a handsomely bound journal with a pen. And the surprise Gloria was preparing at the last moment must have been the small tricolor dog on Karolina's bed. One of the last whelps from the most recent litter, she was three months old.

Karolina's eyes widened when she saw the puppy. The little dog yawned, leaped down from the bed, and pranced over to her.

"This is Kiward Sunday," Gloria introduced her. "We traditionally name the dogs after days of the week. The most famous dog ever born here was named Friday. He belonged to James McKenzie, my husband's father." She smiled. "And he was a famous thief. Like Robin Hood."

Karolina looked up at her, astonished. Gloria returned the girl's gaze. "Sunday is yours," she said.

Karolina made a choked noise. Carefully, she approached the puppy, who eagerly wagged her tail. As Karolina petted her, she licked her hand and snuggled against her.

"I'll show you how to train her," Gloria continued. "She can already do some things. For example, she'll bark when anyone wants to come in. No one will be able to surprise you in here."

A hint of a smile spread over Karolina's face, and a shiver went up Helena's spine. The girl's expression reminded her of when she had shown Helena the war club on the way back from the Maori village.

Karolina then spoke her first words in days. "Will she guard me?" she asked, holding back tears. "Does she bite?"

Gloria shook her head gently. "She'll be a good guard for you, my dear, but she won't bite anyone. She'll only love you."

An hour later, when Helena brought a tray of food up for Karolina—the McKenzies, Helena, and Miranda had eaten together downstairs, but no one had insisted that Karolina join them—the door to her room was ajar. Helena froze when she heard crying. Cautiously, she looked through the crack in the open door. Karolina sobbed and sobbed, her face buried in Sunday's soft fur.

Light

CANTERBURY PLAINS, NEW ZEALAND (SOUTH ISLAND)

JULY 1945–MAY 1946

1

Ahurewa would like to see you."

Moana was visiting for the weekend for a family celebration at O'Keefe Station. She used the opportunity to stop by the McKenzies' briefly and to extend the midwife's invitation to Helena. It didn't sound like the old *tohunga* was giving the pregnant woman a choice.

Helena's reaction was cautious, but Gloria nodded while answering for her. "Certainly. It's smart for her to examine you before the birth, Helena. She'll also want to tell you what to expect. Maori obstetrics are gentler and more natural than those of the *pakeha*. They're better, in my opinion. And believe me: James had a hard birth."

Helena heard that it had taken Gloria McKenzie several years to become pregnant after her marriage to Jack, and James surely wasn't intended to be an only child. Maybe it also had something to do with the experiences of Gloria's youth, about which she wouldn't talk. Helena took it that Gloria had a lot in common with Karolina. She empathized with her as she seemed to with no one else.

Karolina had settled in well over the past two weeks. She still spoke very infrequently, but she followed Gloria like a shadow, making herself useful wherever she could. She seemed to know her way around animals, especially horses. All this, along with her English proficiency, gave Helena the impression that Karolina had come from a wealthy family.

She may have even spent her first years in surroundings like the house at Kiward Station.

"I can drive you straight over to the *marae* now, Helena," James offered, "and give you a ride back, Moana. I need to go to Haldon anyway. I'll pick up Helena on my way back."

Moana had come from O'Keefe Station on foot. Her family was celebrating a christening. The baby's grandmother was Moana's uncle Wiremu's favorite sister, and he had traveled with his family and Moana to celebrate. She would return to Dunedin with them to take her final exam, although most students had already begun their winter break.

The christening celebrations seemed to combine Maori and *pakeha* traditions. Enviously, Helena noted how beautiful Moana looked that day. She wore a colorful flowered wrap dress, which hugged her slender figure and emphasized her waist. She wore her hair down, and Helena thought she looked a bit like one of Paul Gauguin's South Seas beauties. Helena felt as though she was getting fatter every day, though that hardly seemed possible. She was done being pregnant and just wanted to give birth already. The intimacy with her unborn child she thought she'd experienced briefly in Pahiatua had vanished. Helena didn't want this baby, and she raged again and again at her fate. Witold's widow had surely wanted nothing more than a baby with her husband, but instead he had ruined Helena's life and traumatized Karolina.

"All right," said Helena, hoping that no one could hear the reluctance in her voice.

She glanced unhappily in the mirror before following James and Moana to the truck. She hardly even fit in the sack-like maternity dress, but the midwife wouldn't care how she looked.

Helena discovered to her horror that the *marae* wasn't calm as on a normal afternoon. There were several vehicles in the center of town, and between the dirty, run-down pickups, a well-kept Lincoln Continental caught Helena's eye.

"Is that Wiremu's car?" she asked Moana, amazed. "Wow, your uncle must have a good practice."

Moana nodded. "Yes, he does," she said, but it was the other vehicles that troubled her. Parked haphazardly in the central square, some with doors still open as if the drivers had leaped out in a hurry, were a number of moderately nice cars. "What are all these cars from Haldon doing here?" Moana asked. "That Dodge is Bernard Tasier's."

When James came to a stop and they opened their doors, they heard voices. One of them was easy to identify as Tasier. He was shouting amid a group of *pakeha* armed with hunting rifles and facing a group of Maori in front of the meetinghouse.

"Open the door," Tasier was ordering, waving his rifle. "You bring out my son, and I mean now!"

Koua answered just as angrily. "Your brat isn't here, *pakeha*. How many times do I have to tell you? Go look elsewhere. We don't have him."

"You can say that as often as you like, shithead!" roared Tasier. Neither he nor Koua seemed particularly sober. "I don't believe a word of it. The boy disappears, and you're refusing to open up . . . to open up the very building where you had our children before. The whole thing stinks to high heaven."

"Sir, please, be reasonable." A tall man, a slender Maori, stepped out from beside the chieftain. Unlike the others, who wore denim pants, work shirts, and leather jackets, he had an elegant suit on. The fine cloth and his white shirt and neat haircut seemed peculiar in contrast to his tattooed face. Other than him, only Koua had so many tattoos. Helena already knew why that was: Tonga, the old chieftain, had insisted that his sons be given martial *moko*. So this man must be Wiremu, Moana's uncle. "Why would the tribe kidnap your son?" He addressed Tasier matter-of-factly with a calm, friendly tone.

"Exactly," Koua added, smirking. "If there's anything we have too much of, it's children."

Wiremu paid him no mind. "My brother, the *ariki*"—he pointed to Koua—"would gladly show you the building. However, the key to the meetinghouse is missing. My niece—"

"Enough! We'll break it down!" Tasier yelled. "Come on, men. Or we'll burn it down."

"That would kill your son, if he were inside," noted Wiremu.

Tasier raised his weapon and took a step toward him. "Listen, you smart-ass . . ."

"Enough, Mr. Tasier. I have the key."

Moana stepped calmly between her uncle and the angry *pakeha*. She held a key on a string. "I was at Kiward Station and accidentally took the key with me. My father's telling the truth. He couldn't open the meetinghouse for you."

"Whether we have the key or not," Koua interjected, "I don't need to open the damned building for you, Tasier. I'm the owner. This is tribal land; that is our building. And if you want us to let you in, you had better say please." He pointed his own rifle at the *pakeha*.

"What the hell is going on?" James McKenzie stepped next to Moana. "Maybe you should tell us what brings you here, Mr. Tasier. And as a general rule, people talk much more calmly when the man they're talking to isn't waving a gun around. Same goes for you, *ariki*."

Sobered by the intervention of Kiward Station's heir, Tasier lowered his rifle. Koua did the same.

"Marty's gone," Tasier explained, still aggressive but no longer yelling. "My son. My eight-year-old son. He disappeared hours ago. My wife is worried sick. And where was he the last time he disappeared? I'll give you three guesses." He pointed at the meetinghouse.

"But that time he came of his own free will to make a kite," Moana explained matter-of-factly. "There's no crafts class today. There aren't any other children here, and the building is locked."

"But how do I know that you're not keeping Marty in there?" Tasier glared at Koua.

The chieftain made a face. "Oh yes, we Maori are well known for stealing children, aren't we? Unlike you *pakeha*, who never kidnapped Maori children and locked them in missions and those so-called schools to remove them from their tribes. You think we want to make a little Maori out of Marty, do you?"

His men laughed, but Moana ignored them and her father. She opened the door.

"If it will put your mind at ease, Mr. Tasier, you're welcome to take a look around our meetinghouse," she said amiably. "It's just a big room; no one could be hiding here. And I don't think anyone would mind you looking in my aunt's house, either. We're celebrating a christening. Most of the children in our *marae* are there eating, so if Marty came to visit a friend—"

"The boy's not here, Moana," someone interjected. The voice belonged to a well-dressed woman who looked to be both Maori and *pakeha*. Helena hadn't seen her here before; she was probably Wiremu's wife. "When the village men showed up, we looked everywhere and asked the children. The last time they saw Marty was yesterday at school. And it seems they don't play with him much. They said his father tends to say unkind things about Maori people. Occasionally Marty repeats them. He doesn't have any friends here."

Bernard Tasier seemed to want to keep arguing, but the other *pakeha* men with him seemed convinced.

"Forget it, Bernie, he's not here," an older man said. Helena recognized him as Mr. Boysen.

"What would they even want with him?" another asked, the same question Wiremu just had.

"If someone has . . . has him, then they'd want ransom," a third man said, clearly not sober. "Maybe you should wait for that."

"If one of you devils kidnapped him, I'll get you. I will." Tasier raged again, but everyone was already dispersing, and the *pakeha* dragged their leader to his truck. Moana, James, and Helena stayed in front of the meetinghouse until they were alone.

"Where could he be?" Helena asked, concerned. "Could somebody have kidnapped him? Like . . . like with the Lindbergh baby?" Her parents had told her about that in Lwów to keep her from going out alone.

James laughed. "In Haldon? Nonsense. Bernard Tasier makes good money with his hardware store, but he's no millionaire. Marty will turn up. He probably just got lost somewhere."

"How would anyone get lost here?" Moana asked. "This is the Canterbury Plains, James, not the jungle. It's more likely he was playing with a friend and lost track of time."

"Didn't you say that there are at most twenty or thirty *pakeha* children in Haldon?" Helena asked. "I'm sure Mrs. Tasier has already asked the boys Marty's age, even if her husband was too dumb and drunk to think of it. No. If Marty's been gone a few hours, then he either got so caught up playing alone that he lost track of time, or something's happened to him. Do you have any idea where he might be playing? You played around here as children too."

Moana and James looked at each other knowingly.

"The tunnels," said James.

"It's possible," Moana mused. "Let's head there, James. It's worth a look."

She turned back to the truck, James and Helena following, and in a flash the pickup was barreling over the pothole-strewn access road toward Haldon.

"Could we go a little slower?" Helena moaned. Startled, James quickly let up on the gas.

"Sorry," he said. "I'm just worried. If the boy climbed down into the old mines . . ."

"How could he?" Helena asked. "Aren't they locked? And, well, in Siberia it wasn't that simple. You had to get in a hoisting cage." She still shuddered at the memory of the creaking elevator.

"They didn't dig that deep here," Moana explained. "They just dug tunnels into the mountain. When they closed the mine, they sealed the entrances . . ."

"With wood," James elaborated. "It was already rotten when we were Marty's age. And of course we climbed in and explored the mines. It was exciting. We played gold seekers and cave explorers."

"You two never got lost?" Helena asked.

Moana shook her head. "No. It's hardly possible—although Miranda always insisted we take a ball of yarn and unroll it like in that Greek legend."

James laughed nervously. "Right, Theseus looking for the Minotaur. Miranda was constantly expecting a mountain lion or something to appear."

"But if you can't get lost," Helena reasoned, "why hasn't Marty come back?" Just then the pickup reached the paved highway, and she let out a sigh of relief.

"That's exactly why I'm worried," James said. "It's not just the boards on the entrance that are falling apart, Helena. The tunnel beams will be just as rotten."

⚜ ⚜

The old mine was about two miles outside Haldon, toward Methven. The ground was hilly and rocky, possibly of volcanic origin. Helena lost hope of finding Marty all the way out here. A young boy could never have walked that far in one morning. But when James turned again onto a dirt road, still soft from the previous day's rain, they saw fresh horse tracks. A sturdy pony stood near the tunnel entrance, hitched to a manuka tree. It whinnied piteously; it had probably been there for hours.

"Is that Marty's pony?" James asked Moana. "His father said nothing about a missing horse."

"His father is a senseless drunk so intent on blaming the Maori for something that he didn't bother to check the stables first," Moana speculated, going over to the animal and stroking it. Helena had never seen Marty with it, but judging by the length of the stirrups, it had been ridden there by a child. "Otherwise he would have charged us with horse theft too."

James was examining the tunnel entrance; someone had obviously recently climbed in there. The entrance had been boarded up, but one of the boards had been pried loose. James pulled two more out so that they could get in easily.

"Can you get the flashlights, Helena?" he called, as she was struggling to get out of the truck. "They're under the driver's seat. There should be a canteen and a bag with bandaging too, in case he's hurt."

Helena gathered everything and approached the mine. She wasn't sure if she should follow them in. She felt drawn to the manuka tree to which the horse was hitched. Walking past it, she touched the bark and instantly recalled her visit to the Ngati Rangitane, and the manuka tree that had given her strength, whose spirit she had felt.

"Helena, are you coming?" asked James. "Or do you want to wait here?"

Helena tore herself from her thoughts and ran to the tunnel. She didn't want to wait alone outside. She gave a flashlight each to Moana and James, putting the canteen and the first-aid supplies in the old bag in which she had found the flashlights. She put the bag on so that she had both hands free. The ground inside the tunnel was rather uneven, and there were occasional steps. Right at the entrance the tunnel was still wide, but farther down it branched into three narrower shafts.

"Marty," Moana called with her ringing voice. "Marty, are you there?"

"Over here," a weak voice came. "Help!"

"That's him." Moana sounded delighted. "We're coming for you, Marty!" She followed the voice.

"Of course the stupid brat chose the darkest, narrowest shaft." James bent over so his head didn't hit the ceiling. "And the most rotten; all the others are better supported. We're coming, Marty! Holler again so we can find you."

"Here." Marty sounded about to cry.

"We'll get you out of there."

The boy couldn't be far. Helena wondered momentarily whether she should follow Moana and James down the shaft. The darkness frightened her. Then she thought of the shafts in Siberia that were much lower and narrower. Often the overseers forced the smallest prisoners to lie on their stomachs and dig. It wasn't that bad here, she told herself, and went on. She had to duck, but the flashlights showed the corridor was at least six feet wide and five feet tall, and reinforced with wood. Soon they reached Marty. The tunnel wall ahead of him had collapsed, and Marty lay partially under the rubble.

"My leg," he whimpered. "I can't pull my leg out." As if to prove it, he tried to get up, bracing himself with his hands and pulling his lower body against the wood and rocks. He gave up at once, though. The boy was lanky and slight, completely different from his square-built father. "It hurts so much," he moaned.

"But nothing else hurts?" Moana asked. She and Helena kneeled down next to Marty. He shook his head. "You're definitely not badly injured," Moana soothed. "We just need to get you out from under there."

"We'll have you out in a jiffy," James declared, pulling on the broken beam, which lay crosswise over Marty's pelvis. It didn't budge. "I think I need to go back to the truck to get tools," he said. "Can you wait a bit, Marty?"

Marty nodded. He seemed comforted and began to tell the girls about the accident as James made his way back.

"I wanted to carve my name into the wall," he explained, and pointed to his pocket knife, which lay close to him. "And then everything collapsed. First the wall, then the ceiling. It happened so fast I couldn't run away. I was so afraid." He sniffled.

"Didn't you have a light?" Helena asked.

"No," Marty said. "Well, yes, I did, a gas lamp. I wanted to do it right, like the miners, not just use a flashlight. It went out when I fell, though."

Moana illuminated the ground around him, and they found the gas lamp partially buried in dirt. She lifted it carefully. Fortunately, the lamp wasn't broken.

"Well, so it was really scary, huh?" asked Moana.

Marty nodded, almost a little proud. Helena thought him rather brave. She would've been scared to death alone in the dark mine.

Footsteps came once again from the entrance.

"I'm back," called James—and then suddenly curses rang out. "Damn it. These stupid steps."

Helena was startled; James must have fallen. Hopefully he hadn't injured himself too. But the consequence of his fall was far worse than a scraped knee. A moment later, Helena and Marty screamed as a rumbling went through the mine. Support beams broke with a crack, and Helena thought the earth was going to bury them all. A few seconds later, it was all over. Moana, who had dropped the flashlight during the collapse, felt along the ground for it. She found it quickly and shone it in the direction of the exit. But it wasn't there anymore. They were trapped.

2

Helena felt ice-cold panic rising within her. She recognized it from Siberia. The few times they'd pushed her into the cage and lowered her through total darkness into the depths had been seared into her memory.

"We're going to die," she whispered in the dark. "We're all going to die."

Marty whimpered. He felt for her hand and clung to it. Helena squeezed his.

"Nonsense," Moana declared calmly.

At the same time, they heard James's alarmed calls. "Are you hurt? Helena? Moana?"

"No," called Moana. "Everything's fine. No one's hurt."

James said something that Helena didn't understand. She did hear that he'd begun shoveling rubble away. He was trying to free them.

The mine shook again, and Helena screamed. Marty cried.

"Stop, or it might collapse again," Moana called to him. "Drive to the village and get help. The shaft entrance needs to be secured."

Despite her warning, they could hear James start digging again. When another rumble went through the mine, he gave up.

"I'll be back in a jiffy," he called.

Helena began to tremble. "We're all going to die," she repeated.

Moana raised the flashlight and illuminated her pale face.

"Is it true?" Marty asked.

Moana shook her head. "Don't scare him," she scolded Helena. "Of course we're not going to die, Marty. I know that for sure, so just stay calm. James will be back soon."

"Did the spirits tell you that?" Marty asked seriously. "My dad says you Maori aren't real Christians because you believe in evil spirits."

Moana laughed. She appeared truly unconcerned. "We believe in good spirits," she informed him. "But we don't need them for this. We're doing all right. We have water and light, so we'll be fine until James comes back with more help."

That didn't comfort Helena. She was in a blind panic. "What if the mine collapses more?" she whispered. It was possible that the rest of the supports could give way and bury them alive. "Or if the flashlight's battery dies?"

The thought of several hours in total darkness seemed unbearable to her. And then a sharp pain ran through her body. She seized her stomach.

"Moana . . . I think the baby's coming."

Moana gently laid her hand on Helena's belly. "Oh dear, not this too," she murmured. She shone the light on Helena again, and saw eyes wide open in horror.

"I'm going to die," Helena repeated. "I knew it."

"First, we need more light," Moana said, without addressing Helena's remark. "Do you have matches, Marty? You must have brought some."

"Yeah." The boy nodded and pulled a little box of matches from his dirty jacket's pocket.

Moana struck one and tried to light the gas lamp. On the second try it lit. "There we go," she said happily.

Helena kneeled, bent over in the tunnel, as liquid came from between her legs.

"You peed yourself," Marty pronounced.

"Your water broke," Moana said. "Now, try to relax, Helena. Lie down or sit, but it'll be better if you don't lean on the wall. Here, use the bag as a pillow."

Kindly, she tried her best to make things more comfortable for Helena.

"Have you done this before?" Helena asked with a hint of hope. "Helped with a delivery, I mean."

Moana shook her head. "James will be back before it gets serious, though," she said, without much confidence. The baby coming seemed to have shaken even her. "I do have five siblings, and I'm the oldest. They were all born at home, so I picked up some things. We'll manage, Helena, if we must. Try not to get excited. Breathe calmly. Think about something nice."

Helena tried to breathe calmly and to think of James, Kiward Station, and riding in the sunshine. Instead, the memory of her mother's deathbed forced itself into her mind. It had been dark in the barracks in Siberia too, and Luzyna had cried the way Marty was crying. Helena had tried to soothe her then; maybe it would distract her to speak to the boy.

"Don't cry, Marty," she whispered. "You'll make your guardian angel sad." Her mother had always said that to Luzyna. "You know you have a guardian angel, don't you?"

Marty shook his head.

"Is that a spirit?" he asked.

Apparently the boy was fascinated with spirits. Helena wondered if that had to do with the crafts class at the Ngai Tahu's meetinghouse or if his father had scared him.

"Something like that," she answered. "In any case, every child has one, and they watch over us. There's . . . there's a song about guardian angels."

Helena suddenly saw the meticulously decorated stage of the Lwów opera before her eyes. The Christmas program. Luzyna, Helena, and their parents in holiday dress. Humperdinck's *Hansel and Gretel* being performed.

Softly, she began to sing.

> *When at night I go to sleep*
> *Fourteen angels watch do keep*

Moana and Marty listened, spellbound. Helena lost herself in the memory as though in a dream.

"I think Marty's sleeping," Moana said when Helena had finished singing. Helena suppressed a groan as another contraction seized her. "You did that well. You'll be a good mother." Moana stroked Helena's belly.

Helena made a face. "No," she spat out firmly. "I will not. I don't want this baby. I hate it."

Moana looked at her, surprised. Then she shook her head. "You will, you will," she said soothingly. "When it's here, you'll love it. Definitely. It's that way for everyone. Even if you don't want it at first. Believe me, half of the children in the village are unwanted. The women find a job in Haldon or on Kiward Station, a *pakeha* buys them a few drinks, they go along, and nine months later we have another fatherless mixed child. But the mother loves it, and no one in the *marae* is scandalized. The trouble only comes later when the *pakeha* kids call it a bastard at school. Your baby will be white, though. And James will be such a good father."

"What do you mean, James?" Helena asked, dumbfounded.

Moana returned her gaze calmly, but a little sadness seemed to flicker in her dark eyes. "The baby is his, isn't it?"

Helena shook her head forcefully, convulsing at the next contraction before she could answer. "No, of course not. Did . . . didn't Gloria tell you? Or James?"

Helena was confused. After all, it would've been in James's interest to make sure his girlfriend knew. And why hadn't Moana taken him to task for his presumed infidelity?

"Gloria doesn't talk much," said Moana. "And James . . . I thought . . . I thought . . . he said it didn't concern me." She sounded hurt. "If . . . if I'd known . . ." She left the sentence unfinished.

"I was pregnant when I met James."

Helena still didn't understand how Moana could have believed that all these months and not said anything.

"I thought you had known each other in Europe," Moana said. "But it doesn't matter. James is a good man. He'll love the baby just as much as he loves you."

"But he doesn't love me," said Helena, suppressing a cry.

The contractions were growing stronger. She felt like they were tearing her apart, but she didn't want to wake Marty; it wouldn't be good for him to see her like this.

Moana smiled despondently. "Oh he does, Helena. I knew it from the moment he came into the room with you when I was talking to Gloria. I saw at once that he loved you. And when I learned that you were pregnant, it was clear that I had lost him. So far as he was ever mine. Probably he never loved me." She sighed. "It's not something you can force."

Helena was gripped by another contraction and dug her nails into the fabric of her dress.

"You're wrong," she said, after it had passed. "He can't love me. No one loves me, I . . ." She sobbed with pain, with exhaustion, and with fear. "I'm a bad person."

Moana shook her head. "You're a person with a dark cloud over you. I saw that too. And that's what Ahurewa wanted to discuss with you today. It's not good for the baby." She smiled. "It may not come out at all." She thought for a moment. "I'll sing it a song, so it knows that it's welcome. If I can remember how it goes."

Helena thought the baby was forcing its way into the world whether its mother welcomed it or not.

"You see the cloud?" Helena asked, to distract herself—from the pain as well as from thoughts of James. Moana had to be wrong. It couldn't be that he loved her.

"Am I wrong?"

Helena looked at her and shook her head. "It's true. I have darkness around me. And it's only right. I . . . I'm paying for what I've done." She saw Luzyna's face before her again and felt tears welling up within her.

Moana put an arm around her. "Don't cry," she whispered. "Don't frighten the baby." She hummed a melody. Then she seemed to think better of it. Helena wasn't ready; it wasn't yet time to call the baby. "Will you tell me?" Moana asked gently, setting the gas lamp aside so that Helena's face lay in darkness. "What you've been through? Your *pepeha*?"

"What does *pepeha* mean again?" Helena asked, moaning as the next contractions rolled over her.

"Your history," Moana explained. "The story of your past. And more. Your *pepeha* tells what was and what will be."

Helena laughed cynically. "*I nga wa o mua*," she said. "If I hear that phrase one more time . . . but yes, you're right, of course. My betrayal will determine my future. It's ruined forever. That's true, that's right; but I've had enough. I can't anymore."

"But what happened?" Moana asked gently. "Maybe it's not so bad."

"It's very bad," said Helena. Now she really sobbed. "It has to do with my sister and with my mother."

"Just tell me," Moana encouraged her. "I won't tell anyone else. And I won't judge you."

"I already judge myself," Helena blurted out. "And fate has long since passed judgment. I, I have to accept it."

"I don't know how it is in Poland, of course, but in New Zealand everyone has the right to counsel," Moana joked. Her voice sounded encouraging. "Tell me, Helena. And your child. You shouldn't keep any secrets from it. They poison life."

Helena shook her head, rebelling. "The baby doesn't even know what this is about."

"And what is it about?" Moana asked sternly. "Punishment? You think this baby is punishment for what you did to your sister? Isn't that unfair? What can the baby do about it? If I can't be your counsel, Helena, then I'll be the baby's. It doesn't deserve the burden you're placing on it."

Helena bit her lip. Moana was right. She was about to do wrong to the baby just as she had done wrong to Luzyna.

"It was in Iran," she began quietly. "We had escaped Siberia, Luzyna and I. Our lives were no longer in danger, but there was no hope for any kind of future." At first, Helena spoke slowly and haltingly, then increasingly fluidly. In the tunnel's half-light, full of fear, with birth and death before her eyes, she revealed her whole secret. She only paused when she was seized by a new contraction. She described how she'd abandoned Luzyna, broken the promise she had made to her mother. She told Moana how she had given herself to Witold to buy his silence. "I could have fixed everything then," she whispered. "If I had just said no. Then he would have revealed my identity, and Luzyna could have taken my place." She sobbed.

"But you were already in Bombay," Moana objected.

She thought about what Miranda had said several months before. No one would have sent Helena back from Bombay—or, certainly, have organized special transportation for Luzyna.

Helena swallowed again. "When I learned about the baby, I didn't want it. I still don't want it. If I could have gotten rid of it . . ."

Moana rejected this in horror. "Don't say such things," she admonished. "Don't frighten the baby. It will cause you more pain if it doesn't want to enter the world because it feels unwanted."

The baby didn't seem to have any such fear. It was obviously struggling toward the light. Moana supported Helena when she instinctively sat up, and helped her kneel.

Helena moved to lie back down. "It hurts more this way."

"It hurts either way, but it's easier while kneeing," Moana said, holding her up energetically. "The baby slides down. Gravity helps it come out. At Ahurewa's, you would've had to kneel between two posts, pushing against one and pulling the other. That's easiest. But we'd better not do that, so the ceiling doesn't fall down on us. Do you think it's time for you to push?"

Helena shook her head. Exhausted, she hung in Moana's arms, enjoying the short rest between two contractions.

"By the way, I don't think it's so bad," Moana continued. "What you did to your sister, I mean. You said it yourself: Luzyna didn't come to the meeting place. She didn't want to go to New Zealand."

"You didn't see the look in her eyes," Helena whispered. "The . . . the way she looked at me."

"No doubt she looked aghast," reasoned Moana. "She was surprised. And maybe she was a bit angry. She was used to you taking care of everything for her. She thought it wouldn't matter if she came late. That they would wait for her, or you would come get her. For once, you didn't, and of course that surprised her. But she seems to have been pleased with it in the end. Helena, that camp had a telephone, and didn't you say it was an army truck? They have radios. Luzyna could have stopped the truck at any moment."

"She's no traitor," said Helena defiantly.

"She had no reason to," Moana corrected her. "She got what she wanted: papers that made her old enough to marry her boyfriend and leave the camp."

"That's exactly what she wasn't supposed to do!" Helena cried. "She was supposed to come to New Zealand. She was supposed to have a better life. The life our mother wanted for her." She sobbed and convulsed at the next contraction. "I was responsible for her. I should have forced her. I was, I am . . . I will be a bad mother." Helena cried out. She had to push now whether she wanted to or not. And then she felt something between her legs, another stream of liquid. "I'm dying," she whimpered, only to feel immediate relief.

The baby slid out easily. Moana caught it. "A girl," she said softly. "You have a little girl."

Half unconscious, Helena saw how Moana cleaned the baby as best she could with her underskirt and cut the umbilical cord with Marty's knife. The baby cried in shock.

"Don't hurt her," whispered Helena.

Moana smiled. "You see, you love her already," she declared, wrapping the baby in her underskirt. Helena fell back onto her improvised bed and found herself looking directly into Marty's fearful eyes.

"What happened? Are we . . . are we still here?" he asked, confused.

"Nothing bad happened," Moana answered amiably. "On the contrary, something wonderful. Look, Helena had her baby." She held the baby in the light, so Marty could see the tiny, wrinkly red face. "This is her little girl. What do you want to name her, Helena?"

Helena sat up. "Why . . . why not Luzyna?" she managed, exhausted.

Moana rejected this decisively. "No, Helena. You can't do that to her. She needs a name of her own."

"But she would remind me of Luzyna. In case she's dead." Helena stroked the baby's cheek while Marty still stared, fascinated.

"But how did the stork get in here?" he asked, but no one answered him.

"Your living baby is supposed to remind you of the dead?" Moana chided. "That would be doing her a great wrong. Besides, there's no reason to think your sister is dead. Why would she be? She's young and the war is over. You didn't betray her; you only lost sight of her. And that would have been the case even if you'd stayed in Iran and she'd come here. She might have written to you from here because she would've been alone. She wouldn't have had her boyfriend. But she might have had to suffer what you did at the hands of this Witold. Someone like that could've found something to extort her with—you said yourself that something happened on the ship from Russia. And even if he had left her alone, who knows if she would've been happy here, as happy as you?"

"But I'm not happy." Tears ran down Helena's cheeks anew. Even though she didn't want to cry. She wanted to hold the baby she had just given birth to. She wanted it with all her heart. Moana was right: she loved her daughter already. She no longer saw her as a punishment.

Moana laid the baby in her arms. "You are happy," she confirmed as Helena began to rock her baby gently. "The baby is a future grown out of your past. *I nga wa o mua*. Move on; be grateful. What happened was horrible, but it's become a blessing. James loves you."

"That's not true," whispered Helena, feeling renewed pain in her abdomen. "James has always belonged to you. And he'll be yours again as soon as I'm gone."

Moana shook her head. "You're not going anywhere," she said decisively. "And it wouldn't be right anyway. *I nga wa o mua*—that's true of me and James as well. James is a *pakeha*; I'm Maori. We did not come to Aotearoa on the same canoe. James would probably say that doesn't matter, and not long ago, I would've agreed. I wanted to marry him and live with him on Kiward Station—perhaps I would've even fought for the chance to do so, Helena, if you hadn't been pregnant. It was your baby, that I thought was James's, that first made me let go and think about whether I really wanted the life of a *pakeha*. A life like my uncle Wiremu has. He wrestles with a guilty conscience, too. Tonga chose him to be his heir, not Koua, who is entirely unsuited for the role. But Wiremu left. He lives his own life, and, when he's not thinking about how Koua is ruining the tribe here, he's happy. But I wouldn't have been. I want to reignite the traditions of my people. I don't want to sacrifice our past to an uncertain future. I see that clearly in the way the spirits brought you and James together. I will become *ariki* of the Ngai Tahu, Helena. Even though I'm a woman. What the hell. First I'll become a teacher. Then I can offer myself for nomination against my father and try to win the tribe's vote."

"You're a chieftain's daughter, after all." Helena smiled through her tears.

Moana nodded proudly. "And if I have to, then I'll lead my people on the warpath. Against the prejudices and ignorance of the *pakeha*, and against the apathy and misery of the Maori. First, though, I'll build the school. The children of my people should be proud to be Maori again. And they shouldn't be stopped from inviting their *pakeha* friends to conjure spirits with them." She winked at Marty.

"There's no such thing as spirits." Marty remembered his father's claims.

Moana grinned. "Then who let the stork into the mine?" she teased him.

The boy frowned. "Maybe a crow brought the baby instead. Or a bat."

"Don't they teach you anything at school in Haldon?" Moana asked, sighing. "There aren't any bats on the South Island, Marty. *Pekapeka* only live on the North Island."

As she spoke they heard engines coming to a stop in front of the mine, and shortly thereafter voices too.

"That's my dad," Marty cheered. "I hear my dad."

Tasier's voice could indeed already be heard in the shaft.

But the first person to call a name was James. "Helena?" He sounded concerned.

Moana smiled at her friend. "You see? He's calling for you."

Helena returned the smile.

It took a few hours for them to clear an entrance to the shaft. After the rescuers were sure there was no hurry, they worked as carefully as possible to avoid further collapses. The afterbirth came, and Moana said she would bury it in the mine.

"It will anchor your baby's soul in Aotearoa," she said. "Papa's lap will be her *maunga*."

Helena frowned. "But we might not get to stay," she insisted morosely. "Gloria has Karolina now. I should go back to Europe and look for Luzyna."

Moana frowned. "Is that really what you want? Do you really want to go back? Isn't your future here? You don't have to find Luzyna, Helena. Let her find you. She knows she only has to write to Pahiatua to find you. If she hasn't done that yet, then it's probably because she's happy with Kaspar and she's afraid you'll wreck that. Give her time, Helena. Someday she'll remember that you belong to her past, and then she'll have a part in your future."

Helena's thoughts whirled. She couldn't wrap her mind around all that right now. She was tired, but it was a pleasant feeling. She wouldn't think about Luzyna any more that day, but instead find a name for the little girl who was her future. And perhaps James's too. She thought about taking a branch from the manuka tree growing in front of the entrance on her way out. She would carve a *hei-tiki* for James out of it. Surely Moana would help her.

As she rocked her baby, a beam of light pierced the shaft. They had dug through, and soon the entrance would be open again. The light they used as they dug fell directly on the little one's face. The baby squinted into the sudden brightness but didn't cry.

Moana smiled. "Now she has her name," she said. "Turama—'light.'"

3

It felt surprisingly right for James to put little Turama in the elabo-rately decorated bassinet beside Helena's bed in Gwyneira McKenzie's old rooms. James wouldn't budge from Helena's side after he'd helped her out of the shaft and led her back to the light of day. Moana had carried the baby out, but put her right back in Helena's arms as soon as she was safely seated in the truck.

"And how do you like your little daughter?" Moana had teased James with a smile as he looked, enchanted, at the baby's little red face.

Helena had been embarrassed. "He's not—" She'd been about to protest, but stopped when she saw James's happy face.

They hadn't exchanged many words on the way back to Kiward Station. They were just happy to be together. Moana had asked one of the others to drive her back to the *marae*.

Neither Gloria nor Jack spoke much that evening either. They already knew about the successful rescue operation—Helena learned that Jack had come to the mine to help and so learned about the birth. Since he hadn't been needed, he'd driven back to Kiward Station to tell Gloria, who prepared things for Helena and Turama. The bassinet was readied, the sheets changed on the bed, and water heated for a bath.

Astoundingly, Karolina had a lot to say about Helena and Turama's arrival at Kiward Station. The girl was fascinated by the baby.

"What's her name? Turama? That's a strange name, but it's pretty. She's cute, her tiny hands, and that little nose. Later she'll look like you, won't she, Helena? Will she, will she be my sister if, if Jack and Gloria really adopt me?"

Helena had looked at her, at a loss.

"No," Gloria had explained, smiling. "But I could see you being her aunt."

Helena was still chewing on these words when, after taking a quick bath and putting on a fresh nightshirt, she lay in the freshly made bed. She had just gotten Turama to sleep and was dead tired but happier than she had ever been before.

Over the next few weeks, Helena and James took it slow. James visited Helena and Turama several times a day, telling Helena what was going on with the farm and the animals. But with regard to their relationship, he held back. He flirted much more with Turama, who grew cuter by the day. James claimed she already looked like Helena. They definitely had the same porcelain-blue eyes.

"That can still change," Gloria warned.

Helena had told her that Witold's eyes had been brown, and how afraid she was that she might someday recognize him in Turama's face.

James only shook his head, though. "Nonsense, they'll stay blue," he declared. "Or do you think she'll take after me, Helena? They'd have to darken a bit, of course."

Helena laughed at this, but was relieved that James seemed to have no fear that Witold could have passed on his looks—or character—to the baby.

Only when Helena could leave the childbed and came back into the common rooms did James carefully seek physical closeness. He held her up when she first braved coming downstairs, and took her hand gently when they went for a walk. Their hands found each other quite naturally whenever they were together, and at some point, they stood under the glowing starry sky on an ice-cold winter night, and James put his arm around her as they looked at the stars.

A month after Turama's birth, Helena began to help in the stables again. She laid the little one in a basket and took her along outside. The baby had an eager guardian in Karolina. The girl jumped at every chance to watch the baby when Helena started riding with James again. Helena accepted his tender touches as he casually corrected her posture on the horse or came to help her with the sheep, and she saw how happy it made him when she gave him a conspiratorial smile when he did.

And then Miranda Biller came to visit the McKenzies at Kiward Station. She was excited, of course, about little Turama, but also thought that fresh air did everyone good.

"Helena, you're just as much a bumpkin as Aunt Gloria," her friend teased. "It may be more practical to walk around all day in a shirt and breeches"—Helena was just happy that her clothes fit again, and she felt no need to put anything else on—"but just think of James and Uncle Jack. They occasionally need to see you in all your beauty or they might lose interest in you as women. We should go shopping together." Gloria laughed. Jack quite certainly loved her just as she was, she didn't need to dress up for him. But Miranda's teasing landed in fertile ground with Helena. Secretly, she did want to be beautiful for James sometimes, but she didn't want to go to Haldon for fear of gossip. "Tomorrow we'll go shopping in Christchurch," Miranda decided. "Helena, Karolina, Aunt Gloria, and me, no ifs, ands, or buts."

❧❧

Gloria agreed to the excursion in the end. She was reluctant to expose Karolina to a whole day of Miranda's cheerfulness and unending chatter, but Karolina got along with her surprisingly well. She even seemed to find shopping fun. For the first time, it struck Helena how lovely the delicate girl with long black locks could be. Karolina had blue eyes, too, and the dark-blue dress Miranda picked out for her suited her exceptionally well.

"You look like a princess." Helena sighed, unable to help thinking of Luzyna. She was a completely different type of girl, of course, but just as striking as Karolina, and had always loved spinning around in front of the mirror as Karolina did now. Helena hoped her sister had opportunities to buy and wear elegant clothes again. She often thought of Luzyna, full of concern and nostalgia, but the fear that she may no longer be alive had passed. Helena realized that fear had been a product of her guilty conscience. Moana was right: there was no reason to think that anything had happened to Luzyna. The war in Europe was over. Wherever Luzyna was, bombs weren't falling. And even if Helena didn't think much of Kaspar, the strong young man was certainly capable of protecting her sister.

Miranda had the dress bagged for Karolina and sauntered over to a shelf with ladies' pants. She spent the next hour convincing Gloria to get an extravagant pair.

"You do have to go to the breeders' convention. Yes, you do. Uncle Jack was talking about it, and he would love to have you at his side. You could wear pants like these there. The sheep barons will keel over in shock."

"More likely from horror," remarked Gloria. Women's pants still drew attention. "And the women will go first, but all right, you've convinced me. I shouldn't lock myself away in Kiward Station so much. Maybe we'll all go to Christchurch sometime this year: Jack, Karolina, and me, and James and Helena with Turama. It's about time the 'better sort' of the plains got to know our growing family."

Helena also decided on a pair of straight-cut dark gabardine pants, which would be practical whenever she flew with James. Then Miranda dragged her further to the dresses. She insisted on a colorful fitted dress with a wide skirt.

"James will like it," she insisted. "And maybe it'll encourage him to take you somewhere. And I don't mean that stupid breeders' convention. That's boring. Why don't you go to the movies sometime? Isn't there a theater in Haldon?"

There wasn't in Haldon, but Christchurch had one, and James was happy to have an excuse to take Helena there. While Karolina watched Turama—thrilled by this important charge—they saw *A Tree Grows in Brooklyn*. It was the first real movie of Helena's life. James took advantage of the darkness to put his arm around her lovingly, and was happy when she leaned into him. Later, he admitted he had done this on Miranda's instructions. His worldly cousin had told him: "At the movies, you kiss."

They didn't kiss at the movies, though. When they got back, James parked his pickup in front of Kiward Station's stables and opened the door for Helena. As he helped her down, she looked up into his eyes, and the two of them kissed beneath the starry sky. Their mouths found each other tentatively, gently. Neither of them was in a hurry. Everything more would come in time. Helena and James were young, the war was over, and a bright future lay before them. They had no doubts about their love. At some point, they would marry, and one day, Turama might even have siblings.

Epilogue

"H ow much of this should we tell Helena?"
Jack McKenzie played with a big brown envelope. A detective agency was listed as the document's sender. Shortly after Turama's birth, Jack and Gloria had hired the agency to find Luzyna—also known as Helena—Grabowski after Moana had spoken in confidence to Gloria. Naturally, the young woman hadn't given any details, but had told her firmly that Helena wouldn't be at peace until her sister's fate was known. The McKenzies hadn't hesitated to employ the detective agency, but their patience was put to the test. Only just recently, after almost a year, had the agency picked up the trail of Luzyna and Kaspar in Warsaw. They'd collected details by having their people watch the couple, even speaking to them, as well as eavesdrop discreetly at social events. They'd compiled a comprehensive dossier, which lay arrayed in its entirety in front of Jack and Gloria. They had withdrawn to their bedroom and spread the papers out on the bed.

"Well, I'd say just the most important," Gloria opined. "Luzyna and Kaspar took a winding path to Poland."

"Even though many other countries not occupied by the Red Army were open to them," added Jack.

"We also won't mention that they didn't choose the country for patriotism or nostalgia but only because neither of them wanted to learn another language," Gloria said. She laid the conversation transcript she'd learned that from on the top of a second pile. "We can, of course, tell Helena that Kaspar works in a car repair shop in Warsaw and seems to be getting along with the communists in charge."

"Which might have something to do with the way he ignores his girlfriend to meet with officers of the Red Army at night in half-legal clubs," Jack elaborated. "Or are we leaving that out too?"

"Of course," answered Gloria. "We'll only tell Helena that Luzyna and Kaspar aren't married yet. That'll make her happy."

Jack nodded. "And then we'll just give her Luzyna's address. If she wants, she can write and decide for herself how much she wants to tell her sister about her life." He smiled.

"I hope she writes back. If she doesn't answer, I'm sure it'll break Helena's heart," Gloria said, worried.

"She'll write, Gloria, don't worry," James soothed. "Besides, I'm sure Helena will tell her she's as good as engaged to the sole heir of one of the largest sheep farms in New Zealand. That would present her with an alternative if things with Kaspar and the Soviet officers ever stop going so well."

Gloria frowned. Intrigues had always been beyond her. "Do you think she's so calculating?"

Jack laughed quietly. "You might also call it a survival instinct. In any case, clearly no one needs to be worried about this young woman. I'd be more afraid for Helena and James, should she drop in on us here. Let's put away everything but the page with the address. Then we can bring her the good news just before they take off. Where is she, anyway? With Turama still?"

❧ ☙

Helena had tears in her eyes, even though she was trying to sing and laugh with her daughter by way of good-bye. During her first year, Turama had turned into a miniature version of her mother. Her eyes stayed blue, and her hair was a honey-blonde color, similar to Luzyna's.

Her heart-shaped face reminded Helena of her beautiful sister, and Helena hoped that she would grow to resemble her even more.

"I didn't think leaving would be this hard," she said unhappily to James, who was waiting.

He laid his arm around her. "Now, don't be sad, Helena. All that's going to separate you is about three hours in the air. And universities have breaks all the time, not to mention long weekends. Maybe you can schedule your courses so you don't have to be at school on Fridays at all. Uncle Ben isn't exactly working himself to death, you know."

Helena had graduated from high school a short time before. Recently high school correspondence courses had been implemented for children on remote farms. The teachers met with their students by radio, and the lessons came by mail. Karolina went to school this way too, which suited her reclusive personality. She didn't miss having class-mates or group projects at all; she was content with her books and her animals. She was taking strongly after Gloria and worked skillfully with the horses and dogs. Sunday was already proving herself as a sheepdog, and Karolina sometimes offered the world a smile when the shepherds respectfully called her "Miss."

Helena would have preferred to go to a proper school where she could have talked with teachers and fellow students. In that respect, she was looking forward to the university. Helena had decided to study Maori Studies with Ben Biller, to learn more about the natives' language and culture. Later, she wanted to work with Moana, who'd just passed her teaching exam and finished her practicum in Haldon. Though there wasn't really a need for two teachers there, Bernard Tasier and other village notables had worked to create a second position. Tasier was enormously grateful for his son's rescue—he had, with unusual insight, declared that he never would've thought of searching the mine. Marty would've died of thirst and hypothermia if no one had seen his horse at the entrance, and if the horse had managed to tear itself free and run home, no one might ever have found the boy. Tasier no longer talked about mistrusting the Maori, so it seemed that Marty was to grow up in a world where peace reigned between the two peoples.

In the afternoons, Moana opened the meetinghouse to all children. She planned to demonstrate the courses to the *pakeha* parents who were still concerned, so she could win over their children to her project as well. "You'll see. I'll have them convinced the Ngai Tahu haven't smoked the heads of their enemies in a long time," she joked.

Over time, Helena also hoped, the *pakeha* would take more interest in the lives of their Maori neighbors. Moana intended to build an information center that would provide vacationers, travelers, and school groups from other parts of the country a glimpse into Maori culture, and Helena would help with that. But that was a ways off. First would come her studies in Wellington. James was going to fly Helena to the North Island himself.

"It might be you miss Turama's first words," he teased his girlfriend. "And that might be 'Dada' instead of 'Mama.'"

Helena smiled through her tears. "That would be nice, though," she said, kissing her little one once more before giving her to Karolina, who was already patiently waiting for Helena to tear herself from her daughter. Next to her lay Sunday, her tricolored shadow.

"You're supposed to stop by the office before you take off," Karolina said, giving the message Gloria had sent with her. "Gloria and Jack have something for you."

Helena couldn't remember when she had last felt as happy as she did now, leaving Kiward Station's former receiving parlor. Her whole face beamed, and she didn't ever want to let go of the piece of paper with Luzyna's address on it. She would've loved to write to her sister right away, but James was waiting with Pippa. Helena looked forward to the flight. Over the last few months, she had flown with James often, and enjoyed seeing the world from above. Today was a clear day—she would savor the view of the coast and the ocean.

"Everything all right?" James asked, already wearing his pilot's cap and leather jacket. He looked quite rakish in them.

Helena noticed that the little birdman of jade that Moana had given him before he went to war dangled in his cockpit. Around his neck, James now wore a different *hei-tiki*: Helena's first attempt at whittling, carved from manuka wood. It was Tane, the god of the forest, who created a new world by separating heaven and earth and brought Hineahuone, the first woman, to life.

Helena nodded happily and moved to climb in. She was wearing the elegant pants she had purchased with Miranda, knowing that her friend would approve. They would see Miranda when they got to Wellington; Helena planned to live with the Billers during the semester. Besides, she was determined to stop by Elizabeth Street to find out if the Neumanns were back. She had heard that the internment camps for German immigrants had long since been dissolved.

Helena saw Jack and Gloria coming toward the airfield to say good-bye to her and their son, though James was supposed to come back the very next day. "Turama," he'd declared, as they planned the trip, "does need her father."

Helena smiled as she warmly hugged his parents good-bye. Gloria was trailed by a litter of new puppies, who all wanted to be petted. As Helena bent over to scratch them good-bye, something occurred to her, something she had wondered about since they gave Sunday to Karolina.

"You never gave me a whelp," she said quietly to Gloria.

"No?" Gloria smiled and indicated James. "Didn't you get mine?"

"Mom," James moaned.

Helena was still laughing as the plane rolled down the runway.

Afterword

U ntil I began researching this novel, I would never have thought there was a chapter of the Second World War my father hadn't heard about. And even my editor Melanie Blank-Schröder wrote an astonished "Is that true? Did you research this?" on the margin of my synopsis when I reported on the odyssey of the perfectly respectable Polish citizens who, as a consequence of Hitler and Stalin's pact, were sent first to Siberia and then to Iran.

Now, my Helena is naturally a fictional character, but I didn't invent her whole story. It's true that Stalin took eastern Poland, which he annexed after his agreement with Hitler, while the Germans took western Poland. Almost the entire Polish population—a minority in parts of the country annexed by Stalin, alongside Belarusians and Ukrainians—was exiled to Siberia to make room for Russian settlers. Thousands died in work camps. Salvation for the deported only came after Hitler broke the nonaggression pact with Russia in 1941. Stalin joined forces with the Allies, who forced him to negotiate with the Polish government in exile. They demanded an immediate release of the deported Polish citizens, which followed.

The Allies were not acting solely for humanitarian reasons. They also intended to assemble a Polish army out of those men still fit for military service. The prospective soldiers were to receive their training in Iran; the country had been under Allied administration since 1941. On the heels of the future army, the other surviving Poles were sent to Pahlavi, a harbor city in Iran, and later housed in the area around

Tehran. The survivors were malnourished and ill. Many died in provisional hospitals that had been quickly erected on the beach. Hundreds of children and teenagers were left orphaned, and special accommodations were made for them. In one of the Tehran camps, an orphanage was erected; likewise in Isfahan, where the children were particularly well cared for. The administration of these camps lay in the hands of Brits, Americans, and exiled Poles. The refugees were provided for out of army stores. This explains why I have the characters fed with canned goulash and macaroni, a depiction that my editor and copy editor both advised me was "surely not authentic." In fact, however, many of the former camp residents recall precisely this meal in diaries and reports. It received the same praise as the organization of the camps. Long term, though, the refugees lacked prospects. No one saw much of a future in Iran, particularly for the orphans. Thus both the British and Polish government in exile were grateful when in 1941 New Zealand offered to take seven hundred Polish orphans to a camp especially prepared for them near Pahiatua, a small town on the North Island.

The Polish Children's Camp came into being out of a common British, American, Polish, and New Zealander initiative that received strong support from New Zealand's population. Local women's groups lovingly prepared the rooms and common areas. The children and their Polish caretakers were welcomed with much fanfare.

The original intent had been to send the refugees back to their homeland after the war's end. The camp had been consciously conceived as a "Little Poland," with Polish street names and schooling in the children's mother tongue. After the war, when Poland was occupied by the Red Army, however, the goal of repatriating the children was revised. The camp administrators cautiously and successfully encouraged their integration into New Zealand society. The country then also opened itself up to children's family members who had been left in Europe, when there were any such survivors. Many of the orphans found family members believed to have been lost and brought them over to their new homeland.

Less happy at the time in which my book takes place was the relationship between the descendants of the European colonizers in New Zealand and the indigenous Maori population. Indeed, Maori-*pakeha* relations reached a low point in the 1940s and '50s. Following the colonization of the islands by British and other European emigrants, the Maori percentage of the population sank steadily—both by percent and in absolute numbers. Wars and illnesses weakened the tribes. Many were decimated and displaced as a consequence of the land wars. The forced integration into *pakeha* society additionally contributed to the threat of the Maori losing their culture and identity. Industrialization drove them into the cities; squalor and alcoholism were the order of the day. Maori children were segregated in schools and yet so westernized that they no longer understood their own language and could no longer relate to the traditions of their tribes. Unemployment after the world financial crisis of the 1930s, worsened by a local crisis after the separation from the British motherland in 1947, fueled resentments between the whites and Maori. Poorly educated Maori and *pakeha* competed for jobs in the low-wage sector.

A change in this attitude first took shape in the 1950s, when the New Zealand government recognized the problem and began to take corrective action. It encouraged education projects for Maori, and employed social workers to support their families. Within the tribes arose people like my Moana who worked for the reawakening of customs and spirituality.

Massive Maori protests followed in the wake of the international civil rights movement of the 1960s. With newly gained self-consciousness, the tribes fought for the preservation of their language and culture, as well as for reparations for the lands taken from them during the land wars. Many of them used this money to rebuild their *marae*. Today Maori culture has a definite role in the economy as well. Many Maori participate in offering tourists glimpses into the culture. An evening with *haka* and *hangi* belongs on the standard program of any trip to New Zealand. Anyone who wants to know more can book authentic overnights in a *marae* and comprehensive introductions to Maori culture and spirituality.

The relationship between Maori and *pakeha* is still not free of tensions, and it's still the case that, on average, the Maori are more poorly educated and have worse health the European-descended population. But overall the situation has improved, which has benefited the country. Maori organizations, for example, lead the way when it comes to environmental protection and the conservation of natural resources in New Zealand.

I have striven for authenticity in other areas that this book touches on as well. The mine entrances mentioned, which testify to the decades of coal extraction in the area of my fictive little town of Haldon, can still be seen today. You can find some near Methven in the area of Mount Hutt, although the mines there were only closed in the '50s, considerably later than my fictional mine. The economic consequences of the closings for the affected regions were, however, comparable. They resulted in unemployment and further damaged relations between Maori and *pakeha*.

Another sad but true chapter in history is the internment of German-descended New Zealanders during the Second World War. They were locked up in a camp on Somes Island in Wellington Harbour, as well as for a short time in Pahiatua, in the compound that would later become Little Poland. Assignment to the camp occurred without respect to ancestry and political views. Often, Jews who had fled from Germany became the neighbors of fanatical Nazi supporters, who were common throughout New Zealand. The Nazi ideology suited the worldview of racists like my fictional Bernard Tasier very well. People like him agitated against Jews and for the idea of National Socialism, particularly in the run-up to the war and in the first years of it. Ultimately, though, they couldn't influence the overall liberal attitude of New Zealand or its entrance into the war on the side of the British. As in the First World War before it, many volunteered for the war. One hundred twenty-seven Kiwis served in the Royal Air Force, proving themselves daring fighters.

One difficulty in telling James's story, however, resulted from the fact that by far the majority of the airplanes that took part in the carpet bombings were manned by at least two, but often four or more, people. Beyond that, I needed a machine that would combine the functions of a fighter and a bomber. Happily, I found a specialist in my own family. My father assured me that the de Havilland Mosquito was indeed used in the war, armed with bombs but also there to protect bombers. There's nothing like a firsthand eyewitness!

I would like to extend my heartfelt thanks to my test reader, whose geographic knowledge was exceedingly helpful to me. My editor Melanie Blank-Schröder conceived this book together with me. My copy editor, Margit von Cossart, provided many challenges to make it really special. Many thanks as always to my agent, Bastian Schlück—he, too, is always open to new ideas—and to Joan and Anna Puzcas, who for years have taken care of everything that doesn't have to do with my writing.

> *Ka mate te kainga tahi, ka ora ate kainga rua*
> *If you lose a house, another will be found.*

Almost all seven hundred war orphans found a new home in Australia or New Zealand.

—Sarah Lark

About the Author

Born in Germany and now a resident of Spain, Sarah Lark is a horse aficionado and former travel guide who has experienced many of the world's most beautiful landscapes on horseback. Through her adventures, she has developed an intimate relationship with the places she's visited and the characters who live there. In her writing, Lark introduces readers to a New Zealand full of magic, beauty, and charm. Her ability to weave romance with history and to explore all the dark and triumphal corners of the human condition has made her a bestselling author worldwide.

About the Translator

D. W. Lovett is a graduate of the University of Illinois at Urbana–Champaign, from which he received a degree in comparative literature and German as well as a certificate from the university's Center for Translation Studies. He has spent the last few years living in Europe. This is his fourth translation of Sarah Lark's work to be published in English, following *In the Land of the Long White Cloud*, *Song of the Spirits*, and *Call of the Kiwi*.